Where I Belong

Where I Belong

GWENDOLYN HEASLEY

HARPER TEEN

An Imprint of HarperCollinsPublishers

HarperTeen is an imprint of HarperCollins Publishers.

Where I Belong
Copyright © 2011 by Gwendolyn Heasley

Library of Congress Cataloging-in-Publication Data
Heasley, Gwendolyn.
Where I belong / by Gwendolyn Heasley. — 1st ed.
    p. cm.
Summary: When sixteen-year-old Corrinne Corcoran's father loses his job, she
is forced to give up her privileged Manhattan lifestyle and move to Broken Spoke,
Texas, where she discovers that life is more than shopping sprees and country clubs.
    ISBN 978-0-06-197884-5 (pbk.)
    [1. Self-Actualization (Psychology)—Fiction. 2. Moving, Household—Fiction.
3. High schools—Fiction. 4. Schools—Fiction. 5. Grandparents—Fiction.
6. Family life—Texas—Fiction. 7. Texas—Fiction.] I. Title.
PZ7.H3467Whe 2011   2010017847
[Fic]—dc22   CIP
                                                                             AC

Typography by Alison Klapthor
11 12 13 14 15   CG/BV   10 9 8 7 6 5 4 3 2 1
❖
First Edition

FOR MOM, DAD, AND ALICEYN. THANK YOU.

Dear Reader,

Have you ever heard of the Butterfly Effect? I learned about it in science class last year. Probably the only lesson I remember because it's way more relevant to real life than the three types of sediment rock or the properties of noble gases. And it's also not revolting, like dissecting a frog. Basically, the butterfly effect is a chaos theory, attributed to a guy named Edward Lorenz. Here's the CliffsNotes version: A butterfly flaps its wings in Brazil, and it sets off a tornado in Texas. It means the smallest moments of the past, even the ones that don't have anything to do with us, affect our future and our future selves.

When Wall Street nearly collapsed, I didn't pay much attention. I used to care a lot more about the hottest starlet's weight fluctuation than the current prices of stocks. But when the economic problems caused my dad to lose his seven-figure job and me to move to a Texan town that's so teeny tiny it's not even on Google Maps, I realized how seemingly distant events can change your life forever.

This is the story of how I was transformed. How the pieces of the global economy toppled like dominoes and made a teenage ice princess from Manhattan (me) melt and find her long-dislocated heart. So if you hate me at first, keep reading. You might just surprise yourself. I know I did.

And just think, somewhere right now a butterfly might be flapping its wings and altering your future in some peculiar, yet beautiful way.

Sincerely,
Corrinne Corcoran

Chapter 1

Family Meeting

My iPhone loudly sings a little ditty.

She got diamonds on the soles of her shoes.

The Barneys saleswoman, dressed in a hideous avocado green dress, gives me a look of disgust. Maybe she doesn't like Paul Simon's music. Stupid, it's a classic, and I don't have to change my ring tone each time Lady Gaga makes a costume change. Have you ever been to a party where twelve people have the same ring tone? So pathetic, it's almost as bad as two girls having the same signature scent.

From a distance, I am pretty sure the avocado lady is rolling her eyes: Maybe she's one of those people who don't believe in using cell phones in public? Please, isn't that why they were invented? To make us mobile? And look around, Miss Barneys employee; I am the only customer on floor three, the designer collection department. It appears that whole recession thingamajig scared everyone else away.

She keeps staring at me, and I know it isn't my clothes: I am wearing an Alice and Olivia summer white dress and Jimmy Choo pink heels with my mousy brown hair slicked back. And she's the same shopgirl who still hasn't brought me the pair of Hudson jeans that I asked for more than twenty minutes ago. She's probably ignoring me because I am a teenager. I just *hate* age discrimination, but I still refuse to shop in Juniors. First of all, I am a size five in Juniors and only a size four in Womens. Second of all, most of the clothing in Juniors is cheap. I might be only sixteen years old, but I own plastic. That should count for something. The saleslady keeps on glaring at me like it's a new pastime, so I finally silence my phone. It's my mother anyway, and I don't want to talk to her.

I don't want to talk to anyone. I shop alone. Sure, I'll occasionally have lunch with friends at Fred's, the restaurant at Barneys. And I'll be sociable and make a courtesy loop or two of the store afterward, but I won't wardrobe (aka power shop) with them. They'll either move too slowly or claim they spotted that yellow eyelet Milly dress first. And right now, I am shopping for my first year at boarding school. This is serious. There are no Barneys in the middle of Connecticut, and online shopping should always be a last resort. And of course I don't do malls on principle.

When "Diamonds on the Soles of Her Shoes" booms in once more, I silence it again. . . . I mean, really, Mom? We just spent the first two weeks of August in Nantucket, and I have less than three weeks before I need to leave for Kent, my new boarding school. I haven't even finalized my bedding and drapery because Kent has yet to tell Waverly, my best friend, and me if we are permitted to be roommates. Having never shared a room before, I totally tried to finagle a private room by lying and saying that I have a serious snoring issue. But the dean of students said all roommates have to work out differences and mine will just need to wear earplugs or I'll have to wear one of those nose strips. Since a private room isn't going to happen, bunking with Waverly is a better option than some foreign exchange student who doesn't shower daily.

Moving over to accessories, I model shades in the tiny mirror. After trying to remember if I have the tortoiseshell Ray-Bans at home or if I just have the white, the black, and the neon pink, I decide to buy the tortoiseshell ones just in case. I should look at round Jackie-O glasses, too, because I totally hear they're having a revival.

Bing! bounces from inside my neon blue Marc Jacobs purse.

A text message from "her." That's how I put my mom into my phone. Funny, right?

> Her: Family meeting, 7 pm, get home

It's six, and I am supposed to do seven thirty sushi with the girls at a BYOB (bring your own bottle) restaurant in the East Village. My friend Sarita's older brother taught us to frequent BYOBs, so we don't get our fakes swiped because when you bring your own booze, the restaurants don't even card. I guess I'll have to be a little late to my friends' dinner since I'll need to swing by home.

I text her back.

> Corrinne: Fine. The meeting better last only nanoseconds. I got plans.

I bring my purchases—two pairs of Notify jeans, the tortoiseshell Ray-Bans (why not?), and the orange Tory Burch flats—to the counter where Little Miss Bitter Saleswoman sits perched.

"I'd like those Hudsons I asked for," I try to gently remind her how to do her job.

The saleswoman huffs off to find my jeans. After she packages up everything into two Barneys white and black logoed bags, I decide that I am definitely cabbing it. Those bags look heavy! And August in New York is too hot for the subway. Even though I could use the subway-stair exercise since I didn't ride or go to the gym today, I simply can't bear the thought of descending into hot, crowded mugginess. And especially not on a weekday: there are too many sweaty worker bees in tacky, cheap suits.

After I catch a cab outside, I text Waverly and tell her that I might be late.

Waverly: Don't B 2 late, we might drink all the vino. And it's never fun 2 B the sober kid.

I want to call Waverly and say there had better be wine left when I arrive, but the cabbie's blasting the radio news. All I hear is "layoffs" this, "layoffs" that, "another Ponzi scheme." Gross. I am sick of all this bad economic news, and it doesn't even make any sense. Our math teacher, Mrs. DeBord, tried to explain last year when things got really bad: something about defaults, mortgages, shorts. I definitely didn't get it. But hey, I don't even understand algebra. Letters for numbers, really? We might as well learn hieroglyphics. At Kent, I am going to need a math tutor if I want to get into the Ivies. And I for sure want to get into the Ivies because that's where the boys are not only cute but smart and rich.

When the recession first began last year, some kids' parents had to pull them out of school. But it's hard to tell who left because of money fiascos and who left for other reasons, like rehab and divorce. Thank God my dad made it through all the layoffs, and he even still got his bonus. I was scared that it was going to be a pauper's Christmas like Tiny Tim had in *A Christmas Carol*, but everything I asked for, all four pages (single spaced), sat right under the tree.

The cabbie pulls up to my building at Morton Street and the West Side Highway. I bound out of the cab, buzz to open the gate, and jog up to the marble front desk.

"Rudy, favor, please: Hold on to one of these for me," I say, extending a Barneys bag.

Rudy, our hot 6'6" doorman who models on the side, takes the package out of my hands and puts it behind the desk. I always leave one bag downstairs with Rudy so my parents don't know how much I am shopping. Then I retrieve it when I know my parents aren't around. This way, they're only mad at me once a month when the credit card bill arrives versus every time I make a big spree. My mom says my shopping is "O.O.C.," which is an abrevs for out of control; my dad says that "maybe she'll go into fashion, and it's an investment." They argue about it. Actually, they argue about me a lot. Yeah, I've gotten a few detentions and had sit-downs with the parents over learning to filter my comments, but compared to other teenagers I know, I am practically a wunderkind. No mug shot in the *Post* like the girl at school who got busted for smoking pot in a club. Good thing because mug shots, as a rule, find your most unflattering angle and make even celebrities look homeless.

I nudge Rudy with my elbow: "Thanks, Rudy. You

totally help my publicity with the parents," I say, and head to the elevators.

Rudy is awesome; he keeps all my secrets, like the fact that I come in right before curfew, make sure my parents know I am home, wait for them to fall back asleep, and then leave again. And then there was the time I drunkenly threw my keys down the trash chute with the late-night pizza box. Rudy even dug them out for me. If he weren't a doorman, I'd totally marry him. Waverly's doorman will rat her out to her parents for a good Christmas tip, so I know how fortunate I am.

Stepping out of the elevator onto the thirteenth floor, I smell chicken. I haven't eaten all day because I am trying to go vegan to shed some poundage for back-to-school. But still, it smells divine, and I'd kill for a little piece. I am shocked to find the aroma's coming from my own kitchen where my mother, J.J. Corcoran, stands over a stove. She's wearing a seriously unglamorous apron that reads "Kiss the Cook" with a gigantic lipstick mark over her perfectly coiffed clothes, a black Diane Von Furstenberg dress with a full skirt, and a long string of pearls. The black-and-white color combo highlights her naturally honey blond locks. It makes me mad to see that dress because I had picked it out on a rare shopping excursion with my mom, but the store only had it in her size: a size *two*. She told me that she would order me one in my size, but I couldn't bear the depressing notion that I would be Jumbo-J.J. Being fatter than your mom is a common issue for the kids at my school. And even worse yet, my mom told my hairdresser that I couldn't get blond highlights until I am in college. "You have such beautiful brown hair, Corrinne; you'll thank me someday," she said. So I am fatter than my mom and a brunette. I imagine that I will spend a great portion of my adult years on a couch discussing these two injustices with my shrink.

"Corrinne, is something wrong with your phone again? Why didn't you answer when I called twice? You know I don't like texting," my mom says as she stirs the chicken steeped in red wine. She stops churning to take a sip out of a very full glass of white wine.

"Why are you cooking, Mom? And where'd you get that apron? Is Maria okay?" I say, looking around for our fifty-something Mexican housekeeper, who's always at the apartment until at least eight at night. She's worked for our family for years and helps to keep our lives out of madness.

"Maria's fine. She took the train back to Coney Island this afternoon. And I've cooked before, Corrinne. Just not in a while. Besides, I thought it would be nice to have some real food for our meeting."

"Whatever; I have a dinner date at seven thirty, so let's make it quick."

"Corrinne, this is important. Your father's home, um,

he's home early for it," my mom says, and turns back to the stove.

This must be a big deal because my dad and I usually only exchange glances on Saturday mornings.

"Corrinne, one more thing: Set the table."

I give my mother a look like she must not have taken her meds. Yes, we have a kitchen table. And a dining room table. But we don't set them, and we don't eat at them. My mom picks at carrots out of the fridge. I order in miso soup and sit at the counter with my computer. And my little brother, Tripp, uses an end table to eat the grease he's had delivered from the diner while he watches terrible TV. It's what we do, and it works.

But my mother's face goes all desperate in a way I've never seen before, so I put out four plates, silverware, and three wineglasses: hopefully, my parents will at least give me a little vino for doing chores.

"Thanks, Corrinne," my mother says, pushing the hair out of her face. "Go get your brother, please," she adds.

I walk to the hallway.

"Tripp," I say as I approach his door. No answer, so I knock slowly. Tripp's twelve, and ever since the day I found a Miley Cyrus poster in his desk drawer, I no longer enter this room.

Ninety-five pounds of sandy blond hair and blue eyes hop out of the room.

9

"Do you know anything about this meeting?" he asks. He raises his eyebrows, his blue eyes sparkle a little bit (why are mine brown?), and I get mad all over again that he never let me enter him into modeling contests. I could've made a lot of money. He's way cuter than any Disney teenybopper.

"No, it's weird. Who has family meetings?" I say. "I hope they're not getting divorced or having a baby." It's bad enough that I have to share everything with Tripp; I don't feel like getting my inheritance divided into thirds.

Tripp's eyes widen and his mouth hangs open. He looks like he's only eight years old. "You think they're having a baby?" Tripp says slowly.

I feel kind of bad because Tripp is definitely the baby and the favorite, so this would kill him. "Of course not, why would they have another one after what happened with you? It's an experiment gone seriously wrong."

"You're mean, Corrinne." Tripp sticks his tongue out and pushes me aside. "Do you want to hear about my chess game?"

"No." I shake my head. "And in five years, you are going to wish you picked a cooler hobby than chess. Girls don't really dig guys who spend all their time playing with figurines."

Tripp squints his eyes at me. "They aren't figurines; they are kings, queens, knights, bishops, rooks, and pawns.

And I am not taking love advice from someone who is in high school and doesn't even have a boyfriend."

Beelining for the dining room, I don't look back at Tripp or bother to explain to him that being single is a personal choice. Why would I get a boyfriend before boarding school? That'd totally hurt my chances with upperclassmen, who have both cars and muscles, unlike my current classmates.

Tripp and I approach the table at the same time that my father and mother do. It's awkward because none of us knows where to sit. We just stand and wait for someone to make a move even though it shouldn't really matter since it's a large circular table. Finally, Tripp sits down, I sit next to him, and Mom and Dad follow.

We pass around the food on the previously unused lazy Susan. Although I have seen family scenes like this on TV, it feels strangely intimate in real life. All those public service announcements about eating with your children and how it does them good. Wrong. It's actually just awkward. And my wineglass is filled with water. Awesome. If I am late to my girls' dinner because my parents want to pretend we're one of those TV families that sit around a table and ask how everyone's day went, I am going to be ticked off.

"So what's the big announcement?" Tripp implores. "A puppy?"

"How old are you?" I ask. "Do me a favor; don't tell

people we're related." If I had any say in my birth order, I would've chosen an older brother with hot friends. But since I wasn't consulted, I got stuck with Tripp.

"Corrinne, use your filter," my mom says. This is a common phrase in our household. Apparently, my parents aren't aware of the whole freedom of speech deal.

Dad breaks in, "Kids, this isn't easy, but we've got some big changes coming up in the future."

"Not a baby!" Tripp cries.

"Not a baby," Mom answers, and she almost breaks a smile.

"Last week the bank made its final round of layoffs," Dad starts.

I suddenly realize that my fifty-something father, who's already ten years older than my mother, looks about ten years older than the last time I saw him. His gray speckled hair doesn't look classy; it just looks gray in an elderly way. I make a mental note to tell my mom that her hair guy Ricardo should fix this. And Dad's suit is wrinkled. I hope he's not sick.

". . . And so we're going to need to make some changes . . ." My mom trails off as she pushes her chicken around her plate.

My parents just stare at me and appear to be waiting for me to respond. I must've missed something during that whole gray-hair train of thought.

"Sorry, guys, I am way too discombobulated. Can we do a rewind?" I say, checking my watch.

"Honey, I said that I got laid off, and we lost a significant chunk of savings with a bad investment, a Madoff-type situation," my dad says.

"What? Who is Madoff?" I ask. This is getting more *Twilight Zone* by the second.

"What have I been paying your school tuition for?" My mom puts down her fork, grabs her head, and gazes at the table.

"Madoff is a man who said he invested money when he did not. Amazingly, it's happened again," my dad says very slowly as if he is processing it himself. "And it's happened to us. A person I considered a dear friend of mine had a firm where we invested our entire savings. Except he didn't actually invest our money; he embezzled it. We lost nearly every dime, including the cash that we just invested from the sale of the Nantucket cottage, the money we were supposed to use for the new Nantucket house." And my dad swallows hard as if he had just eaten a jawbreaker whole.

"What are the changes for us?" Tripp asks before picking up a leg of chicken and ingesting it almost whole. He's a caveman, but a small one like Bam-Bam from *The Flintstones*. Of course, he got the great metabolism, too.

"Luckily, one of your granddad's old associates who heard about my job situation offered me a job in

Dubai—that's in the Middle East—and it will help us start earning again, but it doesn't pay nearly as much as my old job. We have to make a lot of sacrifices. First thing is that we'll need to sell the apartment," says Dad.

Mom reaches over and puts her hand on my dad's shoulder.

She opens her mouth, pauses, and then starts again. "Kids, we need to save money wherever we can to cover ourselves. I'm sorry, Corrinne, but you won't be going to Kent in the fall, and the three of us . . ." My mom trails off again.

Taking a deep breath, she continues, "The three of us are going to Broken Spoke to move in with my parents. We're doing this because we can't afford to live in the apartment or in New York City in general. It's way too expensive. Plus, we owe a lot of money for the new Nantucket house construction. We have to try to sell the apartment quickly to cover these debts. And we are going to be lucky if we don't have to declare bankruptcy."

At this, I am pretty sure I caught asthma. I can't breathe. I'm not going to KENT!!! How can this be? If we did get to be roommates, Waverly and I had decided we would do coral and turquoise as our color palette. (Fuchsia and lime is way overdone.) Smith Cunnington, the hottest senior at Kent, has already requested my Facebook friendship, *and* the equestrian coach told me that I was varsity material after she saw me ride Sweetbread in my last competition.

"It's a recession, kids," my dad says. "We'll overcome it, but it takes time. I am lucky to get another job at all. Unemployment is over thirteen percent."

Tripp plays with his food a bit and then smiles. "Don't worry, Dad. Texas will be okay. I'll miss you, but I am definitely excited to get cowboy boots."

Wait, cowboy boots? Why are we talking about appropriate footwear for Texas? Holy Holly Golightly! Not only am I not going to Kent, but I am also moving to Texas. This must be an April Fools' joke, except it's August and my parents don't do funny. And Tripp's excited? Why can't he be a normal kid like everyone else and throw tantrums at the appropriate times?

"Tripp, you've never even been to Texas," I argue. "And we barely know your parents, Mom. It's messed up that we're not even allowed to talk to anyone on the subway, and all of a sudden it's okay to live with near strangers in the middle of nowhere."

Fact: We've met Mom's parents on only three occasions, and each time they visited us in New York. Each trip, my mom went nuts trying to convince her parents that they didn't want to do the double-decker bus tour *again* or eat at the Olive Garden in Times Square *again*. Grandma and Grandpa are nice and all, but the only instance that I see the words *Broken Spoke* is when I write thank-you letters for Grandma's homemade blackberry jam.

Mom picks up her fork, goes to eat, and puts it down again. "Well, this will give you an opportunity to get to know them and the town I grew up in," she says.

The town she grew up in? The words *Broken Spoke* never pass my mother's collagen-infused lips. When people ask my mom where she is from, she says, "The Dallas area." I know from getting bored in geography class that Broken Spoke is only in the Dallas area if that area is 175 miles wide and extends to Bumble Fricking Nowhere.

Mom gulps down the rest of her wine and gently puts her hand over my dad's.

"And kids, one more thing: School starts in two weeks in Texas, so we need to begin packing," she adds.

"OMG. This better be a joke. I didn't have a PSAT tutor as a freshmen to get into the best boarding school so I could end up in a small-town school in Texas. Please don't tell me it's a public school. And what about Sweetbread? Won't it be hot in Texas for her? She's used to Connecticut weather. I am going to count down from ten, and before I get to one you guys will let me know that this is a joke."

I push my chair out, and it makes a loud screeching noise. Tripp plugs his ears.

"Ten . . . nine . . . eight . . . seven . . . six . . . five . . . four . . . three . . . two . . ." I count, then pause for a long time. My parents' faces haven't changed except they are now looking at me with raised eyebrows and tired eyes. I don't even bother saying "one." This isn't a joke. This is a nightmare.

"Corrinne, Sweetbread's going to stay at the riding club in Connecticut. I called them. They were nice enough to cut us a deal and we won't have to sell her," Dad says. "We worked hard to let you keep her."

"Not that there's a good market for overpriced thoroughbreds anyway," my mom says softly but loud enough for me to hear.

"Sweetbread's a Trakehner horse, Mom. They are rare purebreds, not that you've ever really paid attention to my riding. I am out of here. Wait, any more bad news, anyone? Is the world ending tomorrow? Actually, that would be great news right about now."

Leaving my uneaten food, I storm to my room and text Waverly.

Corrinne: SOS. Coming to you. Don't drink all the wine. I need it for inspiration to figure out how 2 save my life.

Outside the apartment, I temporarily debate taking the subway since we are apparently now almost bankrupt, but I don't have the energy. I flag down a cab, get in, rest my head against the window, and cry.

Chapter 2

National Sweetbread

INSTEAD OF CONSTRUCTING A PLAN to somehow still attend Kent, I drowned my sorrows with wine and sobbed at the table. And in the following days, I've gotten no closer to constructing a plan. So now it's two days before the day of doom—the move to Texas—and I've decided to launch one last desperate plea. If I am really going to Texas, Sweetbread is coming with me. I walk into the living room determined to convince my parents of this.

"Dad," I start, "I've seen you do business, and I know that sometimes in business you have to pull the ultimatum card. So here it is: I am not going to Texas without Sweetbread."

My parents exchange quick glances with each other and then look at me with this-is-not-up-for-discussion faces.

"Corrinne," my dad starts, "you should try being more grateful."

Grateful for what? My misery? But I keep these thoughts to myself. The one who talks the most in negotiations always loses. Or at least I think that's the rule.

"It could be so much worse, Corrinne," my mom says as she pats my back. "You don't have to sell Sweetbread. Or at least not right now."

And then I lose it: I start bawling. I can't even speak, much less negotiate. If I could talk, I would tell my parents that I would sell Tripp on the black market before I even considered selling Sweetbread. My only worry is that there's not a good market for useless little brothers. According to the news, there's not a good market for anything right now.

"You should go say good-bye to her tomorrow," my mom says, coming over to wrap her arms around me. I don't hug her back. "You'll feel better when you talk to Sweetbread. And you'll see her again soon, Corrinne. Bad times don't last forever."

"When exactly will they be over?" I choke out between sobs.

My mother doesn't answer me, so I retreat back to my room, defeated, and flop on my bed.

Closing my eyes, I imagine running away with Sweetbread, galloping out of the barn and just going. And I'll wear something really cute when I do it. We'll keep riding until somehow we outrun this nightmare. Unfortunately, Connecticut and its surrounding areas don't have good places for a teenager and a horse to hide out. The cops would be on us before we made it to the Merritt Parkway.

Curling up into a ball, I clutch my gold-plated framed picture of Sweetbread, the one with the inscription *A Girl's Best Friend (After Diamonds, of Course)*, and drift asleep.

The next morning, the town car waits for me in front of the building. I jump in, and we head uptown to pick up Waverly. She agreed to come with me to visit Sweetbread at the Blue Spruce Riding Club to say good-bye. I was surprised she agreed because she calls all horses filthy beasts and wishes they would become extinct like the dinosaurs.

Approaching Waverly's town house, I spot her waiting on the stoop. She hops in, and we start the drive out to Connecticut.

"I can't believe I am going to a barn. The only thing I hate more than animals are animal homes." Waverly says. "You remember that I think the only good use for animals is fur, right?"

Of course I know this. Waverly despises animals so much she once even lobbied her building's co-op board to ban all pets. *It's home, not a zoo* was her opening line.

"You sound like Cruella de Vil," I say.

Waverly's eyes light up as she checks herself out in the

rearview mirror. "Really," she says. "That's awesome. I have always really admired her sense of style."

I giggle a little, but then I remember this isn't just Waverly and me on a road trip. This is a journey to say good-bye to my Sweetbread, who I have known since she was a tiny colt. She's practically my own child. I should dial PETA on this: Would some activists please at least consider splashing my parents with blood?

Maybe Waverly notices my sadness because she says, "I am happy to come with you to the barn. I am practically Sweetbread's godmother since you are my best friend. Although I am like a rich, beautiful, distant godmother since I can't stand animals, but she's still my goddaughter."

"Thanks, Waverly," I say, and squeeze her hand. "That means a lot to me even if it's a totally backward compliment."

Waverly squeezes back. "Just one thing, Corrinne," she says, and then pauses. "You don't mind if I don't come into the stables with you, right? I am really not looking for manure to be my new scent."

I roll my eyes and shake on it.

After we park at the stables, I get out and, true to her word, Waverly stays in the car with the driver.

As I am walking away, Waverly shouts out the tinted window:

"Give Sweetbread a kiss for me. Tell her that this separation won't last long. Love is stronger than a recession. Or at least that's what Dr. Phil said yesterday."

Waverly has her moments. I am really going to miss her.

Entering the barn, I think about how many times I've done this exact routine. The smell of the hay, the horses, and even the manure heightens all my senses, and I start to breathe heavily. It's not my personality to get animated about extracurricular hobbies. Here's a secret: I am not actually interested in Global Affairs or Students for Ethical Fashion Merchandising, but I do them for college applications. I dread the meetings, and I would sleep through them if it were appropriate to wear sunglasses indoors. But I don't ride because it's a résumé booster; I ride because I love it. And Sweetbread, well, she's been more loyal to me than any other friend, including Waverly, who missed my fourteenth birthday to attend a mobster-and-flapper-themed party with some douche bag.

Moving slowly toward Sweetbread's stall, I take in the scene. I need to remember everything about it here: This is my happy place, where I'll go in my head when I am in Texas. And hell, I'll add that hot Edward guy from the vampire books. It's my happy place, after all.

With shaky fingers, I unlatch the stall and walk in. Sweetbread neighs when she sees me. She knows; she senses my sadness. Animals are smart like that.

I take a brush out of the grooming kit. Normally, I don't groom Sweetbread since I am so busy with school. One of the stable hands does that for me. But now it seems right because I want to feel as close as possible to Sweetbread even if that means playing horse beautician.

As I brush Sweetbread's honey hair against her chocolate coat, I think about all of our times riding together. Dressage, what I compete in, is basically horse ballet and is an art form that has been practiced since the Renaissance. After five years of us working together, Sweetbread and I get better with each competition. We just scored our first nine (even a score of six is considered great), and we passed into the third level. And now, I am leaving.

As I brush, I softly clue Sweetbread in.

"Everyone at the stable is going to take care of you. Don't you worry, because I will figure out something. Think of it as, like, a minivacation for me, but a staycation for you since you aren't going anywhere."

I also tell her not to get jealous about Broken Spoke: *Travel + Leisure* editors will not be writing a feature on it anytime soon unless it's the last place left after the apocalypse.

And as I tell her these things, I notice how I sound just like my parents when they tried to reassure me. There's both insincerity and uncertainty in my voice. For the first time, I realize that this is actually happening and that it might not end up okay.

I decide not to ride Sweetbread one last time. I am afraid that I'll go into flight mode, start a slow-speed chase, and end up on the nightly news. And then everyone would know: Corrinne Corcoran is not going to Kent; she is moving to Texas without her horse. And she now faces criminal charges.

I wrap my arms around Sweetbread.

"Sweetbread," I whisper, "I promise you that I'll be back soon. And I won't so much as look at another horse in Texas. You are the only one for me."

And she is. Even if there were miraculously a stable that did dressage in Broken Spoke, which I highly doubt, I'd never try it with another horse. Training Sweetbread to respond to my subtle taps and finding our own special rhythm has taken us years. And I am lucky; many people never find the right horse to compete with. There's no horseharmony.com for dressage that matches on twenty-nine dimensions of compatibility.

I rest my head on Sweetbread's chest and feel her breathing. It almost calms me down until I realize that I have to let go. After giving Sweetbread a final kiss between her eyes, I walk out and I don't look back.

When I slide back into the town car, Waverly looks at me with big eyes.

"You know that fraught face isn't your best. You kind of look like some D-list celebrity after one of her bigger benders," she says, and shakes her head.

Grabbing an empty water bottle, I playfully tap Waverly on the head.

"Please," I joke. "Even in the middle of a national disaster like this recession, I never look bad. My looks are unflappable. Really, I should be a war correspondent. In fact, I might consider that."

"Not a good idea," Waverly says, shaking her head emphatically. "You'd be better for E! covering celebrity news, not real news. You wouldn't want to accidentally start a war or something."

No, I wouldn't, I think. Battling the recession is exhausting enough.

And then Waverly directs the driver to Serendipity 3, the best ice-cream place in all of New York. They even have frozen hot chocolate, which is somehow made possible through cooking magic.

"It's not going to change things. But if you can't eat ice cream now, when can you? There are times to diet," Waverly says, and holds her palms up in the air, "and then there are times for ice cream."

With that, I pretty much forgive Waverly for missing my fourteenth birthday.

Chapter 3

Corrinne, You Are Not in the Village Anymore

W E'RE AT JFK AIRPORT SECURITY. The line's long and I *so* don't want to take off my wedges and go barefoot. This is no beach. I could pick up SARS or a fungus. They should at least have those paper slippers they give out at nail places.

"Are you sure you don't want me to go through security with you, Tripp?" Mom asks. "I can get a pass."

"No, Mom," Tripp says. "It's part of the adventure."

"You're such a good sport, kid," Mom says, and I try to remember the last time that my mother complimented me. I think it was when I was eleven and I won my first riding competition. She supposedly used to ride, and maybe she thought riding would bond us. It never did though, and now she rarely even comes to my competitions.

"Mom, maybe you should come with us through security. Isn't it bad enough that we have to go to Broken Spoke by ourselves? Now you're leaving us in the airport with total randoms?" I say.

I look around and wonder if anyone here wants a ticket to nowhere, aka Broken Spoke, because I'd gladly trade mine to go anyplace else. And I can't believe my mother's leaving *me* to watch Tripp. Aren't there professionals called "nannies" that are responsible for caring for children?

My mom puts her finger to her mouth like a librarian: "Hush, Corrinne. You know that I want to go with you two, but we, and our entire country, are in the middle of an economic crisis. Google *recession* and learn something. I have to deal with the interior designers, the architects, and the contractors who all want money for the work they've put into the new Nantucket house, which we now can't afford. And I need to sell the New York apartment. I don't need to remind you again how difficult the apartment market is right now—half our building is for sale."

Yeah, yeah, she's probably right. For a few months now, my apartment building has been going budget on the flowers in the lobby—they are practically carnations. The building even cut the number of cable channels in the gym. No VH1, really? How is anyone supposed to run to CSPAN?

"All right, Mom. Bye-bye." I blow her a kiss, but she

moves toward me and puts her hand on my shoulder.

My mother forcibly hugs me and says, "This isn't easy for me, either. I am scared too, honey."

Her eight-carat ring blinds me a bit. I shrug her off and go for one last blow.

"How about selling the ice, Mom? Maybe then I could go to Kent. But I guess you and Dad don't really value my education."

My mom just looks at me with her Indian Ocean blue eyes and steps back.

"This ring represents a sacrament of marriage, Corrinne. And twenty years of marriage. Your father saved up for two years to buy it. What haven't your father and I given you?"

"Kent," I answer without missing a beat. "The life I am supposed to be living. Do you know that Waverly told me that kids were calling us nouveau poor? This isn't just a cocktail anecdote to laugh about later on. I am not doing a year in Paris, Mom, or even at rehab. Those are things I could spin. I am doing a year in Broken Spoke and moving away from everyone I have ever known. It's going to take forever to rebuild my reputation."

"What's an anecdote?" Tripp wants to know.

"Um," my mother starts, "an anecdote is sort of like a quick story about one inconsequential minute of your life. And Corrinne, you're sixteen. I barely remember who I was at sixteen. This *will* eventually be just an anecdote."

Easy for my mother to say. She escaped a small town for the city and didn't look back. I am being forcibly removed from the city, so all I can do is look back.

My mother kisses Tripp again and then turns like a ballerina in her heels to face me.

"Take care of Tripp, Corrinne. And please try to use your filter. I know it's hard for you, but remember there are things that you say that you should keep to yourself. So think before you speak, especially to your grandparents," she says. "And phone the second you get there," she calls over her shoulder.

Tripp and I watch my mom get smaller and smaller as she walks away. Speechless that this is actually happening, I can't get any last words out of my mouth. When I finally can, she's gone and I quietly say, "Filter this," and hold up my middle finger.

Tripp shakes his head at me. "You're immature," he says, and pretends he doesn't know me as we move through security.

When I get off the plane, my back is aching from my first trip sitting in coach. I think there must be unicycles that are more comfortable than those tiny polyester seats. I am so looking forward to getting fresh air. But when we step outside from the Dallas baggage claim, I feel hotter than I ever have in my life. Despite the fact it's after eight p.m., I get automatic pit stains. So much for wearing white. Maybe I'll sweat out some lbs here. That's one good thing about Texas, and I'm sure it'll be the only thing. Hey, if I go on a hunger strike and pass out, maybe my parents will finally pay attention to the gravity of my desperation.

Grandma and Grandpa sit in an idling old navy truck outside arrival door number one. Grandma, dressed in a denim blouse, waves ferociously. Grandpa tips his cowboy hat. I am happy a) that I recognize them since we haven't actually met that many times and b) that no one I know lives in Dallas to see that I am related to Billy Bo and Sandy Jean Houston (pronounced like the city, not the street). Can grandparents be adopted?

Grandpa jumps out to help with our bags.

"You're a light packer, I see," Grandpa jokes as he tosses my luggage tagged OVERWEIGHT with surprising ease into the back of the rusted truck.

I cross my fingers, hoping that it won't rain.

As if Grandma could read my thoughts, she calls out, "Don't worry, honey, it's the dry season. It'll be safe back there."

"Grandma, you should have seen what Corrinne wanted to bring. She and Mom nearly had World War Three over it," reports Tripp.

Somehow, I made it through the entire plane ride to

Dallas without murdering Tripp, but I am now certain that I won't make it through the four-hour car ride without committing a felony. Hey, jail is an option I have yet to pursue. I am pretty sure they have cable and AC there, and anywhere's got to be better than here. And like Martha Stewart, Paris Hilton, and Nicole Ritchie have taught us, jail totally doesn't ruin you. In fact, it can actually up your net worth. I'll keep this in mind in case things go even further south.

"Do you want a boost, Corrinne?" Grandpa asks. He must have seen me just standing there, staring at the cab of the truck, wondering how to climb up in wedges and a dress without flashing a paparazzi no-no.

"No, Grandpa, thanks," I say as I maneuver into the backseat. After me, Tripp jumps in as if he were on springs.

"This is awesome, Grandpa. I have never, ever been in a truck!" Tripp exclaims, looking around like he landed on Mars. Maybe this is Mars.

"Well, Billie Jean the Second, she is a beauty," Grandpa says. "One hundred thousand miles and she drives like she's gone only half that."

One hundred thousand miles: Manhattan is only thirteen miles long. Where are these people driving? And who names a truck? The only thing we call automobiles in the city is "taxi."

"You know, Corrinne, your mother named Billie Jean

the First when she was about your age. It took her for-ever to think of a name. And then one day: poof, she was inspired." In the front seat, Grandma closes her fist and opens it slowly as she says "poof" and smirks to herself.

"Now, you kids must be tired, why don't you try to get some sleep during the drive?" Grandpa says before start-ing the engine and weaving into the traffic.

Thank God. I was wondering how I could make small talk for four hours. Closing my eyes, I pinch myself to make sure this is happening and fall asleep to Grandpa chirping, "And when you wake up, we'll be in your new home, Broken Spoke!"

Tripp snoring like Shrek jerks me out of my sleep. The kid seriously needs to get his adenoids taken out, or he'll never get a wife. I open only one eye since I am not up for a chat. It's gotten completely dark, and we're travel-ing down a deserted highway. I think I see a cow, but it's hard to tell since we're doing eighty in a rattling truck, and I am using only one eye. Over Tripp's snoring, I hear Grandma whisper "Jenny Jo" and my ears perk up. Jenny Jo was my mother's name before she escaped from Texas and took on the moniker J.J. I know this only from looking at her driver's license. This is a genius time to eavesdrop since my mom never talks about her time in Broken Spoke, her pre-Manhattan life. Maybe I'll even hear some juicy long-lost secret and be able to blackmail my mom into sending me to Kent. Luckily, I have great hearing and my grandparents aren't exactly experts at using library voices.

"You can't still be mad, Sandy. It was twenty years ago," Grandpa says.

"And after fifty-two years of marriage, you can't still be stupid enough to tell me how to feel," Grandma whispers back.

Fifty-two years? Whoa! That's a long marriage. Every married couple I know put together hasn't been married that long. My parents have been married twenty years and that's, like, way weird in Manhattan. But what happened twenty years ago? That's the year my parents got married.

"It's not just what happened twenty years ago. It's what happened during the twenty years after that. Sending checks in the mail, never coming to visit, and now this? She ships off her kids and stays back in the big city herself. I swear, if it weren't for the thirteen hours in labor, I wouldn't think she was mine," Grandma hisses.

"Hush, Sandy, the grandchildren are in the car. You'll wake them. See this time as an opportunity," Grandpa says. I see him wrap his arm around her. Grandma scoots toward him on the bench and rests her head on his shoulder.

"It's just I don't know what to say to people. I didn't

know how to talk about her staying away, and I don't know how to talk about her returning, especially not under these circumstances," Grandma says. "It's not as if she actually wants to come home again, it's just that she has no other choice."

"Don't worry about what people say. It ain't anyone's business," Grandpa responds, and squeezes Grandma close. "And it might even be fun to have a full house."

Hold on. This is big. Something happened twenty years ago, the year that my parents got married. And Grandma, despite all her jam gifting, is apparently still fuming.

And if I heard right, she doesn't want us here any more than I want to be here. If I play this all right, it doesn't look like I'll have to stay long in Texas after all.

"Wake up, Corrinne, wake up." Tripp shakes me.

As I open both eyes, I realize this is no dream. I click my wedges three times, and think, "There's no place like New York." Sadly, it doesn't work and I am still sitting next to Tripp in Billie Jean the Second.

"Welcome to Broken Spoke, Tripp and Corrinne," Grandpa announces like an annoying game show host.

He nudges Grandma with his elbow and says, "How about we *don't* wait until morning for the grand tour?"

"It's late, Billy," Grandma says, and shakes her head.

"Oops," Grandpa says, turning his head to the backseat

to wink. "I made a wrong turn. Looks like we'll have to do the tour."

At the stop sign, Grandpa makes a left onto Main Street. There's only one streetlight, but it's bright enough to illuminate the nothingness of the small town's strip.

"I'm Billy Bo Houston, and I'll be your tour guide," Grandpa says as he mimes a microphone with his right hand and steers with his left. It's sad because he's trying so hard. He reminds me of the dorky kids at school who try desperately to be cool, which just makes them even more unbearable.

"First on your left, you'll see our grocery store. We used to have to drive to another town, but in 1989, we got our own fine Piggy Wiggly. For what we can't grow in the fields or slaughter in houses, it does quite well. On Fridays, they got samples."

I don't want to admit it, but grocery stores have always intrigued me. In the city, we have Whole Foods and some teeny tiny, jam-packed markets. But my mom told me that in small towns sometimes you have the whole grocery aisle to yourself. I've never seen that before. Grocery stores in the city are war zones. That's why I use delivery. Let someone else fight my battles. I am happy to tip three dollars for that.

"And on your right, you'll see Chin's Chinese Restaurant. The Chins have been here for over fifty years. At first, no one wanted to touch the egg rolls, and there were rumors of dog meat. As time passed, people got wise, and now it's our most popular restaurant. There's even a lunch buffet."

"It's also our only sit-down restaurant," Grandma adds.

Great, I think. Do people know how many calories are in General Tso's chicken? It's like a week's worth of food.

Grandpa ignores Grandma's comment and keeps on driving slowly down Main Street. "And here is the hardware store, Hank's Handy Hardware. Hank and I were classmates, Broken Spoke class of 1958. Same year Grandma and I got married. 'Twas a good year.

"And please look to your right; this is where Grandma and I had our first date. Of course, it wasn't a Sonic back then. It was called Peppermint Twist. But the concept is the same. I am sure that you both will be spending a lot of time here in the future because it's where the young 'Spokers' hang out. They even have a happy hour and all the ice cream is half off!"

I look at the deserted Sonic, a fast-food/ice-cream-joint hybrid with its cheesy drive-up order stations and neon red and yellow signs. For a second, I contemplate asking Grandpa to pull over so I can vomit. I have seen Sonic commercials, but in what alternate universe did Sonic become the hub of my social life? And ice-cream happy hours? Please. What makes you happy about getting fat? This is just *fantastic*. While my friends back home are sneaking into clubs because someone's brother is dating the starlet of the month, I'll be getting super-sized eating brownie Sonic Blasts by myself.

"And that concludes our tour," Grandpa says. "We'll save the schools for morning when you can see our football field. We even got a new scoreboard. This one's a work of art, better than any of that fancy, shmancy stuff I saw in New York's museums. It doesn't just sit there looking pretty. The scoreboard has a function and it has a purpose. That's true beauty, in my opinion."

"Yeah, yeah," Grandma says. "Tell that to the teachers who haven't gotten a raise in ten years."

"As you can tell, Grandma's not really a Mockingbird fan. Funny, as she was a Mockingbirdette back in the day." Grandpa laughs.

I don't even bother to ask what a Mockingbirdette is.

"Did you play football, Grandpa?" Tripp pipes in.

Grandpa slams on the brakes, screeching to a halt before putting the car in park. "Did I play football?" Grandpa yanks a large gold ring with a red stone off his right hand and passes it back to Tripp. "Won state in 1958, the last year this town ever did that."

Tripp's face lights up. "Way cool, Grandpa. Our prep school's football team is only for the kids who are too fat for lacrosse. We get killed by all the other schools."

I forgot that football is God in Texas. That must be the other half of the social life, half football, half hanging out at the Sonic. Because I have no desire to see any of this in person, I need to initiate my plan to get out of here ASAP. Even after a few hours, I can already feel myself turning into a loser.

After driving around and seeing lots of teeny tiny houses, more than a few of which need paint jobs, we pull into the driveway of what appears to be a cottage designed for little people.

"Home, sweet home," Grandpa says. "I forgot that y'all have never seen the place where your mother grew up. Lots of good memories here."

"A lot of memories, that's true at least." Grandma sighs. Grandma's turning out to be a total Debby Downer, and I'm loving it.

"You two follow Grandma in, and I'll fetch the bags," Grandpa says.

Grandma opens the unlocked red door, and we step inside.

"I am no tour guide like your grandpa, but I'll show you around the place so you kids feel at home." Grandma stands in the middle of the living room, whose furniture reminds me of *The Golden Girls* minus the Floridian element. Suddenly, I see why they don't lock the door; there's nothing worth stealing.

She points to the right. "That's the kitchen."

She points to the left. "That's the bathroom."

She points ahead. "That's Grandpa and my room."

She points to the left again. "That door, that's my sewing room. Tripp, you'll be staying there. We got a nice daybed for you. Your grandpa insisted on the expensive one."

And then Grandma points to the door to the right of that. "And Corrinne, you and your mother will stay here in the guest bedroom, Jenny Jo's old room."

Hold on: Instead of sharing a room with Waverly, I am sharing a room with my own mother! Wow. This just went even further south. And this entire house is smaller than any of my friends' apartments. I thought people didn't live in the city because they want space. There's no space here. All I see is cramped, old furniture and knick-knacks and an embroidered sign that says COUNT YOUR BLESSINGS. What blessings? No wonder my mom got out of this place. I never knew how poor Grandma and Grandpa were, and now my parents foist their kids on them. How insensitive are they?

But I just smile because I need Grandma on my side if I am ever getting out of here. See, Mom? I am practicing my filter already.

"Scoot. Y'all run off to bed now. It's way past your bedtime," Grandma says, and I am happy to oblige because I have some serious business to attend to.

"Good night, kids," Grandpa says, and he bear-hugs both Tripp and me at the same time. He smells like a construction site mixed with cinnamon.

In my room I don't bother to unpack. First of all, I can't find a closet. There's a tiny door with one hanging rack, but I can't believe that's the closet. I couldn't fit half my suitcase into it. And why should I even bother? I'll be out of here before I know it. I take out my phone and promptly ignore "her" texts.

Her: You make it?

Her: You find your grandparents?

Her: Call!!

Her: At least have Grandma call!!

I dial up Waverly instead.

"Did you make it?" Waverly says, answering on the first ring. "Have you seen any cowboys? Is it really true that everything—I mean *everything*—is bigger in Texas?"

"Yes, I made it. I didn't see any cowboys, but I think I might have seen a cow. And Texas might be bigger, but it *is not* better. I have a plan though, so don't go replacing me yet."

"Please," Waverly says. "I would never un-BFF you. Some people might say mean things about you, but not me. I keep telling everyone that you're not sure about Kent and that you are still figuring things out. No worries: I am totally covering your back."

I sigh and collapse into bed; definitely no pillow top on this baby.

40

"Thanks," I mutter. What are kids saying about me? I've been gossip fodder before, but always for good PR like the time that I lured Octavia Johnson's boyfriend away. Or the time that I managed to throw a Halloween party in my apartment while my parents were away in Bermuda without getting caught. My bribing the babysitter and my brother is legendary. But now, gossip and me in the same sentence doesn't sound good. Ugh, I need to get back to New York and to Kent before this ruins me. Or I need to hire a publicist; they can spin anything. But unless publicists work pro bono, there's no way I can afford one since my parents froze my credit cards.

"I've got to go, Corrinne," Waverly says. "I'm heading to some Chinatown tea place that doesn't card after midnight, but I am thinking of you."

"Maybe pray for me too; thoughts might not be enough," I say, imagining Waverly all dressed up, looking out her bedroom window at the city's lights. She's about to start a night and nobody knows how it'll end. That used to be me. Now I am in a tiny, steamy room in Texas with one small crank window and am about to go to bed at midnight or eleven Central. The only thing the future promises me is misery and Sonic Blasts. But thinking about Sonic reminds me of Grandma and Grandpa's conversation in the truck. What happened twenty years ago and how can I use it to my advantage?

Chapter 4

No Potential Needed

GETTING INTO PRESCHOOL IN NEW YORK CITY is a feat and getting into grammar school in the city is a noted accomplishment. And if your parents can manage those obstacles (aka buying your admission), you need to worry about securing a spot at one of the best boarding schools in the country, which takes a near miracle.

The fear of not getting into the right boarding school has been ingrained in my DNA since childhood. *Don't tease other kids,* our teachers threatened. *We write your recommendations for boarding school.* Or *Don't cheat,* our teachers warned. *We write your recommendations for boarding school.* I promise the phrase *We write your recommendations for boarding school* is the most commonly used phrase by any exasperated private school teacher in Manhattan. It's akin to *Just wait until your father gets home,* which is only scary for girls who don't know how to work their daddy's baby-girl button.

I wanted Kent. My dad wanted Kent. My mom wanted whatever would keep me from prolonged wailing and rebound shopping. But see, Waverly wanted Kent too, which wasn't good since boarding schools prefer to take only one student from each elite private school. Although I am not a fan of admitting it, Waverly was always the A to my A minus. Okay, fine, the A to my *high* B plus. Take, for instance, the ninth-grade science fair: I made a headband that expanded or contracted to fit a head, and Waverly redesigned the entrances and exits of Central Park to better flow pedestrian traffic.

So when Waverly set her heart on Kent, my mom spent weeks telling me that whatever happened, it would be okay. Even my own parents know that I am the princess to Waverly's queen, both academically and socially. Of course, I didn't believe my mother that things would be okay without Kent, especially after I fell in love with the campus and its perfectly manicured stables. And on my visit, I had the hottest tour guide ever: Smith Cunnington, who not only gives tours but stars on the lacrosse team and looks like he walked out of a J.Crew ad. After that day, I became entranced by the idea that my life must play itself out on the grassy knolls of Kent.

And then my Kent interview happened. I had prepared myself for the questions. Yes, yes, I definitely plan on volunteering in a third-world nation *every summer*. (I mean, if Nantucket sinks into the Atlantic, I would think about it. *Not a total lie.*) Yes, yes, I can't wait to balance academics, social life, and extracurricular activities. (I mean, I'll think about vocabulary words while riding Sweetbread and try to use them later in witty social banter.) But then the interviewer hit me with a question I didn't expect: "Why should we allow you in over the far more qualified candidates we get every year?" I stopped, caught my breath, and realized that my perfectly coordinated Elie Tahari suit (black with a pink shirt) alone wasn't going to get me into Kent. I needed to reply with something genius. Raising one eyebrow, just a tad, "I have," I said calmly, "potential. I think Kent's the best place for it to finally mature." When I told my parents my answer, they cackled and said that might just have saved me.

And on April 15, side by side, Waverly and I both opened our thick packages from Kent Boarding School. For the first time in five years, two girls from our school were going to Kent. *Thank you, potential.*

Here in Broken Spoke, there are no private schools. There aren't even mediocre parochial schools. There's only one public high school. All you have to do is fill out a form with your name and your address, and then you just

44

show up. A monkey could do it. Hell, even Tripp, a middle schooler, didn't need help. No potential needed for Broken Spoke High.

"Corrinne, Corrinne, it's almost time to leave," Grandma shouts through the bedroom door, "and you haven't eaten your breakfast."

I put the last details on my makeup. If this had been my first day of Kent, I would have definitely gone for fake lashes. They totally change someone's face; it's the main reason celebrities are so beautiful. Well, that, the Botox, the liquid diets, and the personal trainers. . . . But in this heat, I can't trust that my lashes wouldn't melt and blind me. And who do I have to impress? I am so annoyed that I still haven't been able to convince my father via desperate emails, texts, begging, or threats that I must go to Kent. Hopefully, I'll be able to blackmail my mother into it, but I haven't unearthed any dark and scary skeletons from her past. Although Kent doesn't start for another week, so it's not a total fantasy.

"Corrinne," I hear through the door again.

I try to look myself up and down in the tiny vanity mirror since there's no full-length one. But when I crouch, I still can't really tell what I look like. My first day without a uniform in my entire life, and I am in Broken Spoke. I can't bear to wear what I had planned for my first day at

Kent: a floral Elizabeth and James skirt with a blue cardigan. It's too depressing, so I am going casual and wearing
a J.Crew tangerine cotton dress with wedges, which I've
already worn before to a brunch. Although no one in *Tejas*
knows that, and it's not as if I really care what anyone *here*
thinks.

Adding a final coat of lip gloss, I take one last peek
in the mirror, see that even makeup can't hide depression, and drag myself out to the kitchen, where Grandpa,
Grandma, and Tripp are already sitting around the table.
Tripp's wearing a Yankees hat, which makes me relieved
that he hasn't totally forgotten his roots in exchange for, in
his words, "an adventure."

I spot a gigantic stack of nut pancakes in the middle of
the table.

"Pecan," Grandpa says, catching my stare. "Our state
nut. Eat up; you need your brain food."

I sigh and pull out my red vinyl chair. Pancakes are
totally off-limits unless they are from Clinton St. Baking Co., which serves an out-of-this-world chocolate and
blood orange pancake. And I eat those only if it's a national
holiday.

Grandma and Grandpa keep watching me, so I
serve myself and take a bite just so my grandparents
will stop looking at me so creepily. But then something
in my mouth tingles. I take another bite. More tingles.

Grandma's pancakes are even better than the ones at Clinton St. Baking Co. This can't be. And I can't stop eating. I've got to get out of this place before I will need a crane to lift me out.

"So I'll drop Tripp off at the middle school and then drop you and Grandma at the high school," Grandpa says as he forks another pancake off the platter.

"Why's Grandma coming to the school with me?" I say, and put down my knife.

"She works at the school, so I always drop her off before I head to my work," Grandpa says.

With pancake still in my mouth, I manage to choke out, "You both work? At your age?"

Aren't grandparents required by law to be retired?

Grandpa slaps the table with his hand and grins at Grandma.

"Of course we have jobs," he says. "We're only seventy. Besides, I never want to retire." And he forks another pancake off the platter, "Keeps my metabolism going."

Grandma just stares at me as if I were a unicorn and not her granddaughter.

I try to explain.

"In New York, I know people who are forty and retired. The grandparents I know golf, play bridge, and have cocktails," I say.

"Not us," Grandma says. "We've had the same

jobs since we got married. Work is good for you. I can't believe your mother's never mentioned this. Actually, I can believe it," she says, and looks down at her plate.

Tripp's face twists and he gives me a look, similar to the one my dad often shoots me when I've overstepped some line. "No, Grandma, I knew that. Corrinne has a listening problem when it comes to topics about other people. I know that you do attendance at school, and Grandpa's a mechanic and fixes farm stuff."

Grandpa reaches across the table and puts his hand on my shoulder.

"Don't worry," Grandpa says. "Grandma promises that she won't chaperone prom."

No worries, I want to say. I won't be here for prom. But I keep my mouth closed. I know better than to blab about my plan to find juice on my mom and exit the B.S. ASAP.

With the thought of Broken Spoke prom haunting me, I finish my pancakes. I've always been an emotional eater. There goes my diet.

Grandma forces me to walk into the school by myself.

"I know that you don't want to be walked in like a toddler by your grandmother," she says, and walks ahead of me.

Yes, yes, yes, I do, I think, but I keep quiet. You rode the subway alone at eleven. You once walked into a wine shop in Brooklyn and bought two bottles of wine without being carded. You were fourteen. This is easy. You can handle this.

Outside, the high school looks rather generic: a typical three-story brick building with a football field and track out back. It's nothing like my gated Upper East Side prep school with a park view and an interior courtyard. And at the door, metal detectors greet me. I am not sure what this *Dangerous Minds* metal detector gimmick is about. Maybe it's a public school thing.

After the security guards search my oversize purse (backpacks are for losers), I scan the lockers. Here, one full-size locker is divided into three lockers: top, middle, and bottom. Even the lockers at public school are budget. I search for A15, the number that I got in the mail with my class schedule. Please, please don't be a bottom locker. I wear way too many dresses to have a bottom locker. Of course, A15 is a bottom locker, and I have to squat to open it. Thank God there are no paparazzi in Broken Spoke.

My first class is Spanish I, which is just offensive. I should be in Latin III, but apparently the fine state of Texas has no appreciation for the ancient languages. The classroom number is 305, so I start the trek through the gigantic school to find it. By this point, kids are pouring into the school. There're a bunch of high fives, shouting, and pushing. I keep my head down and try not to inhale the vapors. The whole school smells like a cheap salon. The girls' locks are curled, sprayed, and cementlike. I doubt even a tornado could move a single hair on their heads. And boys, not girls trying to channel Daisy Duke, are wearing cowboy boots. Nearly every guy has boots on, and you can hear them all click on the floor. It sounds like a subway taking off. This is Mars, and I am an alien from Earth. It's the only explanation.

Room 305 is empty, so I take a seat in the back. My dad actually had the nerve to email me this morning: *Good luck, Corrinne. And remember: blank slate. You don't have to be a note passer who sits in the back anymore.* At last year's teacher-parent conferences, Ms. Havisham, the total sellout that she is, told my parents that I sit outside of "the zone." This means that I don't sit in the front-row spots where the students (read: total geeks) that get only A-pluses sit. Only Waverly manages to sit out of the zone and still maintain a 4.0.

As the class fills in, a few kids look at me strangely, but no one says anything. I guess at a school with a class size of four hundred, one new face isn't that big of a deal. For a second, being anonymous does feel good. At my old school, new kids who were rejects at their previous schools would come and attempt to reinvent themselves as popular. *Reinventors,* we called them. It never really worked since someone's cousin or friend from camp would tell someone at my school how the new kid used to be a loser, so their reputation would follow them. And here I am at a new school in a new state, and I could totally reinvent myself because no one in Texas knows me. But why would I? I am awesome. Or at least, I was awesome.

"*Hola.* This is Spanish 1. If you are in the wrong classroom, or if you already speak *español* and are just trying to get an easy A, get out now," the teacher, a good-looking, young Hispanic guy says.

"For those of you who don't know me, I am Señor Luis. I am also Coach Luis, but only on the football field. I expect everyone here, even my players, to pull their own weight. No freebies just because you can toss the pigskin."

Some jersey-wearing students groan.

"I am going to call roll," he continues. "Please answer with, '*Me llamo*' and your name. That means, 'My name is.'"

I pay attention, dreading Señor Luis getting to the Cs. Repeating in my head over and over again, *Me llamo Corrinne. Me llamo Corrinne.* I hate speaking out loud in class. And now the first time I speak at this new school, it's not even English.

"Corrinne Corcoran," Señor Luis calls.

Quietly, I recite, "*Me llamo Corrinne.*" And I don't know how it happens, but a bit of a New Yawk accent slips in, so it sounds like somebody from the Sopranos imitating a Mexican.

"*Donde estás?*" asks the shaggy-haired brunette guy to my right with the green eyes who would be almost attractive if he shaved that five-o'clock shadow. Plus, he's wearing a letter jacket even though the school is like one hundred degrees with the AC blasting.

"Excuse me?" I say.

"What Bubby is trying to say," Señor Luis says, "is where are you from? And Bubby, you say it *'De donde eres?'* "

I sigh. "Manhattan."

Señor Luis looks a bit startled by this news. "Welcome," he says slowly. "Actually, *bienvenidos*. We don't get too many big-city girls in Broken Spoke."

And Señor Luis gives me a heartthrob smile. At my old school, he'd be T.M.F.G., Total Material For Gossip, and I'm sure some student would try to seduce him. Wait . . . that's one way I could get myself kicked out of Texas, but I really don't want to be the subject of a Lifetime movie. At least not for that.

"Kitsy Kidd," Señor Luis calls.

In the front row, a petite girl with massive blond curls (but ones that actually look natural, unlike the rest of the girls, with their ozone-destroying habits) responds, *"Me llamo Kitsy,"* with a Texan drawl.

"Kitsy," Señor Luis says, "you see that Señorita Corrinne doesn't get lost and makes her way to the next class."

"Sí, sí," Kitsy says as she turns around to smile and

gives me a small-town pageant wave.

She looks like a grown-up version of a kid from that *Toddlers & Tiaras* show.

I give my best smile back. Good thing I took all those cotillion classes, which taught me the correct fork for salad and how to pretend to be a lady. I have gotten good at pretending.

Kitsy's probably a sweet girl and all, but I am not shopping for friends.

After class, Kitsy comes right up to me, shakes my hand, and says, "Hi, I'm Kitsy Kidd. I just can't believe you are from Manhattan. I've always wanted to go to the Metropolitan Museum of Art. Have you been there? I really want to see Van Gogh's *Starry Night*." She stops and exhales. "Are you on Facebook? Add me. Be happy to show you around Broken Spoke. But I am warning you, there's not much to show and the leading cause of death is boredom."

I wonder if there's a Starbucks at the school that I don't know about because this girl Kitsy appears to be highly caffeinated. Since I don't know what question to answer first, I just nod.

The kid who sat next to me and harassed me comes up to me and gives me a pat on the back "See you around, Manhattan."

I want to tell him that's an island and a drink, not a nickname. But why waste my time?

Kitsy rolls her eyes and punches the boy on the arm. "Don't worry about Bubby, he's harmless, but he's got enough tongue for ten rows of teeth. . . . He'll probably end up getting a crush on you. Do you have a boyfriend? I bet a girl like you has, like, ten thousand boyfriends."

Tongue for ten rows of teeth? Nobody told me that I would need a translator in Texas. Maybe there's an iPhone app on how to speak Texan.

She breathes, pops a piece of gum, and starts again. "What's your next class? I'll point you toward it."

If Kitsy ever comes up for air again, I'll tell her that I don't have a boyfriend. And I'll never get one since Smith Cunnington will probably find some other less-cute sophomore to make out with since I won't be at Kent. Last night I sent him a Facebook message that I might "spend a year abroad." I figured that Texas definitely qualifies as foreign exchange.

I walk away from Kitsy.

"Thanks for your help, Kitsy," I say over my shoulder. "I am sure that I'll find my next class on my own."

"Okay. Just want you to know it's exciting to have you here. We don't get people from New York City in Broken Spoke, like, ever. The only people that really visit from out of town are the traveling rodeos," Kitsy says, following after me at my heels.

I finally lose Kitsy around a corner. I am not trying to

be rude to her, but I am worried that I am about to burst into tears. Waverly has always been my plus one and while I appreciate Kitsy's offer to be my Texan ambassador, I really just want to be alone in my misery.

Amazingly, I negotiate this large public school without GPS assistance. Can you believe my third-period class is Texas State History? Guess what? The state fruit is the red grapefruit, the gem is blue topaz, and the flower is the bluebonnet. And the state animal is the longhorn. Gripping historical information, I know. Ugh! I am supposed to be in European History, where I'd study about queens and kings, and here I am learning about cowboys and the Alamo. What a waste. This will put me way behind once I get back to real life.

At lunch, I can't force myself to go to the cafeteria. I doubt they went locally organic like my old school did. For the past week, Grandpa raved about the pizza—sometimes he drops by and eats with Grandma. Although I admit I'm curious to see if public school cafeterias are really like the movies where cliques divide the room into war zones. At my old school, there were only two groups: really cool preps and kids that wanted to be really cool preps. But I didn't want to do that whole awkward sit-alone thing or—even worse—the sit-with-your-grandma-and-the-other-secretaries thing. So instead I got my latest issue of *Vogue* out of my locker and I spent lunch hour in the empty library. Maybe Texas won't be so bad for my diet after all.

Bzzzzzzzzzz! goes the school bell.

I've never attended a school with an actual bell. I thought school bells were make-believe and only existed on TV sitcoms. But when that final bell rings, it sounds like angels singing, despite the fact that it's most certainly damaging my eardrums. I don't care because I am saved— at least until tomorrow.

In my past life, I would have had riding or field hockey practice after classes. But here, the only fall sports for girls are cheerleading and swimming. Private schools in New York as a rule don't do cheerleading; it's sexist. Besides, I am not exactly an enthusiastic person. And swimming? Double please. All that chlorine eats your tan and leaves you a pale green-haired monster.

The rest of the students are lingering and chatting in the crowded halls. But not me. I head to my locker, bend, and grab my purse. If I knew I wouldn't trip over my three-inch wedges, I'd sprint out of here.

Just as I pull myself up from the bottom locker and turn around, I smack into that Bubby kid from Spanish.

"Whoa, Manhattan," he says, tilting his head to mirror mine. "This isn't New York. In Texas, we don't do the speed-walking thing. What's the hurry?"

I want to answer that I am trying to make the red-eye

back to New York, but that would involve carjacking and a four-hour road trip through Nowhereville. Oh, and I don't even have my license.

Instead I say, "Just going back to my grandparents' place," and try to move around Bubby.

"Are you going to do any clubs?" Bubby says as he blocks my path. "Today's sign-up day, and a lot of them are having informational meetings in the gym right now. I am on the newspaper staff."

Again, I bite my tongue because I am working on my filter. But all I can think is: *What* news is there in Broken Spoke? What happens here that's worth writing about?

I give my best fake smile. Thank you, cotillion.

"I appreciate you letting me know," I say. "But Texas is temporary for me. It's like a detour."

"Well, where's the final destination? And until you get there, I think you'd be good at newspaper, and I'm a reporter, so I should know. You could do a fashion column and give us some New York–girl tips. Like Carrie Bradshaw. My sister makes me watch *Sex and the City* reruns," Bubby says, and grins.

Oh, I could give some tips, I think. How about: a) keep the boots in the barn, b) keep the hairspray in the bottle, c) the '80s ended twenty years ago, and d) letter jackets aren't seasonally appropriate for August in Texas.

"Thanks, but no thanks," I say, and sidestep Bubby. If

I am forced to live here, the last thing I am going to do is get involved. That would be total surrender.

Heading straight for the door, I don't even say goodbye. In my head, I've already gone to my happy place. And Bubby, the final destination is anywhere but here.

Grandpa drops Tripp, Grandma, and me home because he has one more farm call.

Grandma rushes to the humid kitchen.

"Tomorrow's my day for treats at the office, kids. I need to make my specialty, Cowboy Cinnamon Bread," Grandma says as she takes five sticks of butter out of the fridge. "But first I'll make y'all an afternoon snack. How about peanut butter sandwiches?"

The thought of peanut butter makes my stomach rumble since I am starving from skipping lunch. But I shake my head just as Tripp enthusiastically nods his.

"Corrinne, it wasn't really a question. You need to get off that 'air' diet that your mother and her city friends seem to adore. Hunger doesn't look good on a woman. My parents didn't live through the Depression to see my grandchild choose skinny as a fashion statement."

I want to tell Grandma that the ten extra pounds on her hips don't exactly work with designer sizes, but I am pretty sure that comment might morph Grandma into a Furious Franny.

Grandma takes out Wonder white bread. The last

time I ate white bread I was in elementary school. It's like Mayor Bloomberg outlawed it along with the trans-fats. Grandma toasts, butters, and *then* peanut butters the bread. The sandwich gives my mouth the same tingles that the pancakes did. If only Grandma could find a little style, she could get her own Food Network show and get out of this town.

"How come my mom doesn't know how to cook, Grandma? Why didn't you teach her?" Tripp asks, and I can tell by my grandma's eyes that he's walking into a landmine.

"Some people just don't want to learn, Tripp. Do you and Corrinne want to see how to make Cowboy Cinnamon Bread?" Grandma pulls out a bowl and violently cracks four eggs into it.

"Yup," Tripp says, and moves closer to watch.

"And how was your first day of school, Tripp?" Grandma asks.

"Great. The kids are pretty cool. I need to get some cowboy boots. I was the only person in Top-Siders, so I felt lame."

"Don't let anyone judge you by your shoes, Tripp," Grandma says, which I think is hysterical. Grandma probably doesn't even know what Top-Siders are or how much they cost. But I guess there's no need for boat shoes in a desert.

I really don't want to help Grandma bake, but I also

don't have much homework, there's no cable, and calling Waverly will make me more depressed. She's in the Hamptons, and I am in hell. What would I even say about the first day of school? Imagine a horror movie merged with a reality show. And everyone survives, which makes it even scarier.

Grandma meticulously pours out four cups of sugar.

"So what exactly is Cowboy Cinnamon Bread besides a heart attack in loaf form?" I ask, watching her.

"Cowboy Cinnamon Bread is like a cinnamon bun, but it's bread. Toss in a few raisins and walnuts, and smother on a sugar glaze, and you'd think it's sent by the cherubs," Grandma says, licking the sugar off her finger. "Each lady in the office brings a treat one day of the week. I'm Tuesdays—used to be Thursdays, but then Dot retired and I switched to Tuesdays."

I can't imagine how women can eat like this every day. My friends' moms pride themselves on *not* eating. Waverly's mom is a big-time magazine editor at a *food* magazine, and she still looks like a toothpick with a head. The entire staff draws straws when someone has to go to a tasting for a recipe because no one *wants* to go. Everyone's that scared of getting fat. It's because staying skinny is a sport in New York. Apparently in Broken Spoke, baking yourself fat is the sport of choice—after football, of course.

"You don't need to help if you don't want to," Grandma

says. "I bet you have a lot of homework." I don't, but I figure Grandma must not want me around.

Since I got here, Grandma has been on me to unpack. "Denial isn't just a river in Egypt," she keeps saying. In my room I finally decide to hang up my clothes. Not because I am staying in Texas, but because I don't want my clothes to become permanently wrinkled. Back in New York, we had Maria, our housekeeper, to do this, but I might as well get used to it since there are no maids at Kent, so this will be good practice. Opening the so-called closet, I notice a box on the top shelf. It's all taped up and labeled STUFF I DON'T NEED.

I am a total snoop. I have been one ever since I found my Christmas gifts from Santa hidden in the oven. So the snoop in me thinks, Why not open the box?

Carefully, I rip off the tape. Inside the box, there are three folders, one red, one blue, and one yellow. They're pretty faded, so I imagine they must've been in this box a long time. Each one has a label in beautiful script. FLOWERS. DRESSES. FOOD. What are these? I open the FLOWERS one to find dozens of perfectly cut clippings of wedding flowers from some ancient *Bride* magazines. I open the DRESSES folder and several wedding-dress patterns fall out. Finally, in the FOOD folder, there are a bunch of recipes from *The Broken Spoke Daily News*: Candace Jean's

Pineapple Kebabs, Sarah Ann's Mushroom Turnovers, Adam's Ribs. And there are also photocopied recipes from *Betty Crocker's Cookbook*. In the margins, there are notes like "perfect for a bridesmaid lunch" and "perfect passing hors d'oeuvres." Reaching into the bottom of the box, I pull out one more yellowed clipping. It's a newspaper engagement announcement. It reads,

> *Mr. and Mrs. Billy Bo Houston proudly announce the engagement of Broken Spoke darling and Rodeo Queen Jenny Jo Houston to New York City investment banker Cole Corcoran the II. The pair met when Jenny Jo moved to New York to pursue a career in modeling. The Houstons are hosting the September 15 wedding at their home. As we all know, Mrs. Houston is a domestic wonder, so the wedding should be newsworthy.*

But my parents got married in New York City. I know this because I've seen the albums, all six of them. There was even an ice sculpture of my parents! According to my mom, in the 1990s, ice sculptures were the crème de la crème. My parents' wedding still gets referred to in bridal magazines as the one that changed marriage from a sacrament into a soiree. The late Evangeline Corcoran, my father's very rich mother, had no daughters, so she spared no expense on the lavish Plaza wedding for her favorite son, Cole. So if I add 1 + 1 + 1, I know that Grandma Houston had wanted a Broken Spoke wedding and didn't get it. *This* is what happened twenty years ago and *this* is what she and Grandpa had whispered about in the car from the airport. My mom chose a glamorous New York hotel wedding even though it seems her own mother had lovingly spent years clipping, plotting, and planning a hometown backyard wedding. Of course, I understand my mom's decision—who makes her daughter's wedding dress? That's so 1800s. I am sure Grandma knows how to sew, but why compete with Vera Wang? And who serves wings at a wedding? That's bar food. But still, I feel a bit bad for Grandma Houston, considering all her hard work. Even though my mother never tells this part of the story when recounting her wedding, this news is unfortunately just not blackmail worthy. I carefully put it away and tape the box back up.

I am totally depressed that this isn't the dirt I needed for a ticket to Kent. To cope, I find my iPod and earphones and listen to my most emo playlist. As I cram two suitcases' worth of clothes into a closet that must've been designed for doll clothes, I wallow in my misery. Just as I am wondering if anyone—even these emo rockers—have ever hurt as bad as me, I spin around to find Grandpa opening the door.

"Sorry, Corrinne, I didn't mean to startle you. I

knocked, but I don't think you heard." He points at my iPod. "You young people and your music. All tuned out of the world. The radio used to be something we shared. . . . Anyway, I want to hear more about your first day, and it's time for supper. Hurry now, because I have a surprise," Grandpa says, and winks obviously for about ten seconds. He looks like he has twitch.

Glancing at my watch, I see it's only ten minutes past five. I am not sure if this is an elderly thing or a Texas thing, but I can't imagine eating right now. Sighing, I take off my iPod and join everyone at the table anyway.

When we are all seated, Grandma says, "Let's say a prayer for the first day of school." She pauses and bows her head. "Thank you, God, for bringing us another school year and bringing us our grandchildren to share it with."

I mimic my grandma's gesture and look down at my plate. My parents don't do religion, and this dinner-table grace is the closest I've been to formally talking to God.

"Before we dig into Grandma's brisket and get all dirty, I have something to give Corrinne," Grandpa says, and he plucks a folded-up piece of paper out of his pocket. "I got this at the DMV."

The pamphlet reads, "Parent-Taught Driver Education Program." I am not sure what this means, so I look at Grandpa for an answer.

"In Texas, we teach our kids, or grandkids in our case,

to drive. And I taught your momma in Billie Jean the First and now I am going to teach you in Billie Jean the Second."

Hold on. I have no plans to get a license ever. Mostly because it's illegal to drink and drive. My only future automobile plans involve taxis and drivers, not pickup trucks with rust stains and Grandpa.

"Oh, Grandpa, thanks," I say. "But in New York, you don't need a license. We pay people to drive us."

"Corrinne," Grandma starts, "this isn't New York. You will get your license. We can't be driving you all over the place. And besides, women worked hard for all their rights, including the privilege to drive."

"You'll love it," Grandpa says as he tussles my hair. "You're just having first-time jitters."

Tripp's eyes get really big. "And then, Corrinne, when you get your license, me and you can go to Sonic!"

I smile at Tripp as I imagine shaking him, and I think the only place that I am heading if I get my license is due northeast. There will be no stops made at Sonic. Hey, maybe I should learn how to drive. . . . It might be my only escape route now that blackmail seems to be out of the picture. But I'll need to ditch Billie Jean the Second before I make it to Manhattan. Cruising New York's streets in a pickup truck would make for horrendous public relations. What if the paparazzi or my friends spotted me?

"First lesson will be Saturday, Corrinne," Grandpa says. "Eight a.m. sharp!"

"And Corrinne, you need to call your mother," Grandma says as she dishes out huge portions of something called brisket, which looks like a vegan's worst nightmare.

"Yes, Corrinne," echoes Grandpa, "I think she's lonely in the city with you kids in Texas and your dad in Dubai."

I try not to gasp. *She's* lonely. *She's* at home, surrounded by everything familiar—our apartment, the restaurants we go to, the shops we shop in, and the city that we love. And *she's* lonely? Please.

"Guess what, Corrinne?" Tripp says with a mouthful of brisket. "Mom says there might be a buyer for our New York apartment, and if there is, she's coming to the Spoke soon."

A buyer? Mom coming to Texas? I take a big breath. It's all really happening. This recession has destroyed my life. My sprawling apartment with its Hudson River views, my hunky doorman, and all my memories are being sold. And I am about to become roommates with my mother and not Waverly. There really will be no Kent, no Smith, no equestrian team, and no promising future. So much for my potential.

A single tear suddenly rolls down my face and splatters onto my plate. I quickly wipe my eye and blink frantically to stop more tears from falling.

Looking up, I see my grandpa staring at me with his kind brown eyes. Oh, *that's* where I get brown eyes. Thanks a lot, Grandpa!

"Cheer up, sunshine," Grandpa says. "This Friday is the Mockingbirds' first game."

I bite my lip hard enough to distract myself from tears and spear a blob of brown meat. What the hell is brisket, anyway?

P.R., pre-recession, I could've shopped my way out of this funk like the time that Carlton Sanders told everyone I kissed badly. Not enough tongue, he said. How much tongue did he want? Kissing shouldn't feel like a trip to the orthodontist. The shopping spree that followed lasted an entire weekend. I even went to *Brooklyn* to harvest their boutiques. And at the end of it, I *did* feel better, and my new wardrobe distracted everyone from Carlton's insane comments. But now, with my credit cards frozen, I can't even online-shop my way out of this.

Well, there's always greasy brisket, and like everything else from Grandma's kitchen, it's shockingly delicious. I hope I packed my sweats because I might need an elastic waistband soon.

Chapter 5

If That Mockingbird Doesn't Win, Broken Spoke's Going to Have a Breakdown

SOMEHOW, I MAKE IT TO FRIDAY, the football season opener. The chocolate-chip, apple, granola, and blueberry pancakes, the casseroles, the pound cake, the rhubarb pie, and the snickerdoodles—they all greatly helped me survive. I am going to need to cut this eating orgy out. Between eating at Grandma Sandy's Road-to-Diabetes kitchen and not having a gym or Sweetbread to ride, I am so not going to fit into my clothes by Thanksgiving. And it's not exactly like I can go shopping for new clothes because a) it's A.R., After the Recession, and b) where would I go?

Oprah is definitely onto something with that emotional-eating concept. When Oprah asks, "What are you truly hungry for?" my answer is: "I am starving for New York, for Barneys, for Bleecker boutiques, for dinners at Il Posto with friends, for sneaking into clubs, for getting ready for Kent, for falling in love with Smith, and for living the life I am supposed to be living. I am so hungry, Oprah." Perhaps I could get on her show as a guest: She could be my sponsor, right? I've seen her give away free cars. So why not restore people's lives to their rightful place?

And to make life worse, it's a Friday without a social itinerary except for a Saturday driving date with Grandpa in the a.m.

After Spanish class Kitsy approaches me.

"*Hola, Corrinne,*" Kitsy says, and moves from one foot to the other, "*¿Como estás?* Wait, I am talking in *español* after class? That's really lame. So anyways, what are you doing this weekend?"

I shrug, even though I know the answer: driving Billie Jean the Second and eating leftover brisket.

"Are you going to the game?" she asks.

I shake my head.

"To tell you a secret," she says, lowering her voice, "I get sick of football too, but I'm a Mockingbirdette, so I'm required to go. I'm sure you guessed that with me wearing the uniform and all."

I don't respond, but Kitsy keeps going.

"Anyways, the good part of game night is there's always a party afterward. If you want to go, find me."

For some inexplicable reason, I nod. Nodding, I believe even in Texas, is the universal sign for yes. I think the heat is going to my brain.

"Great," Kitsy says, and saunters away in her gray Mockingbirdette cheerleading uniform, holding her pompoms in one hand and her books in the other. Broken Spoke Question of the Day: Why does Kitsy bring her pom-poms to class? Best guess: so she can cheer effectively if there was ever an emergency situation.

Señor Luis must be forcing Kitsy to take me on as some charity project. Or maybe this is one of those teen movies where the kids lure the new student into some trap. Because on top of me and Kitsy having nothing in common, I gather that Kitsy's actually popular at Hairspray and Cowboy Boot High. Unlike me, she's not exactly lacking for friends, which makes her attention all the more confusing. Maybe she's looking for a free place to stay if she ever gets to Manhattan. But if our apartment sells, it looks like even I will be staying at a hotel.

Despite Grandma's protests against the unfair allocations of time and money on the football team, she still dons a steel-gray Mockingbird sweatshirt and hops into

Billie Jean the Second with Tripp, Grandpa, and me for the kickoff game.

"Of course I am going, Corrinne," Grandma says. "Season opener is like prom for the whole town. And everyone's been on me to make my Mockingbird cupcakes since last season ended."

And with good reason. Grandma's Mockingbird cupcakes beat out any of New York's famous Magnolia Bakery cupcakes: Each is a perfectly moist red velvet cake with a tiny lifelike mockingbird shaped out of mascarpone perched on top. Grandma has baked enough for the whole town and probably the rival town's team, the Bolston Bluebonnets, as well.

When we arrive at the game two hours before it's actually going to start, the entire parking lot's filled with people. It looks like a gray sea. Everywhere people are wandering around the parking lot, and every car's trunk is open and every pickup's tailgate is down. There are enough portable grills and coolers to feed and quench the entire state of Texas, the second largest state in America, mind you.

Tripp squeals, "Tailgating—just like on TV. Awesome. Dad promised to take me to a Jets game to tailgate even though he hates football, but, you know, work came up. This is way cooler than I thought."

Grandpa pulls into one of the last empty spots. Jumping out, Tripp hollers back to us, "Got to go find my friends. See you after the game."

Ah, so this is tailgating. The all-American ritual of hanging out in parking lots and eating unidentifiable grilled meats out of pickup trucks. In the city, we would never do this because we use cars to get from place to place, not as party furniture. The whole scene seems rather disgusting, and I hope that it forces me to lose my growing appetite.

I am relieved to see that the young people dress up somewhat for the event. Getting ready, I worried that my outfit—a soft gray linen dress with a pink cardigan—might be too extreme. Because I lack pride or any feelings other than hatred toward Broken Spoke, I had no desire to wear gray. But ultimately I decided there's no use in sticking out more than I already do, so I wore it anyway.

I need to iPhone this tailgate scene to my father in Dubai. Seeing me here might change his attitude. He says football is for meatheads; real gentlemen golf and play polo, games of skill, not brute force. I don't exactly agree, but I am willing to use anything to my advantage. Of course, the eight-hour time difference is making it a bit difficult to get ahold of him.

Since Tripp galloped off with his friends, I am left with Grandma, Grandpa, and their group of friends, which appears to include the entire town.

Grandma pulls me up to a large group of ladies wearing Mockingbird gear.

"Here, have a cupcake," Grandma says, and hands them out to the group. "I just know how y'all have been waiting for one. And this, this is my granddaughter, Corrinne. She's enrolled at Broken Spoke this fall. And her little brother, Tripp, is at the middle school. He bounded off with his new best friends. You'll recognize him; he's the one who looks like he belongs in a cereal commercial."

The entire group's eyes get big, almost in unison.

"Jenny Jo's daughter?" someone mutters in my direction.

"Last time I saw her was in *People* magazine at some gala," another one remarks.

"She's the one that got away," laments another.

"How is she?" one lady asks, and looks in my direction.

I don't know how to answer, so I just raise my shoulders and say, "You can ask her yourself; she'll probably be here in a few weeks."

And then the group chuckles, and again it is almost synchronized. Creepy.

"No way, Jenny Jo's not coming back to Broken Spoke ever," replies a heavyset lady wearing a red sweatshirt with a gray sequin mockingbird patched on.

I want to tell this woman that this is the fall of surprises. And if Corrinne is here in the Spoke, *Jenny Jo* better show up too.

At this point, Grandpa approaches the group, puts his arms around my shoulders, and saves me.

"How about we go taste some of Broken Spoke's finest BBQ?" he says, steering me away from the Gossiping Grannies.

And as we leave the group, I can hear my grandma yakking about recession this, recession that, and yes, twenty years is a long time.

With Grandpa and his buddies, I get to relive Broken Spoke's last State Championship season, game by game, play by play. Although it occurred fifty-two years ago, these men talk in the present tense as if it were days ago rather than a half century.

Grandma, Grandpa, and I eventually settle into front-row seats in the senior citizen section and the kick-off occurs. I sigh. Finally. An eerie, deadly silence takes over the Broken Spoke crowd until they score the first touchdown. I swear to you no one even breathes until the Mockingbirds are up by seven. Soon after, that kid Bubby from my Spanish class intercepts the ball and scores the second touchdown. Our section erupts into deafening applause; I've heard sirens that are more pleasing to the ears.

Grandpa points to number twenty, Bubby.

"You meet that boy yet, Corrinne?" Grandpa asks when the thunder of applause dies out. "They say he's going to make it big-time. Division one, Longhorn scholarship, maybe even the NFL one day. We haven't ever had a Spoker make it to the NFL. All talk right now, of course, but I think he's got it. Real good kid, too. Academic as well, so your grandmomma says. Way back when, your momma knew his father."

I don't tell Grandpa that he's the Neanderthal that calls me Manhattan, one of only two people at the whole school who talk to me. The game, despite the fact that I am the only teenager seated in the geriatric section, passes by quickly enough. For a few seconds, when the Spoke temporarily falls behind the Bluebonnets, I find myself clenching my fist, holding my breath, and praying that Broken Spoke wins. When I realize that I might actually care about the outcome of this barbaric game, confusion overcomes me. Newfound school spirit? Hardly. I chalk it up to the fact that this town's depressing enough; I am not sure what a loss would do to it.

After the game, I see Kitsy skipping, yes skipping, toward the grandparents and me as she pumps one white pom-pom up and down. I wonder what kind of uppers she is on and if she can get me some.

"Can you believe it, Corrinne? Big win. Huge win. And did you see those lame Bonnets totally mess up their cheer? Amateurs. You ready to go? Oh, excuse my manners. I've seen y'all around town, but we've never actually met. I am Kitsy Kidd, and it's very nice to meet you, Mr. and Mrs. Corcoran."

"Houston," Grandma quickly corrects. "Mr. and Mrs. Houston."

"Hello, Miss Kitsy," Grandpa says. "Any chance you are related to Amber Kidd?"

Kitsy pauses. "She's my mom," Kitsy says quietly, and bends down to tie her shoe.

Grandma nudges Grandpa in an obvious way, and I feel myself blush even though I don't care what Kitsy thinks of me or my grandparents' manners.

Kitsy stands up tall and takes a deep breath. "I promise that I am very responsible. My boyfriend, Hands, the quarterback, is an excellent driver. Corrinne will get home at a reasonable hour, and I'll see to it. I can't believe Corrinne's from New York City. I have never met a New Yorker before and want to hear what it's really like versus how it is in the movies. Someday I am going to move there. Or I hope so."

Grandpa steps forward, shakes Kitsy's hand, and says, "I didn't realize that Corrinne had made such a nice friend."

"And I didn't know that you were going anywhere, Corrinne. We haven't even discussed a curfew yet," Grandma says as her eyes trace Kitsy's frame.

Curfew? I wouldn't even know how to convert New

York time to Texas time. After all, they eat dinner at five p.m. here. Does that mean I need to be home by nine thirty p.m.?

"I'll get her home by twelve, ma'am," Kitsy says. I want to laugh. Midnight? Really? That was my middle school curfew.

"All right, Corrinne. I have your cell number, so go off with your friend. Try to have some fun," Grandpa says, and Grandma turns to him, opens her mouth, but then closes it.

"No drinking, Corrinne," Grandma yells.

I say nothing. Actually, I have said nothing during this exchange, and now Kitsy's dragging me by the hand toward a very tall football player with reddish hair and his perfectly waxed banana yellow two-door pickup truck. I wonder what his truck is named. Yellow Submarine?

"I'm Hands, Kitsy's boyfriend," he says. "You must be Corrinne. Kitsy keeps yapping about you. '*Hands,* there's a new girl from New York City. *Hands,* she's like a real-life *Gossip Girl. Hands,* I want to be her friend.' Kitsy's seriously obsessed with all things New York, including you."

And then he extends his hand, still sweaty from the game, and I suddenly understand the name: His right hand alone is the size of a large pizza pie.

Hands opens the door for me, which is something Grandpa always does too.

"Let's get wasted," Kitsy says, and jumps in after me. "You drink, right?"

Wow, I thought Kitsy was a front-row do-gooder. At least it turns out the one person who likes me in Texas takes me to parties rather than study groups.

Driving down dirt road after dirt road, I can barely believe that this is still Broken Spoke. And my bladder keeps jiggling. There'd better be a bathroom when we get there. Or maybe a magical Starbucks will pop up out of nowhere; they always have bathrooms.

Finally, Hands turns on his high beams as he pulls into a field where a bonfire is raging and about half a dozen trucks are already parked. *Not another tailgate.* And there's not even a Porta-Potty in sight.

"Is this like the pre-party before the house party?" I ask Kitsy. "I really have to go to the bathroom," I whisper.

Kitsy moves her index finger in a circle. "*This* is the party," she says.

I try not to let my mouth gape open.

"Not to worry, I always carry TP in my purse," Kitsy says.

"TP?" I ask as Kitsy starts digging around in her bag.

"Toilet paper," she says as she hands me a wad. "I'll take you to the woods."

Woods? I am not about to pee on my satin heels; they cost four hundred dollars, and I don't know when I can get another pair. They sold out within hours of going on sale.

"Don't worry, Corrinne," she says, catching me staring at my shoes. "I'll show you the cowgirl method."

I look down at my iPhone: no service. I can't call Waverly, I can't call Dubai, I can't call Grandma and Grandpa, and I can't even call 911. So I guess I will have to pee in the woods, cowgirl style. My parents will have to pay for my hypnosis; I can't live life with these memories.

Kitsy takes her pom-poms in one hand, grabs my wrist with the other, and drags me toward the woods. I find out that the cowboy method means throwing one leg on a fallen tree branch and squatting like a ballerina. Hopefully, no one can see the other full moon—mine—in the night sky. But no pee winds up on my heels or my leg, so I guess the method works. This would so get you arrested in the city though!

"Beer time," Kitsy says when we reemerge from the woods.

Beer? Does Kitsy have any idea how many carbs are in that? I can't handle any more carb overloads after everything I've been eating at Grandma's. But with only kegs in sight, I follow her. Bubby is filling up red plastic cups.

"Manhattan," Bubby says. "Didn't think I'd see you here. I thought you'd have some private jet waiting to whisk you to the Hamptons for a white party."

"I summer in Nantucket," I correct him. "Anyway, it's

now totally acceptable to wear white after Labor Day, so white parties are kind of over."

"What's a Nantucket?" Kitsy wants to know.

Bubby hands me a cup with no foam. Apparently, he's done this keg thing before.

"Nantucket's an island for rich people, Kitsy. So Manhattan, what's a girl like you doing in Texas? Is this like rehab for you?" Bubby says.

I gulp down the beer. It tasks like urine, which is just perfect since I probably smell like urine after the woods. "Yup, rehab." Holding my cup in the air, I tip it toward him. "Cheers."

Kitsy winks at me. "Corrinne's just spending some time with her grandparents, but you seem awfully interested. You wouldn't be sweet on the new girl, would you?"

Sweet on? Is that like Texan for having a crush? I wouldn't even accept Bubby's virtual friendship much less let him be sweet on me. Not that there's anything *sweet* about me.

"Kitsy, Manhattan's a bit uptight for me. I prefer a cowgirl," Bubby says, and pours me out another beer.

I decide *not* to tell Bubby that I've already learned the cowgirl method about five minutes ago. Taking the cup from Bubby cautiously, I remind myself to take it slow, or I'll have to go to the woods again.

"And I prefer gentlemen," I say, which is a lie since

I've never met a gentleman in my life. My past love interests thought offering pills to go with my cocktail counted as a grand romantic gesture. Smith was supposed to be my first gentleman, but this fall is turning out to be the season of supposed-to-bes. I was supposed to have a life of potential, supposed to go to Kent, supposed to room with Waverly. I was supposed to make out with Smith.

"So why don't you guys have house parties?" I ask, turning my head both ways to look at this so-called party, which more accurately resembles a grassy parking lot.

"*We guys* don't have houses big enough for house parties. Even if we did, our parents are home. There isn't much to do in Broken Spoke after nine p.m. It's a dry county, you know. So most of the parents that aren't beating the Bible in their living rooms are drinking alone in their living rooms. *Not* exactly the kind of parties we'd want to crash. Besides, the field's cool. Teams have partied here for years," Bubby says, and I look around to realize that I am the only one not in a Mockingbirdette uniform or Mockingbird football jersey.

Broken Spoke and the city couldn't be more different. Here, the parents' social lives revolve around the kids and their sports. Everyone in the town was at that game tonight. There were generations upon generations rooting for the kids. In Manhattan, parents can barely make their kids' extracurriculars fit into their overscheduled work and social schedules. And on the weekends, most parents often stay out as late, if not later, than their children. But I guess it makes sense that Broken Spoke is different. No wonder Bravo's not rushing to film *The Real Housewives of Broken Spoke.*

"I am going to leave you lovebirds at the watering fountain." Kitsy says. "I've got to find Hands."

And Kitsy, with her pom-poms, scampers off toward Hands, who's still throwing around the football with a couple of jocks by the fire.

I want to run away, but heels aren't good for that—even if they are Nike Air Cole Haans—and I have no idea where I am. This field with only kegs, trucks, and a few pine shrubs makes Broken Spoke look like a metropolis.

Bubby pulls down the tailgate of a truck and sits on the edge.

"Take a seat," he says.

I hand him my cup and try to gracefully push myself up, but my arm muscles fail me. Bubby reaches down, clasps my hand, and pulls me up easily.

"So, Texas isn't some sort of Manhattan princess rehab thing. Why are you really here, then?" Bubby asks, and turns his head to make eye contact. "Not exactly a place where many people decide to relocate."

That's for sure, especially not by free will, I think.

"My grandparents live here. My grandpa said that your

dad actually knew my mom. She grew up here. J.J. Corcoran? I mean, Jenny Jo Houston?" I say.

"No way. Your mom is Jenny Jo Houston?" Bubby
bends forward and lets out a belly laugh. "I can't wait to
tell the old man. I've been hearing stories about Jenny Jo
since I first started throwing the pigskin with my dad. You
ever see their prom pictures?"

"Whose prom pictures?" I ask.

"Your mom never told you?" Bubby asks back.

"Told me what?" I reply. This kid is beginning to
weird me out.

"Your mom. My dad. They dated, like, all of high
school, and then some," Bubby says, and drains the rest
of his beer.

The thought of my mom dating anyone, let alone this
hick's dad, makes me almost spew my beer. I swallow hard
to keep it down.

"Um, my mom doesn't talk much about Texas. I never
visited Broken Spoke before, like, ten days ago," I respond.
"And it wasn't exactly something I planned on ever doing."

"Yeah, I know that part of the story too. Some banker
guy swept your mom off her feet when she was modeling
in New York. The story goes that she always thought she
was too good for this town. Or at least that's what my dad
says, but he could just be bitter."

Yes, my mom *is* too good for this town. So am I, but it's

not exactly like I have anyone else to talk to here, so I filter.

Or rather, I semi-filter.

"Hold on. I am not usually in the business of coming to my mom's defense since she's the whole reason that I am in this *hellhole*. But it's not your place to be talking about someone you don't know."

"So what happened, then, Corrinne?" Bubby says, making eye contact.

"I said she doesn't talk about Texas, and I am beginning to see why."

I scoot toward the edge of the tailgate so I can hop down, find Kitsy, and get out of this place. So much for this party!

But Bubby blocks me by sticking his arm out. "Why exactly are you here, Corrinne? It's obviously not to make friends."

"I don't know if you guys have newspapers other than your silly school one, but the country's in a recession. New Yorkers are having a particularly tough time. We are the home to Wall Street, after all."

"Oh yes, that recession. Go ask a couple of kids over by the fire if they've heard about it," Bubby says, pointing across the field. "Farming's been in recession for decades. And they closed the farm equipment factory over two years ago. It used to be the biggest employer in town. But there are no plans for a new factory. Our economy is not like the stock market; it can't just bounce back up when people hear some good news. We're used to bad news here in Broken Spoke. Not that a princess like you would know anything about Main Street and how it is."

"Excuse me, my father lost his job because of the recession and we lost all of our savings in a scam, so don't say I don't know anything about bad news," I say, crossing my legs to face away from Bubby.

And it's the first time, I realize, that I have said the truth out loud. To Waverly, I only implied it, and I lied to everyone else. It feels strangely cathartic, so I continue. "And my father had to move to Dubai—that's, like, practically in Iraq—for another job."

"Tough life, Corrinne. By the way, Dubai is in the United Arab Emirates. It's like the Las Vegas of the Middle East—not exactly a war-torn country. Not that I would expect you to know that since you obviously don't have any idea about anything aside from your Prada shoes and Gucci sunglasses. You only see the small picture, the self-portrait." And with that, Bubby releases me. "Go ahead, go. You've already made up your mind about this town and its people. No need for you to be here."

At least we agree on something, I think, before I quickly shove off the edge. I want to add that they aren't Prada heels, they are Cole Haans, and I am not wearing any sunglasses, much less my Gucci pair. I decide not to bother.

Just because I have to live in Broken Spoke doesn't mean I have to mix with its locals.

Marching to the keg, I pour myself another beer.

I am so angry, my filter has disappeared, so I decide to go for the final last word. "The reporter act is lame, by the way," I say from the keg. "Go back to just playing football."

"Actually," Bubby says as he comes down from the truck, "I like reporting. I learned pretty early on that your dreams don't usually work out. I could blow my knees and have nothing. So I am pretty conscious to use my brain as well. It's something you should try more often yourself."

I open my mouth to answer, but no words come out, so I walk as slowly and steadily as I can to Kitsy.

"Kitsy," I ask quietly, "can we go?"

"Ohmigod," Kitsy says, "I am a terrible friend. I haven't even introduced you to anyone. There're a bunch of people over there. Let's go talk to them. I thought you were having fun with Bubby; he's totally sweating you. Everyone agrees. Here, I'll introduce you now. I am so sorry."

"It's just that I don't feel well," I start, and hold my stomach. This is true: I feel like I am dying. I hate my life, and now one of the only two people that I know in this godforsaken town hates me for no reason.

"Oh, of course, Corrinne," she says, "Ugh, I am sorry.

I thought this would be fun. I'll get Hands. He doesn't drink 'cause he hates being hungover at eight a.m. practice. He can take us home."

Eight a.m. Oh yes, I have driving lessons with Grandpa. There is yet another circle of hell; someone should tell Dante. I finish my beer and throw the cup on the ground.

"Thanks, Kitsy," I say, and I mean it. She really is a nice girl. Maybe when I get out of this place, I'll raise some money to get Kitsy out too. She's too good for the field, the Spoke, all of this.

After a bumpy truck ride home, I tiptoe into my grandparents' house, where I drunkenly eat three Mockingbird cupcakes, which does nothing good for my queasy stomach. Hiding under my covers in my room, I call Waverly three times: no answer. I don't leave any messages. I am embarrassed to even tell my best friend how pathetic my life has become.

Chapter 6

Her Name Was Billie Jean,
She Caused a Scene

MY IPHONE WAKES ME UP TO THE SONG "DOWNTOWN." *You can forget all your troubles, forget all your cares, and go downtown.*

Never was there a truer song, I think. If I could just somehow make it back to downtown. At the very least, I need to go back to bed. My head's pounding. Nothing is worse than a hangover when you didn't even have an ounce of fun or a remotely good story to make up for it. Wasted calories, too. I feel like a marching band is using my head for a bass drum and using baseball bats as drumsticks. And I can't exactly ask Grandma and Grandpa for some Advil. It would be a bit Captain Obvious that I am Hangover Harriet, especially after Grandma told me not to drink.

"Corrinne," Grandpa beckons through the door, "breakfast is on the table. Don't forget, driving lesson afterward."

What I need: three more hours of sleep and a long brunch with Waverly, followed by a bad-reality-TV marathon. What I don't need: a driving lesson with Grandpa.

I figure my pajamas will work for driving clothes. While I am not usually into that whole the-homeless-look-is-the-new-chic mentality, I can't bear to style an outfit with percussions playing in my head.

Diner smells invade my nostrils as soon as I step out of the door. Tripp's already digging into the mountains of scrambled eggs, bacon, and sausage.

"Corrinne," Tripp says, "Grandpa calls it the Saturday Sensational Special. *Way* better than any diner. Grandma, you need to open a restaurant."

At Tripp's comment, Grandma, for the first time since I arrived, beams. "Stop talking silly. I can just follow a recipe."

Grandpa carefully folds up his newspaper. "Don't be so modest. You could open a restaurant. We'll call it Sandy's Sensations. I can be the dishwasher." Grandpa then chucks the paper in the recycle bin. "Corrinne, how was that party? Meet any nice young fellows?"

"Yeah, Corrinne, next time can I go with you?" Tripp asks with a piece of bacon still in his mouth.

"There's not going to be a next time, Tripp. I had a

miserable time. If you don't mind, Grandpa, I am too homesick for driving lessons." Homesick, hungover, and hungry for New York. This is all true. At least I have my bacon and eggs.

I fall into my seat, somehow resisting an overwhelming urge to put my head onto my plate.

Grandma moves from the kitchen stove to the table and looks me in the eyes. "Corrinne, your grandfather cleared his day for this. You *will* be learning how to drive." She unfastens her apron. "I am not sure how it is in the city, but here we have manners. When someone offers you a favor, you accept graciously."

Staring at the shag, Brady Bunchesque carpet, I do not dare to look up at Grandma. "Yes, ma'am," I say.

I am not accustomed to being yelled at, and I am not sure how my grandmother thinks she can get away with telling me what to do. Mental reminder: Dial my dad on this one. The one and only time in my life I was ever punished lasted for ten minutes because my father came home and said, "She's just a child, J.J. We both hated our parents for disciplining us like that. Let's be different." And since then, my mom and dad have been what my economics teacher would call laissez-faire parents.

Grandpa picks up his keys off the table and jingles them.

"Sandy Jean, I think Corrinne's just tired. Don't

worry, Corrinne," Grandpa says. "We'll only do a half day to start. Your momma took out two mailboxes on her first day, so I am a veteran at this."

Grandma looks like she's about to start on me again. I am desperate to get out of this house and away from her.

So I smile and say, "I am nervous. There have been a lot of surprises in the past month. I just never imagined this day."

Or this life, I add in my head. Hey, I am getting better at this filtering thing.

"I know, honey," Grandpa says, and he pats my head. "Eat some food; we'll leave in ten."

I pile a ton of food onto my plate. Hopefully, grease can cure this hangover. I look for a coffeepot, hoping caffeine will soothe my headache. Normally I drink skinny mocha lattes with three Splendas, but I would take anything right now, even just plain black generic coffee.

"Is there coffee?" I ask.

Grandma stares at me as if I just asked her for meth to give a baby.

"Corrinne, caffeine is a drug. I can't believe that your mother would permit you to drink coffee. Well, I *can* believe it, but I won't tolerate it here," my grandmother scolds.

I don't tell her that coffee is the new water for successful New Yorkers. Although Grandma has *no* problem clogging my arteries, it appears I will not be getting a cup of Joe to help me over this hangover. So I am going to learn to drive in a rusty, blue pickup truck named Billie Jean the Second while I am hungover, tired, and miserable. My life keeps finding ways to suck exponentially more each day.

Grandpa drives Billie Jean the Second to some deserted dirt road by a bunch of cattle farms. I am relieved to see the cattle are fenced in. The last thing I need to deal with is mad cows.

"Okay, Corrinne, let's get out, switch spots, and go through the basics."

And so for the first time in my life, I sit in the driver's seat as Grandpa details the truck's anatomy: the third pedal, the gearshift, the RPM dashboard, and the red line. Can't someone invent iStick that will do this all for you? All the pedals at my feet feel like potential land mines. One wrong move and it will all be over. . . .

Grandpa must've recognized the confusion on my face because he places his hand on my forearm and says, "You know, Corrinne, very few people, and fewer women, drive stick these days."

And then Grandpa theatrically wags his finger at me. "Someday, you are going to impress the dickens out of a man with your beauty, your smarts, and your dry sense of humor. And then he'll propose on the spot when you tell him that you drive a stick."

I smile at Grandpa and laugh. "I think boys are into different stuff than they used to be."

"Not the good ones," Grandpa says. "You ready for this? Remember, you won't go anywhere unless you work the clutch."

"If my friends could only see me now . . ."

And just when I think I know what I am doing, my mind goes blank. Do I put my foot on the brake then the clutch? And which one is neutral on the gearshift? There are too many numbers on it; it's like a math test. Since I am not one to ask for directions, I just fumble my foot on the clutch and I quickly shift into what I think is first gear.

Errrereg! Billie Jean the Second lets out what must be a truck's equivalent to a human's scream for bloody murder, and then we lurch forward before we sputter to a stop. I lean my head on the wheel . . . and then of course, Billie Jean the Second honks back. Ugh! Screw my life, screw driving, and screw you, Billie Jean the Second.

"Grandpa, I don't want to do this," I whine with my hands over my face. "What just happened?"

Grandpa is actually laughing as if this were funny. "You just stalled, Corrinne; it happens to every beginner. You can't start in third gear, sweetie; you have to start in neutral."

Grandpa points to the correct position on the gearshift.

"Billie Jean won't let you get ahead of yourself, that's why you stalled. Now let's try it again."

"Try it again?" I balk. I am looking out the window, estimating how far the walk is back to the grandparents' or even better, New York. I am pleased that Converses came back in style last summer, and I am even happier that I am wearing them now. Checking out the door handle, I wonder if Grandpa would try to chase me. I hope I don't give him a heart attack.

"Corrinne," Grandpa says, holding up his index finger. "Just one more try and then you can give up. Remember, start in neutral, then move her to first." Grandpa pantomimes the action.

It looks hot and dusty outside, and I worry that a cow might charge me. With the way that people eat beef here, the cattle must be plotting for revenge.

I have done stupider things than try stick more than once. Like how Waverly and I steal a golf cart every summer in Nantucket and get caught every summer so we can flirt with the caddies. Given that record for repeat mistakes, I figure I should at least try again. And I do everything just like Grandpa said, clutch, neutral, first, gas.

Screech! After Billie Jean the Second lurches to a more horrifying stop than the first time, she even starts to smoke from underneath. I am positive that the car's on fire, and I look at Grandpa with panicked eyes. Maybe now he'll realize how teaching a city girl country tricks is a bad idea. I quickly unbuckle my seat belt. I am ready to stop, drop, and roll out of the car.

But Grandpa doesn't move an inch. He just remains buckled in.

"This one is my fault, Corrinne," he says calmly. "I forgot to tell you less is more. You only want to use a teensy bit of gas. It goes a looong way. Don't worry. It's just smoke," Grandpa says, looking out the window, where the smoke is slowly disappearing.

"What about that saying, where there's smoke, there's fire?" I ask, looking out my window for flames.

"Oh, Billie Jean just likes blowing off some steam. No worries," Grandpa says. "Okay, Corrinne, one more time. I promise I won't ask you to do it again. Remember, clutch, neutral to first, and a tiny bit of gas."

I roll my eyes at Grandpa. There's a reason that even professional drivers like cabbies drive automatic. Shouldn't we just quit now and be happy that the car never exploded?

But Grandpa just smiles at me and says, "Come on, Corrinne, a city girl like you is afraid of an old lady like Billie Jean?"

Talking about the car as if she were human is just getting creepy. I rebuckle my seat belt, fumble for the clutch, release it, slowly go neutral to first, and give the gas pedal a tiny tap. And I realize that I am moving. Holy shit,

I—well, Billie Jean—is moving.

"Grandpa, Grandpa," I yelp with my white knuckles gripping the steering wheel. "What next? Help me."

Grandpa laughs and laughs. "Okay, step on her and take her to second, remember just a tiny bit of gas," he says.

"I am scared," I say, and I find my knee shaking.

"You are going seven miles an hour." Grandpa slaps his knee and shakes his head. No wonder taxis are always honking and swearing. This is fricking terrifying.

I look down at the joystick—gearshift, whatever it's called—and move it to second. A huge dust bowl swirls up behind me.

"Great, girl, great. You're a natural," Grandpa says. "Now let's get this baby to thirty miles an hour."

And I did. Apparently, there is a bit of rhythm to this whole stick thing.

Grandpa yells above Billie Jean's engine, "Roll down the windows. Feel what flying is like."

Now it isn't exactly like taking a heli to the Hamptons or skydiving in the Alps when I went to Europe, but it isn't all horrible. With the windows down, my hair swirls in the wind as Billie Jean the Second soars her way down the country road.

"Okay," Grandpa yells, "stop this girl on a dime. The clutch, downshift, and then the brake!" Somehow, I manage to follow his directions in the right sequence, and with the jerk of a taxicab, Billie Jean the Second comes to a sudden halt and a brown dust cloud surrounds the car. Thank God for seat belts.

"That was cool, Grandpa," I say, breathing for the first time since Billie Jean the Second took flight. "I can't wait to tell my dad. I don't think he knows how to drive stick." Because he grew up in the city, my dad didn't even get his license until he graduated college.

"Your daddy's got many fine qualities, even if he doesn't know how to drive stick. I feel bad for him, though. It's one of the simple pleasures of life, driving stick on the open road." Grandpa reaches for the ignition and turns it off. "You doing okay, sweetheart? I know that you miss your parents. Was the party really that bad?"

I don't want to disappoint my grandfather and tell him that I miss shopping more than I miss my parents. Or that the party was worse than a school dance with your own mother as a chaperone. Luckily, my mom only did that to me once. Two weeks of silent treatment and she learned her lesson.

"It was kind of bad," I say, and frown. "That Bubby kid is a loser. Did you know that my mom actually dated his dad? My mom never mentioned any of this."

Although I don't say it in front of Grandpa, my mom rarely mentions anything about Texas, including her own father. I feel a bit nauseous thinking of my mom dating anyone but my dad. I don't even like to see my own parents kiss. But I am nosy and I need to know the details.

"Bubby's probably just tainted by his father's teenage broken heart. His daddy really loved your momma," Grandpa says, and looks away out the passenger-side window.

I guess this is awkward for him, too.

"Dusty even loved her enough to tell her to go to New York and try out the modeling thing. I think he thought she'd be back though. Spokers who leave, the few that do, they come back," Grandpa says, still looking out the window.

I seriously wonder if they drug Broken Spokers immediately after birth. Who would leave this place and then come back? I wonder if there is a cult here that I don't know about. I'll have to be extra careful around any Kool-Aid. But I use my filter since Grandpa's been nice and patient, even though I almost killed him and Billie Jean the Second twice today. . . . And my mom had a boyfriend named Dusty? If page six only knew . . .

"Dusty?" I start to cackle until my head feels dizzy again. "My mom dated a *Dusty*. And then broke his heart? Really?"

I almost snort, which reminds me that I have forgotten what it feels like to laugh.

"I always thought Mom was boring as a teenager. I didn't know that she dated, let alone was some high school heartbreaker."

I pause and think how to phrase this.

"When Mom does actually talk about Texas, she makes it out like she was the perfect girl who never did anything wrong, who never hurt anybody."

"Dustin's his full name," Grandpa says as he fidgets with the radio. "Your momma was quite . . . well, quite exciting, though Grandma didn't always think exciting was a good thing. Boring girls don't move from Broken Spoke to New York to become models, Corrinne."

"Is that why Grandma's mad?" I ask as Grandpa flips from one country music station to the next. "Because Mom left you guys behind to become a model?"

"No," Grandpa says. "The modeling was your grandma's idea. She always wanted more for Jenny Jo, until she found out that getting those things meant leaving us and Broken Spoke behind forever. Grandma's not mad just at your mother, she's also mad at herself for pushing Jenny Jo to go." Reaching over the stick shift, Grandpa turns up the radio really loud.

"Really?" I shout over the radio, trying to put these details together. All my life, I thought it was my mom who carefully concocted her escape from Texas and that's why she never talked about it. I knew she came to New York to model, but she only did a few catalogues for swimsuits. "Didn't have the heart for it," she always said. I thought she meant she couldn't take the constant rejection like you

see on shows like *America's Next Top Model,* where even your forehead is never perfect enough. But maybe Mom quit because it wasn't her dream ever—it was Grandma's.

"Really, sweetie," Grandpa says, turning down the radio. "Your momma cried like a baby the whole way to the airport when she left. She was twenty-one, and I felt like she was my little girl leaving for the first day of kindergarten again. Dusty cried the whole way back to Broken Spoke. Men don't usually cry in front of other men." Grandpa focuses his attention back on the radio. "Enough of the past though. The past is the past. Let's find a good driving song."

I didn't feel like driving at that moment. My mom crying? She never cries. She didn't even cry A.R., After the Recession. And crying because she didn't want to leave her parents, Dusty, and Broken Spoke? Who was this Jenny Jo Houston? When I leave, I am not going to even look out of the rearview window.

Grandpa opens up the glove compartment, and he pulls out what I believe is called a cassette. "I found this in Billie Jean the First before I sold her. It's your momma's old mix tape. I haven't listened to it in years."

"I only know what a mix tape is from eighties movies," I say. "Let's hope it's not a makeout sound track."

Thinking about my mother making out makes me want to puke. Turning toward the passenger seat, I see that Grandpa's blushing too. Filter, Corrinne. Filter.

"You know what song this is?" I ask, changing the conversation.

"It's her song," he answers, and turns up the volume.

"Mom's?" I ask.

"No," he says. "Michael Jackson's 'Billie Jean.' Oh, Jenny Jo, how she couldn't get enough of this song. She even named the truck after the song and she'd make me drive around town while we listened to it over and over," Grandpa says. "And this is back before there was a repeat button. We'd listen once and then have to rewind it to listen again. She'd dance for hours in the kitchen and it drove Grandma crazy because she danced a lot more than she helped cook and clean."

"Danced?" I repeat. I've never seen my mom even sway.

Grandpa laughs.

"There are lots of things you don't know about Jenny Jo," he says. "And I reckon there's a lot she doesn't know about you."

He jingles the key chain—a longhorn, University of Texas mascot charm.

"Let's get Billie going again because she hates to idle, especially when we're playing her song," Grandpa says.

Grandpa even lets me put her into fourth. And when I do, he holds his hand out for a high five.

I might even miss him a little when I wake up from this nightmare.

Grandpa drives back since he didn't think I was quite ready for the *one* stoplight in town or interference from other cars. In fact, I never actually made a right- or left-hand turn, but I still can't wait to text Waverly about driving. For once, since I arrived in Texas, she might be jealous of me.

Tripp's skateboarding in the driveway when we arrive home. Leaving his board behind, he runs toward the car.

"Hey, Corrinne," Tripp says, sticking his head through the car window. "How many accidents did you get in? Next time, I am coming with you, but I will wear this for protection." Tripp knocks on his helmet. "Someone in this family needs to have brains that work."

I ignore the brains comment.

"No helmet required," I say. "I am an excellent driver—even Grandpa thinks so."

Grandpa nods at Tripp. "It's true, especially for a city girl. Tripp, what did you and Grandma do today?"

"We went grocery shopping, and I am going to the skate park to meet up with friends later. That's why I'm practicing. And guess what?" Tripp says, and raises his eyebrows.

"What?" Grandpa indulges.

"I learned what we're called." Tripp smiles like he's in a TV commercial. "A grandfamily. I heard it on the *Today* show."

"Grandfamily," Grandpa repeats. "I like that, Tripp." Turning to me, Grandpa says, "Great job, Corrinne. Next time we are going to take her on a spin to Main Street."

I smile, get out of the car, and walk into the house. Grandma's at the stove, baking something that smells like Dylan's Candy Bar on the Upper East Side. I feel friendly enough to give her a wave and a "Smells great" before darting into my room, where I find my phone. Four new texts.

Mom: Call me. I miss you.

Dad: How's my little girl? I hope you are being good for your grandparents.

Waverly: How's my cowgirl? Sorry I missed you last night. Beach party, totally wasted. College guys. Wish you were here.

Waverly: You'll never guess who just Facebooked me. *Smith!!* How's the plan to still make it to Kent? Time is running out. I don't want a weirdo for a roommate.

Smith never even responded to my message about "my year abroad." And now he's moved on to my best friend? Besides why would Waverly tell me that when she knows

I claimed him first? Sometimes I feel like she's missing a sensitivity chip.

I turn from feeling like a Driving Diva to a Deflated Debbie. I know that calling Waverly would just be a sink-hole into a deeper depression. I'd have to hear about her actually exciting life; then I'd remember that Driving Miss Billie Jean the Second isn't remotely thrilling unless you are an ex-Manhattanite trapped in small-town hell.

Lying down on my bed, I glance at my nightstand picture of Waverly and me at the beach in Nantucket. And my mind drifts back to this past summer.

Click, clack, click, clack, echoes through the entryway.

"That must be Waverly," my mom says.

And I roll my eyes. Of course it's Waverly. Some people make their presence known with a signature scent, like my friend Sarita, who goes through a bottle of Gucci Rush a month. You can smell her from blocks away. It's Waverly's gold charm bracelets, stacked up her arm, that announce her arrival. She has a charm for her first step (a foot), her first day of school (an apple), and even her first kiss (lips). She's only fifteen, and she already has four charm bracelets. By the time she's ready for college, she'll have run out of room on her wrists and need to wear charm anklets, except Waverly would never wear something that tacky.

"I am here," Waverly says, emerging into our blue and

white living room. She's wearing Bermuda shorts and a cardigan. For being totally un-conservative (she got that first kiss at eleven), she dresses more like a mother who summers than a girl who summers.

"Did you miss me, Mrs. Corcoran?" Waverly asks.

My mom fakes wiping sweat from her brow. "Those four hours you were gone were unbearable, Miss Waverly."

"I missed you, Waverly," Tripp says, looking up from his lighthouse puzzle. Of course Tripp would do a puzzle. He even started the chess club at his school. If he weren't so good-looking, I'd be sure that he was switched at birth.

"Okay, Mom," I say, standing up from the rocking chair. "We're going to touch up our makeup, and then we are going to bounce."

"Wait, Corrinne," my mom says. "Maybe you girls would like to have some lemonade first and then tell me exactly where you are bouncing to." My mom stands up and heads to the kitchen.

"Mom," I say, "I don't drink lemonade. Empty calories. Besides, the island is only fourteen miles long. Does it matter where we are bouncing to?"

Waverly just gives her best parent smile and says, "Aren't you going to the Barefoot Gala?"

My mom looks down at her jeans and white T-shirt. "Nope, Waverly, my date is working, so I am going to take it easy with Tripp."

The truth is that my mom's not much for galas. Despite being beautiful and glamorous, she's always sidestepping opportunities to hobnob. I think growing up in small-town Texas socially stunted her. Other Manhattan parents have known one another since the days of elite nursery school.

"Oh!" Waverly says. "My mother will be so disappointed. She hasn't seen much of you this summer!"

I lock eyes with my mom: We know that the only thing that disappoints Mrs. Dotts is when someone is slow to refill her drink.

Holding up the pitcher, my mom asks, "Are you sure about the lemonade?" Waverly and I shake our heads.

"Okay, no lemonade. I got it. You are too old for that. But I do remember just a few summers ago when you and Waverly made a killing with your lemonade stand."

"Ugh, don't remind me. We were so juvenile," I say, thinking back to our curbside stand where we harassed every biker and jogger into paying a dollar for a cup of Country Time Lemonade.

"Hey, Mom," Tripp says. He doesn't even bother to look up from the puzzle, which he's completing in record time. "Can I do a lemonade stand?"

"Sure, Tripp," Mom says.

Waverly tucks her long, blond hair behind her ear. "Good luck, Tripp. No one's going to buy lemonade in this shaky economy, even from a heartthrob like you."

Tripp immediately blushes, highlighting his already apple-colored cheeks.

"C'mon, Waverly," I say, itching to get out of this living room. "Let's go see these outfits in a full-length mirror."

"Corrinne," my mom says, and she stands to block our path upstairs. "First you will tell me where you are going and with who."

"Whom," Tripp pipes up, head still in the puzzle.

"A small gathering at Bronson McDermott's," I say, which is the truth.

"Will his parents be home?" my mom retorts with the sentence I most dread.

"Yup," I lie, and look my mom in the eye so she thinks I am telling the truth. I learned that in psych class.

"Waverly?" my mom asks.

"Totally true." Waverly confirms my lie.

"Okay, girls," my mom says, opening the way for us to pass by. "I want you to remember a thing called island mentality. Just because we are on Nantucket, thirty miles to sea, doesn't mean that the rules don't apply. It seems that children and adults get on this island and think it's high school all over again."

"But Mom," Tripp says, "they are in high school."

"Yes," my mom says, sitting down again, "that's exactly what I am afraid of."

❧❧

Bronson lives way out in Madaket, which is known both for its sunsets and the fact that the dump is there. Luckily, Bronson's brother, Dennis, at twenty-four, has yet to become employed, so he drives us around for free. I think it gives him purpose, which he lacks as he eats up his trust fund.

We meet him in town near Orange Street and jump into the back of his hunter green Jeep Wrangler. There are more SUVs in Nantucket than anywhere else, even Colorado. I am sure of this.

"Hey, ladies," Dennis says. "Looking good for underage girls." Dennis often says creepy things like this, but he's totally harmless.

"Thanks, Dennis," I say. "You are looking good for being Bronson's brother."

"Hey, hey, Miss Corrinne," Dennis says, and looks back at me from the front seat, "as I remember it, I caught you and him making out on our couch just last summer."

"Last summer," Waverly says. "That's a lifetime when you are fifteen."

I can always count on Waverly to say the genius thing and defend me. She's been like that since we were little girls playing in our fenced-in nursery school sandlot.

"Okay, then," Dennis says. "You girlies are going to have to get a professional driver for the way back. I am going to the Box tonight."

No shocker there. Everyone goes to the Box, the local dive bar. Everyone, that is, with a really good fake ID that will scan *or the privilege of actually being legal.*

"Think you could sneak in two hot girls?" Waverly asks as she locks eyes with Dennis in the rearview mirror.

"Not a chance," Dennis says, gunning the car once we hit the main road to Madaket. "I am in enough trouble there for a bar fight that my friend started."

After a few more minutes of banter with Dennis, he pulls up to the seashelled driveway to their house.

"I'd tell you girls to be good," he says, "but I know you won't listen."

We both laugh and jump out of the Wrangler. Walking toward the front of the house, I see that a bunch of our summer friends are already there and hanging out on the porch. On the side yard, croquet's been set up, and a drink cart is overloaded with top shelf booze.

"Hello, lovely ladies," Bronson says, approaching in madras with a denim button-down. He looks decent, and I can almost see why I made out with him last summer. "How about a life-is-good?" Bronson says and points to the drink cart. "As you may know, it's the signature drink of the island."

"Sure," Waverly says, and grabs my hand. "After all, life is pretty damn good to us."

Bang!

The sound of pots and pans clanking around snaps me out of better times, B.R., Before the Recession. Glancing at the photograph of Waverly and me one last time I realize that times like those might never happen again. If I want to feel happy, my memories might be the only place to go. Searching out a mysterious smell—a cross between street chestnuts and the cotton candy at Yankee Stadium—I get up and go to my grandparents' kitchen.

"There's Texas's newest driver," Grandpa announces in his game show host voice.

"Your grandfather says you're a natural," Grandma says from the stove. "I guess you and your mom are different, because she cost us a fortune to get insured. Three accidents with a learner's permit. Maybe she always was a city girl in her core."

"What are you baking, Grandma?" I ask.

Tripp pipes up from the couch, "Cherry-chestnut cobbler."

"Your grandmomma has great news, Corrinne. She just called up an old friend of your mom's, Ginger," Grandpa says.

I do not believe that Grandma, "news," and a woman named Ginger mean anything good for me. But I indulge my grandfather.

"Really? What is it?" I ask.

"I got you a job," Grandma says as she douses the crumble with brown sugar. "It isn't healthy for you to just mope around the house after school. You need some fresh air."

"I don't remember saying I need a job," I remark with my hand on my hip. "It's not exactly like I have anywhere to shop."

Only my friend Sarita worked. That's because she had to buy a second cell phone. Her parents were monitoring her every call and even had a GPS detector put in her phone. If she never got her own cell phone, her parents were going to ruin her life.

"It's a job with horses," Grandpa interjects as he turns the TV volume down. "We know how much you miss your horse. You've got his picture plastered all over your room like he's a movie star."

"Sweetbread is a she," I whisper. "Thanks for the concern, but I don't want a job even with horses—unless it's my horse and it's in Connecticut." Saying Sweetbread's name loudly would cause a breakdown of epic proportions.

Grandma stops her sugar dousing. "Corrinne, I know your parents let you do pretty much whatever you want, but in this house you will do as we say. *We're* in charge here."

She takes a step closer to me and locks eyes with me. "So you will be helping out at Ginger's stables, and you will start Monday. Otherwise, you'll be grounded."

"Grounded from what?" I challenge as I inch toward her. "You mean I won't be able to see my totally awesome Broken Spoke friends and go to happy hour at Sonic?

Being grounded sounds just fine. This whole place is a prison; I might as well just stay in my cell."

"You are being dramatic, Corrinne," Grandpa says, and stands up from the couch. "Maybe this winter you'll try theater, but this fall you will try working at Ginger's. Your momma used to ride there."

"I think cleaning stalls and shoveling manure might do you some good," Grandma says, and turns her back to me. "You'll build some muscles and maybe even some character while you are at it."

"Shoveling manure? Don't they have stable hands that do that?" I spit.

Grandma spins around. "That's the job I got *you*. You are the newest hand. Hope you brought some clothes that you can get dirty in."

Without another word, I hightail it to my room. I slam the door extra hard to make sure even my grandparents, with their declining hearing, can feel the vibrations of my anger. Shoveling manure? Sick. While I am not afraid of getting manure on my boots now and again, I—okay, my parents—pay people to shovel Sweetbread's manure. I don't shovel *other people's* horses' poop for a few dollars. This is not happening. Isn't there, like, a hoof and foot disease I could catch?

I lie back on my bed. And no matter how hard I try, I can't get back to B.R. even in my daydreams.

Chapter 7

This Is My First Rodeo

I SPEND SUNDAY IN BED. Grandpa brings me in trays of food and laughs at his own room-service jokes.

"Room service here," Grandpa says. "Is this like the Plaza, Corrinne?" he asks.

No, I think. Grandma's food's way better. But I don't say it. Even after a day, I am still fuming at Grandma about this job thing. First I am driving. Now I am working. Does she also have me in an arranged marriage that I don't know about? Am I adopting a child from a foreign nation? She's got my life on total fast-forward, and I don't like it. I didn't plan to work until after college except for some internship where I could somehow still manage a good summer tan.

After dinner, Grandpa returns to my room to collect my tray.

"You know that your momma used this same tray when she stayed home from school with a cold. She said she could only eat pancakes; that was the only thing that'd make her feel better. I think that might have been a white lie though, just so she could eat pancakes for dinner."

Uncurling myself from the fetal position, I sit up. "I am not sick, Grandpa," I say. "I am grounded."

"There're a lot of ways to be sick," Grandpa says as he sits on the corner of my bed. "Homesick is real sickness, sweetie. It's okay to be sad, but moping doesn't do anything except make it worse. And you aren't grounded if you go to your job tomorrow."

"There's no way I am working there," I say.

What would I even wear if I were insane enough to do it? I mean, my dressage clothes would be totally ridiculous. It would be like going to a dive bar in a ball gown. You don't shovel poop in beige jodhpurs, a blue jockey skullcap, and a hacking jacket. And I never got into that whole grunge trend, so I don't have any boyfriend jeans or flannel shirts.

"How about we make a deal?" Grandpa says, reaching out his hand for a shake. "This house is small, and we need peace. You go tomorrow and see if it's truly unbearable. And if you find it's not and you keep at it, I'll let you have Billie Jean the Second when I get a new truck. Hard to resist, huh?"

I think this offer over: If I am willing to shovel manure in extreme heat, I can become the lucky winner of a junky jalopy. Even in a recession this sounds like a bum deal.

"I'll think about it, Grandpa," I say because I am too exhausted to argue, but I don't shake his hand.

"That's all I ask, Corrinne," Grandpa says as he gets up from the bed. "Grandma thinks idleness is the door to all the other vices. And I tend to agree. A pretty girl like you shouldn't be locked up in her room watching TV on a computer," Grandpa says. Opening the door, Grandpa mutters to himself, "Never thought I'd live to see the day that there was TV on a computer."

After he shuts the door, I put my earphones back on to continue watching *Gossip Girl*. It's the closest I can get to my old life right now.

Just when I am so immersed in the world of Chuck, Serena, and Blair that I forget about Texas and my impending employment, Tripp flings open my door without knocking.

"I know that you are a mutant and don't know social norms," I say loudly without even taking my earphones off, "but on planet Earth, we knock, even here in Twilight Texas."

Tripp leaves and shuts the door behind him, and I sigh.

A second later, I hear a loud knock.

I do a calming countdown from three to two to one.

The knocking persists.

"Come in," I finally grunt.

Tripp then leaps onto my bed without an invitation. I decide to just let that one go.

Yanking out my earphones and pausing *Gossip Girl* midscene, I roll my eyes at Tripp. "What business do you have in my room?"

"Grandpa says you are homesick," Tripp says. "And you know what? I am too. Well, just a little. I am really bored without chess club. Do you want to do something together? Grandpa and I are watching the Yankees later."

"I am not homesick," I lie. "It's not home that I care about. Or Mom or Dad. I miss my life. That's different. And you didn't have a life, so you have nothing to miss besides chess, which is lame anyways."

"Corrinne," Tripp whines, "you never hang out with me. I thought Texas would be different, especially since it's not like you have friends here."

"Out," I say, and shove Tripp off the bed. He lands with a thud, dusts himself off, and retreats.

Tripp's right, I don't have friends, but hanging out with my annoying little brother won't make my life any less pathetic.

Monday at school reminds me why Monday is the most psychologically damaging day of the week. People should just stay home to protect their mental well-being, and the government should enforce the rule.

Bubby totally harasses me in Spanish class.

"Manhattan," he whispers, "you were gone in a New York minute from the party last Friday. Hope it wasn't anything I said."

I whisper back, "No, it's who you are."

Bubby hoots at this. Apparently he doesn't even get how to take an insult.

After Spanish class, Kitsy grabs my hand and says, "Please forgive me about the party. Sorry you didn't have fun. I feel terrible. Did some girl say something? Girls here are super jealous, especially over football players, and everyone knows that Bubby's got it bad for you. Can I make it up to you? Let's go shopping for Saturday's dance together. Please? I want your opinion on my dress."

Like always, Kitsy's monologue has left me totally confused. Bubby, who verbally assaulted me, has a crush? A dance? Shopping in Broken Spoke?

"I don't know, Kitsy, because I am not totally sure how much longer I'll be here," I reply, and Kitsy's permanent smile disappears. "Could be just a few more days," I elaborate, feeding my own lie.

Kitsy totally deserves an A for effort, but I am not in the business of giving out congeniality awards. So I walk away without even thanking Kitsy for asking me to go shopping.

After school, I had prepared to continue my grounding and watch more *Gossip Girl* episodes. While Grandma and I wait for Grandpa to pick us up, I don't say a word. Total silent treatment. Grandpa smiles really big when we get into the truck.

"Surprise, Corrinne. I got you something!" And he pulls out a big shopping bag with a shoe box inside.

"Open it," he says. Grandma just rolls her eyes at him. And out of the box I pull a pair of totally faded, worn, caramel brown cowboy boots. They look like they're a total gem from a vintage store in the East Village.

"They were your momma's. She left them here when she went to the city," Grandpa says. "I guess she thought she'd be back for them."

And I have to admit that they're wicked hot. Posh might even lend me Beckham in exchange for these.

"They'll be great for your first day of work," Grandma says, and reaches for another bag. "I did you the courtesy of packing some more—uh—appropriate clothing. They used to be your mom's too."

I guess my grandma didn't think a yellow sundress would be appropriate for manure duty, but I hadn't actually planned on shoveling manure.

Peering into the bag, I see there's a totally chic pair

of ripped Levi's, dark but faded, and a gray T-shirt with BROKEN SPOKE HIGH SCHOOL in navy letters.

"So let's get Tripp and then we'll drop you off. Before you know it, you'll be able to drive yourself," Grandpa says, and turns to wink.

I have two options: a) watching TV in a barely air-conditioned room or b) shoveling poop. I am for sure going to choose a) until I realize that b) might just make me enough money to get a ticket out of this town. At this point, I am willing to take the Greyhound bus if it means escape.

"Okay," I say, "I'll try it. But just today."

And I swear, Grandma almost cracks a smile.

GINGER'S STABLES, TURNING GIRLS INTO RODEO QUEENS SINCE 1975, the sign reads. TOURISTS WELCOME. TRAIL RIDES DAILY. The facility is astonishingly dilapidated, complete with a chipped red barn and white fences mended with duct tape. They are nothing like the Martha Stewart–inspired stables where I ride back home. And tourists in Broken Spoke? That is laughable. The only tourists who would make it here would be very lost tourists. But the horses, mostly quarter horses and paints, look beautiful in the pasture. After noticing my prickly goose-bumped arms, the effect I get from being around horses, I desperately miss Sweetbread, which reminds me that I need to email my barn to make sure she's getting her exercise.

"What's a rodeo queen?" Tripp asks.

"Your mother was a rodeo queen, Tripp. It's a pageant for beautiful, smart girls. A little like Miss USA, but with a four-legged friend," Grandpa says.

"Not exactly." Grandma laughs, and she looks pretty when she laughs—it's those same Indian Ocean blue eyes as my mom's.

"Are there rodeo kings?" Tripp wants to know. And both Grandma and Grandpa chuckle.

"No, Tripp," Grandpa says, regaining his composure. "Although there was one young fella last year who petitioned that there should be rodeo kings or boy queens or whatever it was. Gee, that got people talking around town."

Grandma interrupts Grandpa. "Corrinne, you change in the car, and we'll take Tripp to meet Ginger."

After a few minutes of wiggling into my clothes, I am dressed, and Mom's cowgirl clothes fit perfectly. She must have been bigger in high school because I definitely can't wear her clothes now. For going casual, I think I look pretty damn good. Mental reminder: Wear this outfit when I get back to the city. It'll be totally uncopyable.

Even from a distance, I can tell that Ginger is appropriately named. A woman of about Grandma's age, she has fiery red hair and is wearing a pink cowgirl shirt and red boots. Apparently she didn't get the memo that redheads aren't so pretty in pink. (Unless of course, it's retro, like Molly Ringwald.)

"You look just like her!" Ginger exclaims.

"Who?" I say, walking up closer to Ginger, Grandpa, Grandma, and Tripp.

"Your momma. I mean, your hair's different, your eyes are different, but oh, you got that same glamour," Ginger effuses.

Me? Look like my mother? That's new. And I'm glamorous? While this part may be true, I can't say that many people have articulated it before. I might just like this Ginger lady.

"We're so happy to have you working here," Ginger drawls. "Your grandmomma told me that you're quite the horsewoman. We're lucky to have you."

"Actually," I correct her, "I ride dressage; it's a bit different from rodeo. I don't do any other kind of riding. And I don't ride any horses but my own, Sweetbread. We're in a monogamous relationship. No offense to any of your horses or anything."

"I know dressage—it's like *Dancing with the Stars* but for horses. Here we're more horse circus." Ginger giggles at her own joke. "We do a bit of everything: barrel racing, steer roping, bareback bronco riding. Pretty wild stuff. Your momma was the best barrel racer we've ever had."

"Barrel racing?" I repeat. She has to be joking. To me,

riding's an art; here it's a carnival.

"Barrel racing is like a slalom skiing course. I imagine you ski?" Ginger guesses correctly. I've skied since I could walk. "You ride as quick as you can as you navigate a series of barrels. It takes a really good relationship with your horse, just like your dressage."

The words *your horse* sting. *My horse* is alone in Connecticut. We've been forced into a long-distance relationship by my tyrant parents. And now I am here to shovel manure and watch people rope cows. Ugh. Feeling like I am suffocating, I debate making a run for the car. At that moment, Grandma, Grandpa, and Tripp back away from our circle and wave.

"Good luck, we'll pick you up at six," Grandpa calls out quickly, approaching the car with rapid speed.

There goes my escape plan. I am stuck here.

"Did your grandmomma mention the pay?" Ginger asks.

"Nope," I say. "She's more of a director than an explainer." I want to say *dictator,* but I know Grandma and Ginger are friends.

"Seven fifty an hour," Ginger says. "And if you like, I'll exchange your pay for lessons."

"Seven dollars and fifty cents?" I repeat. That's two slices at Bleecker Street Pizza. That's less than what a Serendipity sundae costs.

"That's more than most people in this town—including adults—make, Corrinne. Those lucky enough to have jobs, that is," Ginger says, and topples a pile of dirt with her boot. "And you'll find it will get you a lot more in Broken Spoke than in New York, especially when you buy only what you need."

Deciding there's no use arguing with Ginger, I shrug and say, "Tell me where to start."

"Let me introduce you to your coworker," Ginger says, and she whistles like a construction worker. "Rider!"

Out of the barn walks the hottest guy that I have ever seen. And I used to live in the breeding ground for models and actresses. Pulling a white T-shirt over a tanned washboard stomach, a boy with moppy brown hair jogs up. I swear the '70s song "Blinded by the Light" starts playing in the background. The only breeze in Texas, which I've yet to experience, tousles his hair.

"Rider," he says, holding out his hand.

"Corrinne," I stammer.

"So you're our city girl. You look just like your mom. Ginger told me Jenny Jo's daughter was coming to work here. Her pictures are all over the Rodeo Queen Hall of Fame. I haven't seen you at Broken Spoke High this year yet. Ginger told me you're going there," he says with a grin.

"I'm new and I sort of keep to myself," I say, blushing.

"I haven't seen you there either."

"Usually you can find me in the music room, practicing with my band. I've been working at Ginger's to pay the fee to enter the Battle of the Bands in Dallas. And it keeps me in shape."

Indeed it does, I think.

"Y'all two get into those stables and start cleaning. The girls will be arriving for lessons soon," Ginger says as she shoos us with her hand.

Of course, this isn't how I imagined meeting my soul mate. I definitely didn't think I'd be wearing denim and cowboy boots. In my fantasies, I was at a posh hotel lobby bar, wearing an LBD (Little Black Dress) and holding champagne. But isn't this how it happens in the movies? Love finds you in unexpected places. Rider could be the cosmic reason behind this whole move to Broken Spoke. That's it; Rider has to be my destiny. And he's in a band, so it's a modern-day fairy tale. I might just be able to endure this job long enough to get Rider to choose me for his muse. He'll write love songs about me, and then we'll be rock royalty. The recession will just be the entry point for our love story rather than my demise.

As we walk into the stable, Rider grabs a shovel and tosses it to me. Amazingly, I catch it.

"You do that one," he says, pointing to a stall heaping with fresh manure, "and I'll do this one."

So much for my plan to work side by side and gaze into each other's eyes.

Rider tunes the radio to a hard rock station and turns it up so loud that I can't even make conversation. At first, I just look at the piles of manure, wishing I had a magic wand to make them disappear. The piles don't get any smaller despite the curses and spells I put on them. I attempt to shovel up the largest pile while holding my breath. With my hands shaking at the weight, I manage to raise the shovel to the height of the wheelbarrow before I drop it all right back where it was. This happens about four more times before I finally manage to get it in the wheelbarrow. Obviously, I wasn't born for this type of work. Before long, my arms and back are aching.

"How about a break?" I yell, peeking my head into Rider's stall.

"No," he yells back. "Gotta get out of here as fast as possible so I can practice with my band."

"What's your band called?" I shout back. This Rider might be a bit more difficult to rope in than I previously thought.

"Friday Night After the Lights," he responds, and stops shoveling for a second. "Pretty genius, huh?"

"Totally," I answer. "When's your next gig?" I am feeling pretty smart for remembering the music lingo. My friend Jason's father is a total music mogul, and he signed two of the biggest boy bands. Unfortunately for me, all the guys were gay, so I couldn't use that angle for fame. Maybe Rider's into guys? He certainly doesn't seem that interested in me.

"We're playing at the school dance this Saturday," he says, "Lame, but we'll take anything we can get and student council is paying us fifty bucks."

Oh yeah, the dance. Mental reminder: I need to accept Kitsy's offer to go shopping ASAP and ask her if I can tag along to the dance. This will help set the new plan—the one to establish myself as Rider's number one groupie—into action. Band guys love groupies, right?

"Awesome," I say. "I am really looking forward to it."

"Really?" Rider says as he moves into my stall to help finish it. I follow him. "I thought you stuck to yourself."

"Well," I say, watching Rider effortlessly finish my stall. "Maybe it's time for me to branch out." And maybe, just maybe, I can swing this recession and year in Texas into the story of how I met my rocker boy and became the next Nicole Richie. Maybe I could even get my own record deal out of this. And I can so already imagine us on the cover of *Us Weekly*.

I rinse three times with Kiehl's body wash until I am convinced I no longer smell of manure. After getting dressed, I sit down at the dinner table, starving. Shoveling manure is a better workout than the Bar Method, Pilates, and running in Central Park combined. I might just write the *Why Stable Hands Don't Get Fat* diet book. It's a good thing, because dinner looks especially calorie-packed tonight.

"You've got that industrious glow to you," Grandpa says. "You might be a worker yet."

I didn't tell Grandpa that my flush is more of an "I just met a total hottie" glow than a "I love shoveling manure for minimum wage" glow.

"I would agree," Grandma says as she brings dinner— more dead cow—to the table. "Did Ginger ask you if you want to take lessons?"

"She did," I respond, "but I don't think that rodeo is my style, and I'm faithful to my partner, Sweetbread. I saw Mom's pictures, though. Where'd she get all those bedazzled tops? So ridiculous." Ginger's Hall of Fame had big, cheesy color glamour shots of all the past rodeo queens. Mom wore turquoise shirts with magenta rhinestones. Yikes.

"Actually, Corrinne, I made those for your mom. That's the traditional style for rodeo queens," Grandma replies as she sits down and stabs into the roast beef.

Oops, I'm right back on Grandma's bad side. So what's new? Oh well, I have to focus on how to get Rider. He totally ignored me for the last two hours that we worked, and didn't even check me out when I bent down in front of him when I was shoveling. I mean, really? I saw how my Levi's fit. But I am determined. If I can't get New York and Kent and Smith, I will get Rider. It's justice. Those who are wronged will find justice. That's, like, in our constitution, right?

"Big news, Corrinne," Tripp says with his mouth full. "Mom said the person who was thinking about buying the place is definitely going to make an offer. So if it all works out right, Mom will be coming to Broken Spoke soon. And then I told her about you driving and working. She was in total shock. I could actually hear her gasp over the phone."

Oh yes, my mother, my middle-aged roommate. Sweet. I definitely needed to get a boyfriend and get out of this tiny cottage because it's not big enough for Mom, Grandma, and me.

After dinner, I spend alone time in my room and do the little homework that teachers assign. The best part of Broken Spoke High: Teachers give normal amounts of homework. Unlike my teachers back home, they understand that kids have lives. Of course, I have no life here, but I appreciate the courtesy.

Logging on to Facebook, I search for Kitsy Kidd. Her picture—in her Mockingbirdette cheerleading outfit— pops up. I think for a second and click ADD AS A FRIEND. Not much later, I get a confirmation notice. I officially have one friend in Texas. After searching for Rider on Facebook, his picture pops up—all dark, blurry, and emo (how hot!), but I don't friend him. I can't be too Stalker Stacy.

Rummaging through my closet, I try to find something that I could wear to the dance. Isn't the whole point of dances to buy something new? That's what it was like with events in New York. If Grandma actually liked me, I could get her to alter one of my dresses into at least looking somewhat different. But on second thought, she'd probably bedazzle it. Never mind.

Maybe I will go with Kitsy to the mall. I have watched the show *Dress for Less* enough times, and sometimes they find something inexpensive that doesn't look like it came from a mall in Kansas—or Texas. Rarely, but it has happened. With my style and accessories, there might be a dress out there decent enough to wear while watching Friday Night After the Lights. Plus, I saw on TV that shopping makes us happy because it releases endorphins. It's also ingrained in our hunter-gatherer pasts. We need to gather to feel happy. Let me gather, let me be happy, and let Rider pull me onto the stage and ask me to star in his first music video.

Chapter 8

Is This a Mall?

PEOPLE SAY IF YOU PRACTICE SOMETHING VERY OFTEN, you develop muscle memory. I have practiced shopping in NYC a lot, so I am strong at it. And I know how I do it best: alone and with plastic. So thinking about shopping in tandem with Kitsy gives me major anxiety. Will I even know what to do? It also makes me remember the last time I shopped with someone and that disaster.

"You do not need this dress, Corrinne," my mom says. "Do you really get how much money a thousand dollars is in the real world? That's how much a wedding dress should cost, not something for a high school charity function."

After I unzip the zebra-print full-length dress, I step out of it, pick it up from the floor and put it neatly back on the hanger.

I don't want it to get wrinkled, and I won't have time to get it dry-cleaned before the event.

"Mom," I say, "this is exactly why I like to shop alone so that I learn to make big decisions on my own. How else can I grow up? You won't always be here, you know."

My mom starts to laugh, and then she realizes that I am not joining in. Pursing her lips, she takes the hanger with the dress off the wall.

"Corrinne," she says, "you need help. Your version of reality is seriously skewed."

Placing my hand on the hanger, I tug on the dress to get my mother to release it. My mom just holds on and stares back.

"Mom," I say in my I-sound-calm-but I-am-internally-freaking-out voice, "listen to me. This is not just a party, it is a fund-raiser for the Children's Zoo at Central Park and we're supposed to dress accordingly. Waverly claimed cheetah print because of her complexion, which I do admit is too ruddy for zebra. So I got screwed and got zebra, which is apparently going extinct in the fashion world. This is the only not-metallic-or-pleather zebra-print dress in Manhattan. Unless you want to go to the Bronx Zoo and get me some zebra fur, you will unhand this dress."

My mom shakes her head. "When I was your age, I used to fight with my mother about getting a new coat once every two years. This is ridiculous. You are fifteen and going to some charity function when you should be watching TV and ordering

pizza with your friends. Fifteen is too young for galas. Really.
I am so sick of Manhattan," she says.

I pull the dress from my mother's fingers, and she finally
relaxes her white-knuckled grip. She sits back on the blue plush
dressing room chair and slowly hits her head against the wall.

Hopefully, knocking her cranium will get her to think
straight.

"Mom, your shoes cost a thousand dollars. I see the red bot-
toms; they are Louboutins. This dress means a lot to me. And
Grandma was right, why would you even need a coat in Texas?
I actually have a purpose for buying this. Don't hate on Manhat-
tan just because you are antisocial and get anxious over events."

After stepping out of the Saks dressing room with the dress,
I go to the register and charge it. My mother and I ride silently
in the cab home.

And the day of the gala when all the parents come over for
cocktails beforehand, my mom snaps my picture and smiles all
the same when everyone compliments her daughter's good taste.
Typical.

Thinking about how much I hated shopping with
someone—even back when I had plastic power—makes
me super nervous about how dress-hunting with Kitsy is
going to end up. I even break into a cold sweat. Or a hot
sweat, rather, since it's Texas, and it's never cold here.

～∽

Before Spanish class starts, Kitsy skips into the room and starts one of her signature monologues.

"I am so glad you Facebooked me. Now I can totally tag you when we take pictures. Do you want to come to the mall with me tomorrow after practice?"

Tagged in pictures? I am not sure I want to go *that* public with my year in Texas. And Facebook is permanent public record. I know kids who have gotten expelled for pictures they posted. Photographs of me in Texas will not be good PR . . . except if Rider's in them. Waverly would flip out; Rider's so much hotter than Smith!

"Hey, Kitsy," I say, "you know Rider?"

Kitsy throws her bag on her front-row chair and comes to sit by me in an empty desk in the back.

"Rider Jones," she says. "Of course. He's going to be totally famous. He's in a band, but he's kind of stuck-up and he won't go out with any girls from Broken Spoke. So when he makes it big, they won't be able to go on the *Today* show and flash old pictures and say, 'Here's me and Rider at prom.' It sucks because that would probably be my only chance to get on TV," Kitsy says, and frowns. "Not that I would ever dump Hands, though. We've gone out since, like, the sixth grade."

Sixth-grade sweethearts. Wow. New Yorkers only commit to that type of monogamy with the Yankees or the Giants.

"I got a job," I say, which sounds strange. "And I work with him at Ginger's stables. I am totally—what do you call it?—sweet on him."

I use Kitsy's lingo because I want her to understand that I am serious about me and Rider and our fate. After all, I am a big believer in going straight after what, or whom, you want.

"You work at Ginger's stables?" Kitsy says as she stands up to walk back to her desk. "I totally wanted to be a Rodeo Queen because of the scholarship money, but the lessons are hella expensive. Rider would probably make an exception to his no-dating rule for you since you're a beautiful city girl and not a hick like us."

I smile at Kitsy; she's shockingly sweet. None of my friends back home ever compliment me. They'll say "Nice dress" or "Nice shoes" or "Nice hair" but never "You're beautiful."

"You know, Kitsy, I'd love to go to the mall," I say to her before she makes her way back up to the front. "And how does this dance thing work? Do I need a date?"

"Ohmigod," Kitsy says, and I swear she shakes an invisible pom-pom. "I am so psyched that you want to come. After the field ordeal and our last conversation, I was worried that you were leaving Broken Spoke. . . ."

Just then, Señor Luis walks in, so Kitsy starts talking even faster, "We usually go as couples in a big group. I'll find someone to ask you. Did you know Rider's performing? Maybe he'll come to the bonfire afterward. That'd be perfect. I promise I'll help you with this because I love playing matchmaker. I just wish you liked Bubby. Then we could hang out more." With that, Kitsy slips into her front-row desk and focuses her attention on Señor Luis.

Then class starts so I don't have any time to get more dirt on Rider or to figure out who Kitsy has in mind to be my date to the dance.

Hands and Kitsy pick me up from Ginger's stables on Wednesday. Hands's practice jersey is caked in mud and grass. And the smell of his truck makes even the worst taxicabs seem like they were just freshly cleaned.

"Hands is just dropping us off. He's going to eat his weight at the pizza buffet while we shop. He knows what are girl things and what are boy things. That's why I love him," Kitsy says, and rubs his shoulder, then shrieks and pulls her hand back.

"Ewww, you are sopping wet. Ugh, dating football players is the worst," Kitsy teases, and then pecks Hands on the cheek.

Hopefully, there's a shower at the pizza buffet. Otherwise, I might just lose my lunch on the ride back.

"Just call me Mr. Chauffeur," Hands says before

peeling out of the stable's parking lot. "You have those in New York, right?"

"Oh," Kitsy squeals, "I found you a date for the dance. You might not be happy, though. See, you need to go with someone in our group so we can drive together, eat together, do pictures together and all that. And all the guys on the team asked their dates last week because they are totally hunted. It's like deer season for girls who are total football jersey chasers. It's pathetic; these girls' main goal in life is to get a football player for a boyfriend or at least get one for a night." Kitsy rolls her eyes and pauses. "And so the only person in our group without a date is . . . Bubby. You see, Bubby won't go out with jersey chasers; he says it's like finding a fish in an aquarium. Too easy. Of course, it wouldn't be, like, romantic or anything. And Bubby promised to be nice or at least nicer."

Hands raises an eyebrow as he floors the truck down the backcountry road.

"Bubby agreed to take me?" I ask, trying not to freak out about Hands's driving. Just today in Spanish class, Bubby asked me if I popped my collar to remind everyone how stuck-up I am. Doesn't he know that's what you do with a collar? He takes any chance to be a jerk. It's like he's bitter about what happened, like, twenty-five years ago. My mom dumped your dad. Get over it. I don't even know who my mom was back then. She was an entirely different person who wore bedazzled shirts. I can't be responsible for her past actions, especially her fashion faux pas.

"Of course he did," Kitsy says, and playfully slaps Hands on the back of the head. "It's too bad that you heart Rider because it would be awesome if you had a boyfriend in our group."

"You like Rider?" Hands says, taking his eyes off the road long enough to look at me like I am an alien.

He focuses back on the road. "Good luck with that. I am not sure he's into girls. He only talks about music and his band and hitting it big. He wouldn't notice a hot girl if she bit him. Why try to be all rock star without the scoring-hot-chicks part? Isn't that the entire purpose of it all?" Hands says, and shakes his head.

My face flushes when Kitsy outs me about Rider, so I look out the window for a second. Breathe. Remember that Rider is the one thing that might make this situation all better. What's that New Age philosophy? Put your thoughts into the universe and you'll get what you want.

"Yes, Rider's totally cute," I underplay. I don't mention that he's an eleven on a scale of one to ten. "I don't think he's gay. He's just career-driven, which I am used to since I am from New York. And I am going to be the first girl he goes for. But yeah, I'll go with Bubby to the dance because you two are my only friends in Broken Spoke, so I want to be with you guys."

" 'You guys,' " Kitsy mimics. "I just love how you say 'you guys.' I am going to use that. Okay, *you guys*, we're at the mall. Let's do this, *you guys. You guys* are great."

"*Y'all* are annoying," Hands jokes as he pulls into a parking lot.

The mall is actually what I believe is called a strip mall. We drove at eighty miles an hour for twenty minutes to two towns away and this is the best we can do? Finding a dress is so not going to happen. Hands jumps out and opens our door.

"See you guys in an hour," he says, and jogs to the pizza buffet.

Kitsy and I walk into Charlotte Russe, a store with a serious overload of fluorescent lights. There are racks of clothes everywhere from floor to ceiling. Tons of the merchandise has fallen off the rack and is lying on the floor. There's also a huge line for the dressing rooms. I long for the days of DJs and free champagne at Barneys. I'd even put up with age discrimination right about now.

"Where do we even start?" I murmur as I check prices. A dress for $24.99? Is that a payment plan $24.99 now and pay the rest later? How can an adult dress cost $24.99? Well, the dress does have boob cups and a very oddly placed flower. In my purse, I have sixty-five dollars— forty-five of my own from work and twenty that Grandpa slipped me this morning. While I might have plenty of money for this type of shopping, I am not convinced that there's anything in here that I even want to touch my skin. I think I saw a *Dateline* special about someone who got a rash from places like this. Or maybe that was a massage parlor. I can't remember.

"Here's the deal," Kitsy says, scanning the store. "Most of the dresses are horrendous. And then there's ten percent that are banging. Luckily, most girls can't tell the difference, so we should be able to find some good stuff. Let's just both pull what we think might work, and we'll bring it all into a dressing room."

For the sake of my sanity, I pretend that I am the host of *Dress for Less*. Remember, I tell myself, there are great deals to be found everywhere, especially in a recession. Keep it simple; a little black dress always works as a good base. You can then accessorize with more expensive pieces. Mix high and low. With my motivational monologue running through my head, I spot a few potential winners: a black bandage dress, a sequined gold mini, a bright blue halter dress, and a red strapless number. I meet up with Kitsy, whose petite frame is weighed down with about twenty dresses. She might topple over.

"Wow," Kitsy says, "great finds. I knew that this would be fun. Okay, let's get a dressing room and have ourselves a fashion show. I picked out some dresses that I thought would work well on you too."

After waiting forever in the dressing room line, Kitsy and I start trying on our stash. This whole experience violates my shopping rules: no malls, no shopping with friends, no clothes that cost less than an order of sushi. But when in a strip mall with no other options, do as your only Broken Spoke friend does.

Kitsy throws me a backless black dress with a high neck.

"This will be hot on you. You've got a great back. I would say it's the shoveling, but you've only worked three days. Did I tell you I work at Sonic? Just on Saturdays when we don't have games. The manager's awesome and he lets me work around my mom. Sonic's cool, too, because everyone hangs out there when they aren't at the field."

I apply my filter and don't say that I hope Sonic is a Broken Spoke rite of passage that I can skip.

As I examine the dress Kitsy gave me, I am shocked that it's surprisingly attractive. "Are you sure that you don't want this dress, Kitsy?" I ask, admiring the gold studding on the hem and sticker price of $24.99. "You found it."

"No way!" she says. "I got it thinking of you. Besides, I want to do red. I am so bored with gray. What kind of school color is that?"

"Here." I pull the red dress out of my pile. "Try this. And I've been wondering about that school color thing too. Maybe you could start a revolution and get the color changed. You are the captain," I say.

"Thanks," Kitsy says, taking the dress. She thinks for a second. "Actually, we can't change the color. It's *always* been gray. We don't mess with tradition, not in Texas, and especially not when football is involved."

Kitsy helps me pull the dress over my head.

"Thanks," I say as the dress slips down over my shoulders.

Although the room has what I refer to as "cellulite-enhancing lights" and "fat mirrors," I have to admit that I look fierce and Kitsy is right—my back is getting sculpted.

"Hey, Kitsy, what do you mean by the manager lets you work around your mom?"

"Oh." She pauses as she looks into the mirror. Red is definitely her color. "I thought your grandparents would have said something already. People talk a lot. My mom's not exactly stable. She tries, she really does, but it's up to me to take care of my seven-year-old brother, Kiki, a lot. Did you know that he's the town's champion mutton buster?"

"Mutton buster?" I repeat, avoiding talking about Kitsy's mother since I don't know what to say.

"It's a rodeo sport where little kids ride sheep. Really pretty hysterical since sheep aren't that big on being ridden. Kiki's even on YouTube doing it."

I laugh. "I'd like to see that." I feel bad for Kitsy. My

mom's got her problems what with being incredibly annoying and ruining my life, but she's relatively stable and she only made me take care of Tripp that once on the plane. I wonder how Kitsy stays upbeat all the time. Maybe her pom-poms have magical powers. . . .

"You will see mutton busting in person" Kitsy says. "The town rodeo's not that far away. Kiki's favored to win again." She turns to face me. "So what do you think? Is the red okay? I know I don't look like your city friends. But will it do?"

"You look beautiful," I say, and mean it. After all, most people can't pull off a $24.99 dress. I guess it's like that saying, the girl should wear the dress; the dress shouldn't wear the girl. Maybe wealthy women in New York do pay too much money for clothes.

Taking in the compliment, Kitsy blushes and looks away to her reflection.

"Saturday's going to be awesome," she says. "Rider's going to need a defibrillator when he sees you in that. Oh yeah, I think we're going to Chin's beforehand. You know, the only other restaurant besides Sonic."

"Great," I say, and I almost mean it. Having something to look forward to makes Texas—and life—more bearable, even if it does involve Bubby, who I still haven't forgiven for being such a jerk. Most important, I get to see Rider onstage. You always remember the first time you see someone perform live, especially when you plan to date him. I can't wait to recount that first concert when Rider and I get interviewed after he makes it big and tells everyone how I am his muse.

Chapter 9

Not Just Another Day at the Spa

To: corrinnec@gmail.com

From: waverly@gmail.com

Subject: WHAT HAPPENS WHEN YOU LEAVE ME

Message: I am at Kent!!!!! And I got an exchange student for a roommate. Her name is Vladlena. I am not even sure I can pronounce it. She better shower daily. First you leave me, then this. What happened in my past life that makes me deserve this?

To: waverly@gmail.com

From: corrinnec@gmail.com

Subject: Re: WHAT HAPPENS WHEN YOU LEAVE ME

Message: VLADLENA! Where's she from? She speaks

English, right? Keep covering for me. There's always second semester. And whenever you think your life is bad, remember Corrinne's in the middle of nowhere Texas living with her grandparents. That'll give you some perspective.

I try calling Waverly to get updates and see if there have been any Smith spottings, but she doesn't answer. She just texts back:

> Waverly: Wish u were here. This isn't how it's supposed 2 B.

I think it's whack that she blames me for messing up our rooming plan. She should be mad at my parents and the government but not me. I am an innocent bystander to the recession's slaughter.

The week passes quickly despite the fact that Waverly doesn't call me back and Rider says only about two words to me at work. But I caught him humming once, and it gave me goose bumps. I totally think he has it: the star factor. After thinking over Rider's nonchalant attitude toward me, I have an epiphany: Rider isn't that into me at the stables because he must believe in the separation of work and play. The dance will be another story.

The Broken Spoke football team wins on Friday, so the whole town is on natural uppers. At the game, I sit with Tripp and his friends. I am not sure what's worse: sitting with seventh graders or seventy-year-olds. His friends seem decent enough for hicks. He seems happy, but Tripp always seems happy, which is something I definitely don't share the genetic disposition for. He even said to me after the game, "Thanks, Corrinne, that was awesome that you hung out with me. You wouldn't ever have done that in the city." He's right about that, but in the city I would have never gone to a football game, never mind one with my little brother. But when in Broken Spoke, do as Broken Spokers do, I guess.

I wake up on Saturday, completely sore from working for an entire week. No one's more baffled by that than me. Thinking of it, I should make sure that's legal under child labor laws. And I only have seventy dollars to show for it. Hopefully, Bubby will pay for my dinner at Chin's tonight. Really, it's the least that he can do after pestering me all week. "Looking forward to Saturday, Manhattan," he said. "I hope a city girl like you knows how to two-step." Two-step? I doubt Friday Night After the Lights will be singing do-si-dos. At least, I hope not. And I am certainly *not* dancing with Bubby. The last thing I want is to have Rider see me with that meathead—even if Bubby did score two touchdowns yesterday.

My pre-party routine *used* to consist of an early work-out, manicure, pedicure, a ten-minute massage while my nails dried, a blow-out, makeup, and if I was lucky, a pre-cocktail or two. In Texas, I haven't seen any nail or hair places, not even at the strip mall. I guess I am now my own personal hairdresser and stylist. Just call me Ken Paves meets Rachel Zoe. Remembering Waverly and me sitting side by side at Bliss Spa, getting pampered and not even thinking twice before paying extra for the spa pedicure, makes me depressed.

In my room, I can smell breakfast brewing, so I decide it's time for some emotional eating. The beauty of a backless dress is that it's the back—not the arms, the stomach, or the legs—that are on display. I don't even need to wear Spanx, which is awesome since I enjoy oxygen. Breakfast this morning is an egg casserole with chorizo. It's amazing. Thank God for the shoveling; otherwise I'd really start to look like a corn-fed farmer's daughter.

"Are you excited for the big dance, Corrinne?" Tripp wants to know. "In three years, I'll get to go to one if we still live here. I am totally okay with that as long as Dad moves here too."

"That would be quite the full house," Grandma says, and raises her eyebrows.

"Uh, Tripp," I say, "we aren't going to be here *that* long. This total up-and-coming band is playing, so I am somewhere between remotely and slightly excited for the dance. I don't know what to do all day, though, since I don't have work. This job stuff is messing up my lazy genes."

"Well, how about another driving lesson?" Grandpa says, and folds up the newspaper. "You still need to master the stoplight."

"Okay," I say. "That'd be nice." I really need to get on this driver's license thing so that Grandma and Grandpa don't drop me off at work every day. I want Rider to know that I am worldly, independent, and know how to drive stick.

I imagine that driving will also distract me from thinking about what I would be doing to get ready if I were in NYC. When someone else gets you ready, it takes a whole day. That's why celebrities are so busy and look so good. It probably will only take me two hours to do it by myself, so I have time. Of course, I won't be red carpet ready, but it's not exactly like the Broken Spoke High School dance is going to be broadcast on HDTV.

After my driving lesson, which I rocked even with other cars around, I get a text.

Kitsy: I'm fixin to get ready. Want to come over?

Why not? It'll almost make the DIY approach fun and less pathetic. I hope Kitsy's house is bigger than Grandma and Grandpa's, and that she doesn't share a bathroom with a twelve-year-old boy with seriously questionable hygiene. And I am not just talking about forgetting to put the cap back on the toothpaste.

I text back,

Corrinne: Sure, let me ask the grandparental units.

I walk back into the kitchen where Grandma is—guess what?—baking.

"Grandma, can I go to Kitsy's to get ready for the dance?" I ask, and I walk over to taste the brownie batter.

Grandma shields the bowl with her hands.

"No, and use a spoon if you want to taste this," Grandma says.

"Why not?" I ask.

"Kitsy's mother is always around, but never there, if you know what I mean," Grandma says as she passes me a spoon.

I dip it deep into the batter.

"Yeah, Kitsy said something like that. But we're just getting ready for the dance," I argue before licking a gob of brownie batter. "Besides, I am sixteen; I don't exactly need adult supervision."

"How about this, Corrinne?" Grandma says as she continues to stir. "You can have Kitsy here. Y'all can play with makeup or do whatever you crazy teenagers do."

"Okay," I say. I have been fighting enough battles lately, no reason for an unnecessary spar with Grandma.

Kitsy seems relieved to come to my grandparents' even though I told her that the bathroom is small and infested with prepubescent boy cooties. When she arrives at the door, she is carrying her dress and what I think you call a tackle box, a red one with a silver latch. My dad has one in Nantucket for fishing stuff.

"You didn't just come from fishing? Did you?" I ask, trying to sniff her for fish guts. Is there even water in Broken Spoke?

"No, no, silly. This is makeup. Some of my mom's and all of mine. I just didn't have anything else to put it all into, and I found this in my garage. It used to be my dad's. Hi, Mr. and Mrs. Houston," Kitsy says.

"Hello, Kitsy," Grandpa says. "You girls have fun. Don't know why you need to get all dolled up. You both already look beautiful. And one thing I'll never understand about women even after eighteen years with your momma: What do you girls do in the bathroom before going out?"

"We'll never tell," Kitsy says. "That's part of the magic, Mr. Houston."

After Kitsy and I have both showered and blow-dried, we discuss hairstyles. I tell Kitsy to go crazy and straighten her locks. She helps me curl mine. The results are surprising in a good way; my hair now has a natural, beachy wave that looks like I belong on a resort-wear runway.

"Do you want me to do your makeup?" Kitsy asks as she bends down for her tackle box.

I would normally say no because unless you pay someone to do something for you why would they have any incentive to do a good job?

But I know that Kitsy isn't the type to sabotage, so I say, "Sure, but don't be insulted if I wash it off. I am just used to doing things my way."

As I sit on the toilet with the seat down, I pass Kitsy my polka-dotted makeup bag.

"Let me do it with mine," Kitsy says as she reaches into the trays filled with what's clearly drugstore makeup. Maybelline. L'Oréal. Wet n' Wild? Ohmigod, this is going to be scary, but I shut my mouth. After twenty minutes of Kitsy penciling, shading, blushing, and glossing, she finally lets me look into the mirror. I brace myself, expecting to see a MTV reality show star, but what appears in the mirror is more like an airbrushed magazine advertisement: flawless skin, cheeks the color of peaches, and brown eyes that don't look like they belong to a puppy dog. Kitsy's a miracle worker.

"Holy Holly Golightly, Kitsy!" I exclaim. "How did you get so good at this?"

"Please," Kitsy says. "I just had a beautiful canvas. You have killer bone structure."

"No, really," I say, feeling like Cinderella, even though my story is more riches to rags than rags to riches. "How?" I stare intensely into the mirror, and I am very pleased with my reflection. My brown eyes finally match my complexion; for the first time, I no longer lust for blue eyes.

"Well, my mom's got a lot of makeup, and I always liked art. We didn't have many art supplies, so I have been playing with makeup since I was pint-size. Eye shadow, blush, and mascara were like my Crayolas growing up."

"But it's *drugstore makeup*," I blurt.

Kitsy just laughs and packs up her stuff. "Sometimes cheaper things, Corrinne, are really just as good as the expensive ones."

"I wouldn't go that far," I say, still checking myself out, "but thank you. You should do this professionally."

"Like in a department store?" Kitsy says. "Really? Even in New York?"

"No, not in a department store," I say. "Those people are annoying—always forcing you to take free perfume samples."

"Wait a minute." Kitsy pauses as she relatches her box. "They give away free perfume in New York?"

"Never mind about that," I say, not wanting to explain the vulture perfume salespeople and their guerrilla tactics. "You need to do it in salons and at rich people's apartments. You'd make a killing. A lot of rich people aren't naturally attractive, so they really need your services." And Kitsy just laughs and beams.

When Kitsy and I emerge from the room, all dressed up in our bargain purchases, Grandpa lets out a big whistle. Kitsy and I giggle, but inside I am happy—no one's ever whistled at me except for construction workers.

"Corrinne," Tripp says from the couch, "guess what the word of the year is? I just read it in the newspaper."

Tripp, at twelve, is already such an old man.

"What, Tripp?" I say, pleased enough with my DIY spa day to be nice to him.

"Recessionista," Tripp says. "That means someone who makes the best out of this economy and finds cheap, alternative ways to live and save money. We are recessionistas."

Grandma laughs from the kitchen as she cuts the freshly baked brownies into perfect squares.

"I think only girls can be recessionistas, Tripp. But you are right; Corrinne is turning into a recessionista. You, my friend, are my little recessionor. Now you girls have fun. And Corrinne, home by midnight. No ifs, buts, or ands about it."

Recessionista. I'd prefer fashionista, but it sure beats nouveau poor. After all, I am wearing a $24.99 dress and drugstore makeup, and I still look rocking. Now if I can just survive dinner with Bubby, I can make it to my dream boy: Rider.

Chapter 10

After the Lights

I SUPPOSE CHIN'S IS THE CLASSIER CHOICE OVER SONIC, but only because Mr. Chin isn't on roller skates and there are place mats on the tables, albeit paper Chinese calendar ones. While getting ready with Kitsy somewhat enthused me for the dance, arriving at Chin's for a pre-dance meal reminds me just how far out of my area code I am. Back in New York in the 212, we'd pick the most expensive restaurant that might not card and enjoy parent-sponsored vodka sodas and lobsters. Now in the 806, I am about to eat at a place with an orange neon sign whose *H* doesn't even light up: Here's to a night at C IN'S.

Stepping inside, Bubby holds the door for me.

"C'mon in, Manhattan," he says. "I know it isn't the Palace Hotel, but I've got to tell you the egg rolls are amazing. And I hold the record for the number per sitting: fourteen."

"Yeah, thanks a lot for that, dude," Hands says. "That's part of the reason the football team is now banned from the lunch buffet. You were literally eating the Chins's profits."

Arriving at a four-person table in the back, Kitsy puts her hand over the seat next to her.

"Corrinne," she says, "sit here. We'll save each other from listening to the playbook for the entire dinner. Honestly, I think I could coach y'all after listening to you yap for years."

Immediately I feel nauseated, but I can't pinpoint if it's from the MSG smells, the fourteen-egg-rolls story, or the entire situation.

Behind me, I feel Bubby pulling out my chair and I sit down.

"Don't worry, Corrinne," he says, leaning down toward me. "It's a Texan thing. I don't want you getting the wrong idea. We're on the same page. You want to be with Kitsy, and I want to hang with Hands. It's like a business alliance."

"Good," I say. "And I appreciate the gesture, but in New York girls are equals. From now on, I'll get my own chair."

Kitsy raises her eyebrows but says nothing.

"And who says that Yankees aren't friendly?" Bubby

jokes, and Hands high-fives him.

Filter, Corrinne, I think. For Kitsy's sake.

I order broccoli and fried rice because I think that's got to be safe anywhere, even in Texas.

After the food arrives, Mr. Chin asks, "Okay, kids, how many forks and knives?" Kitsy, Hands, and Bubby's arms shoot up. Mr. Chin walks off to retrieve them.

"C'mon, guys," I say. "You've got to eat Chinese food with chopsticks. It tastes better. And if you don't, well, that's like eating cereal with a knife."

"Actually," Kitsy says, getting a bit pink, "Mr. Chin prefers if we don't; we always get the table disgusting and the floor becomes a rice field. And as a waitress, I get it because it's pretty gross to clean up others' messes."

"And what makes you the expert in chopsticks?" Bubby asks. "Did you learn it at the Chinese Embassy or something?"

"No," I say, and shake my head. I don't mention that at cotillion we did learn the proper way to eat pasta using both a spoon and a fork in case we were ever invited to an Italian villa.

"Well," Bubby says, waving over Mr. Chin to get a round of chopsticks, "How did you learn, then?"

Taking chopsticks from Mr. Chin, I say: "It's embarrassing."

156

I unravel, snap, and hold up my chopsticks. "My friend Sarita did a chopstick diet," I confess. "Someone proved that you eat, like, forty percent less if you use chopsticks, so we all went through a chopstick phase. I can pretty much eat anything with them, even ice cream."

Bubby rolls his eyes: "Is there anything New Yorkers won't do to get skinny?"

Kitsy smiles and looks over at me. "Okay," she says, "I am ready for a lesson. Then if I come to New York, we can go to Chinatown, eat, and buy fake purses."

I let that one slide. No way, even in the recession, am I getting caught with a knockoff.

"If you can hold a pencil, you can use a chopstick," I say. With my hand over Kitsy's, I show her how to grasp one chopstick like a pencil and practice "drawing." Then I show her how to use the other as the fixed stick.

"Okay," Kitsy says, looking down at a dumpling. With a swoop motion, Kitsy picks up the dumpling.

"Can you teach her again?" Hands says. "That was surprisingly hot."

Kitsy playfully pokes her elbow in his chest. "Now teach the boys," she says. "If you can teach these jocks, we won't have any more rice fields issue. And then Mr. Chin won't have any more conniption fits."

Bubby turns out to be a natural, and even Hands, despite his large-fingers handicap, gets it after a while.

After Mr. Chin clears our table, the boys pull out cash to pay the check.

"Another formality?" I ask, feeling sorta bad that Bubby has to pay for me even though we're not actually a real couple. "I can pay my share. I do have a job these days."

"No worries," Bubby says, and he even maybe smiles at me. "This is for the chopstick lesson."

Once he puts down cash, Bubby pitches each of us a fortune cookie.

Kitsy tosses hers right back.

"I am done with fortunes from this place. I've never gotten a single good one. Why would they even make bad fortunes?"

"Who needs a good fortune when you got me?" Hands says, and kisses Kitsy on the cheek. "You can only ask for so much luck in a lifetime. I am opening mine, though—it might say something about us winning State."

"Fine," Kitsy says, grabbing hers back. "We'll all open them. Maybe for once I'll get a halfway decent one."

Filtering, I don't say the only good fortune to receive in Broken Spoke is "You will soon move somewhere better."

Reading over Kitsy's shoulder, I see her new fortune: "Accept life's struggles."

Wow, she really does get bad fortunes. I didn't think those even existed. Usually I get the one that says "You like Chinese food."

Kitsy crumples it up without even reading it aloud. "Typical," she mutters.

Cracking open mine, I find the best fortune ever: "Everything will come your way." Score: I am a believer. This must mean that my life is going to be restored, I will get Rider, this will be my only meal at Chin's, and my time in Texas will soon be just an anecdote. Catching Kitsy's eye, I notice she looks seriously depressed, shocking since it's a football-win weekend and a pre-dance Saturday. That's about as good as it gets in the B.S.

"Hey, Kitsy," I say. "Do you guys play white elephant with fortunes?"

I can't believe I am about to do this, but seeing Kitsy upset is like seeing a kitten frown.

"What's that?" Bubby says. "Is it some New York society game?"

"No," I say. "It means that everyone reads their fortunes—"

Hands interrupts, "And adds 'in bed' to it. Yeah, Texans do that too."

Bubby and Hands grunt and elbow each other.

"No," I say, and roll my eyes. "That's not the game. That's like a seventh-grade game. White elephant is where everyone reads his or her fortunes silently. You can either keep or give away your fortune, which of course is a gamble since you don't know what anyone else has."

Quickly retrieving her fortune, Kitsy extends her hand. "I'll switch," she says. "Anyone, anyone . . . ?"

Both Hands and Bubby look away. "We can't be taking any chances with your bad fortune," Hands says. "This is our year for State."

"I'll switch," I say. "I'm not much of a believer in fortune anyways. Plus, I like a gamble," I lie, reluctantly handing Kitsy my royal flush of fortune cookies.

Reading the slip aloud, "'Everything will come your way,'" Kitsy squeals. "Thanks, Corrinne. But God, I feel bad. My fortune's awful, and now it's yours."

"Read yours, Corrinne," Bubby says, eyeing me strangely.

"'Accept life's struggles,'" I say, pretending to be surprised and disappointed. Grandma would so want to embroider that one on a pillow.

"What's your fortune?" I ask Bubby. "I bet it says, 'You are a life struggle.'"

"Funny, Manhattan," he says, and pauses. "It says, 'Someone is not who you think.'"

"That's creepy," I say. "Does that, like, mean someone you know is a serial killer? You'd better sleep with one eye open."

"Maybe it's not a bad fortune," Bubby says. "C'mon, y'all, let's get out of here. There's a dance waiting. Let's hope that the amps break and we don't have to listen to that Rider kid whine."

OMG, *Rider*. All that MSG must have distracted me. Even if I did give my awesome fortune to Kitsy, I am still looking forward to the one good thing in Texas: Rider. And something tells me tonight's totally going to be our night.

Inside the gym, gray and white crepe paper haphazardly strung encompasses the bleachers. Cutout Mockingbirds of all sizes and varying artistic accuracy hang on the walls. I am used to theme parties: astronauts and aliens, bungles in jungles, Madonnarammas. But the theme at this dance is the same tired theme of Broken Spoke in general: There is one god in this town: Mockingbird football. To top it all off, there's a balloon arch where you can get your photo taken with Mack, the Mockingbird Mascot. And there's already an extremely long line for this photo op when our group arrives. I try to forget my old school dances where passed hors d'oeuvres and mocktails in the theme colors were staples and where professional party planners carried around walkie-talkies to make sure the party unfolded perfectly. Those parties didn't have Rider; they had pretty boys who prided themselves on their father's portfolios and access to prescription pills.

Trying not to look too obvious, my eyes scan the room for Rider and his band. On a makeshift stage, I spot Rider playing with the amps. Unlike Bubby and the rest of the football boys all dressed up in what seem to be their fathers' suits, Rider looks positively rock star in a pair of jeans and a black Hanes T-shirt.

I grab Kitsy's hand. "Let's go say hi."

Rider barely looks up when Kitsy and I approach the stage.

"Hi, Rider," I say a bit too loudly.

"Hey, girls," he says, looks away, and turns the amp way up. When I imagined this very scene—about a hundred times in my mind over the last week—this outcome never occurred to me. In my mind, Rider would nearly fall off the stage when he saw me. Or do a little solo dedication right then and there. But never ignore me. Maybe he really isn't into girls. Or maybe as the one good thing in Texas he doesn't need game. I see Bubby watching, so I turn up my own prowess. Corrinne sees, Corrinne gets. This whole recession isn't going to ruin my love life. I can control at least that, right?

"You going to the field tonight?" I ask, and turn to my side, hoping to show off my sculpted back.

"Maybe," Rider says, and he doesn't even look up.

"Y'all playing your new stuff?" Kitsy asks.

Rider stops fiddling with the amps, picks up his guitar, and is suddenly totally engaged. "Yeah, we are practicing our new set for the Battle of the Bands," he says.

Bingo. I should've remembered that trick from Waverly: Talk about what they like, Waverly says. She got a ton of boy advice from her late grandmother, Wilhelmina, one of the first gossip columnists for the *Post*. Even *the* Marilyn Monroe took heartbreaker lessons from Wilhelmina. Whatever the boy situation, Waverly has always had good advice.

I think quickly. WWWD? What Would Waverly Do? Waverly recommends pretending that talking to a boy is just a pit stop on your way to somewhere better.

I push out my chest for effect. "See you later," I call over my shoulder. Declarations versus questions, Waverly also always says. "You like me," not "Do you like me?" I flex up my muscles a bit. I don't look back, but I am pretty sure I feel Rider's eyes following me to Bubby and the rest of the football squad.

"You ready to dance, Manhattan?" Bubby says before he attempts an only somewhat accurate Justin Timberlake Sexyback move. Except Bubby isn't bringing sexy back; he's bringing lame back.

"I am not much of a dancer, Bubby," I lie to avoid any up-close-and-personal moments with him.

Not only did I take ballet, tap, and jazz as a child, but I

am also well versed in the waltz and the tango from cotillion.

"But I am sure there're plenty of jersey chasers who would love to get up close and sweaty with you," I say, pointing to a flock of girls checking him out. "I am more into the artistic type."

"Your loss, Manhattan," Bubby says before making his way to the cookie buffet.

Kitsy and I spend the next ten minutes in the bathroom drinking wine coolers out of Gatorade bottles.

"The one benefit of having a mom on the sauce," Kitsy says, and cringes.

Because I don't know to respond to that, I just put my hand on Kitsy's shoulder.

"Red really is your signature color," I say, changing the subject.

"Thanks," Kitsy says, and passes the Gatorade bottle back without taking a sip.

The pink wine cooler (tropical fruit flavor) isn't Dom, but it makes my head fuzzy all the same.

When we reemerge, Rider's on the microphone. "We're Friday Night After the Lights. Enjoy us while you can. Soon we'll be out of this two-star town."

"They started in Rider's garage," Kitsy says as we edge up to the front. "What if they do make it? And you are his girlfriend?"

Kitsy and I play groupies for a couple of songs and hang out at the front of the crowd. But as it turns out, Friday Night After the Lights music is one hundred percent undanceable.

"Um, Kitsy, do they have any songs that you can—as my grandpa calls it—groove to?" I ask.

"No." She shakes her head. "But everyone hires them for all the dances anyway because they are cheap and Rider's hot."

Ugh. Even though I've never been to a séance or a human sacrifice, I am pretty sure this would be the type of music that'd be played. This is terrible music for a dance, even a humdrum Broken Spoke one.

I give up trying to dance and start to just sway back and forth, but even that seems too energetic.

So I focus my attention on the words. Maybe Rider's genius is in his lyrics. Let's hope because he's most definitely not going to have a song that anyone ever requests in da club.

I look up at Rider, whose eyes are completely closed as he alternately croons and yells into the microphone:

"It's over
There ain't any cover
I don't have even a lover
This world's nothing but a heartless abyss
HEARTLESS ABYSS."

Wow. You would think that Rider grew up on the streets without shoes rather than in Broken Spoke. Don't get me wrong, Broken Spoke is torturous, but these lyrics have even me, a refugee from the recession, wanting to tell Rider that the world's not *that* bad. But so what if the music's a total downer; no rocker girl ever chose a musician for the music. It's the lifestyle that's sexy. Plus, Rider looks good, even when he's playing the wounded soul role.

After an hour of slow swaying with a few bathroom wine cooler stops, Kitsy and I are still standing up front and I'm still unsuccessfully trying to get Rider to open his eyes and notice me. Then Bubby and Hands make their way up to us.

"Okay, girls, we're out now. Let's listen to some *real* music rather than this suicide sound track," Bubby says, and he grabs my hand. "As Kitsy would cheer, P-A-R-T-Y time."

I want to argue to stay and watch Rider, but WWWD? Waverly advises never to wait on anyone and to be sure to leave before the curtain falls, so I follow the group out.

We climb into Hands's truck and head to the field, the same one as before. It's not even completely dark when we arrive; a bunch of kids have already beaten us there and are gathered around the three kegs. Apparently, the school dance is just a front for the actual party. At least that's one common thing between here and New York.

"All right, Manhattan," Bubby says. "Let's get our party on."

Figuring that I might as well loosen up a bit before Rider (hopefully) shows up, I head to the migration of students at the keg and collect a warm beer.

Bubby walks up to Hands's truck and pulls out a bag from the cab.

"What about horseshoes?" Bubby asks.

"Horseshoes?" I ask.

"Yes," Bubby says. "It's croquet for the common folk. No manicured grass courts or whites required. But you probably wouldn't want to get your fancy dress all dirty, would you, Manhattan?"

I don't bother to tell him that it's a $24.99 bargain-bin find. Let him think I am a snob, what do I care? And I get that he's not a fashion critic, but it's still awesome that he can't tell that it's not expensive.

Stepping up to Bubby, I take a horseshoe from his hand.

"I like anything that's a competition, especially when it means I can beat you. How do you play again?" I ask, examining the horseshoe, which is twice as large as a real one.

Bubby walks about fifty feet away and twists a post into the ground.

He walks back and puts his hand on my shoulder. "It's me against you," he says. "I'll go first. Watch this because you are going to want to copy it."

Bubby, with an underhand toss, hurls the horseshoe toward the stake. It lands close, but not at the stake.

"Don't worry," Bubby says. "You're a beginner and a city girl, and so I won't laugh. Or I won't laugh too hard," he says.

With a horseshoe in my hand, I look to Bubby and Kitsy, who's now standing next to him. "I am used to adapting; I think I've proved that," I say.

I toss it and it lands almost on the stake.

Pointing at it, I say, "Pretty sure that means I win. Like they say, close only counts in horseshoes and grenades. By the way, I have played horseshoes, like, at least a dozen times in Central Park. Guess I am not the only one with stereotypes, Bubby."

"Touché, Manhattan. And I'll admit you're not bad for a girl," Bubby says, and taps me on the butt. "Especially a city girl," he adds.

The liquid's making me feel nicer, so I decide not to break Bubby's arm. "And you aren't so bad for a Neanderthal," I say, and give Bubby a little hip check.

A few horseshoe wins later, I spy Rider's car drive into the field. Parking among the trucks, his two-door Honda sticks out. Perfect, I think, it's just like him—standing out in a crowd. I don't walk over to him right away; I stay by the keg and wait for him to get thirsty. Finally, he walks over.

"Hey, girl," he says. "You left early."

I stumble as I sip my beer. "I was hoping that I'd get a private concert later, so I figured it would be okay to leave early. Want a beer before the football team empties the kegs?"

"I don't drink," Rider says. "It's too generic for a musician because it's totally expected and it eventually ruins your career or your life. I am sober."

"Oh," I say, dumping out the rest of my beer in the grass. "Me too, really. I was just thirsty." I figure Rider's no-drink policy must also keep those washboard abs intact, so I am grateful for his sobriety.

And then Bubby walks up and edges between Rider and me. "So you don't drink now, Manhattan?" he says, tousling my hair.

Please, Bubby, I think, go back to your cave. Didn't we both agree that it was an arranged date and haven't we both fulfilled our contractual duties?

Rider looks Bubby straight in the eye and says, "How about that concert, Corrinne? I got my guitar in the car." And as if we are in a movie, he takes my hand and walks me away. Ohmigod, it's all happening. I can hear Bubby making puking noises behind us, but I pay no mind. Corrinne's finally got her groove back.

Rider collects his guitar. We sit down around the deserted bonfire; Rider even lays out his corduroy coat for me to sit on.

"Don't want you to ruin your pretty dress, darling," he says.

"Oh, this old thing?" I drawl before I wink at him.

"I wrote you a song," Rider says, pulling his guitar out of the case.

"W-what?" I stammer. I want to say I thought you were gay or blind or both, but I pull it together. Never look surprised that someone wants you, Waverly says. Why should that be a surprise?

"Only one person's ever done that before," I lie between my teeth.

"Well, you inspired me. The girls here are boring. No one thinks about anything besides the next game or the next party. Everyone seems content to just get old and die here," Rider says as he starts to strum the guitar. "You seem different."

I look around: Where is a camera when I need one? I don't care that I am wearing a cheap, beer-stained dress. I am being serenaded by the hottest rocker ever. Talk about a new profile picture! My new Facebook status update needs to be, *Sometimes your life figures out how to get amazing, See y'all on the next cover of* Us Weekly.

Rider keeps strumming. "This isn't really my usual style, but I want to go solo eventually."

Brilliant, I think. Rider is already about to pull a Nick Jonas and drop his band. Smart Rider, because going solo will just get him more name recognition and he won't just be the hot guy from that After the Lights band. He'll be Rider Jones. And then we won't have to deal with the band being jealous of the girlfriend—that Yoko Ono thing. . . . Enough talking, Rider. More singing about me. I cock my head to one side and gaze into Rider's eyes.

And in the telltale tune of "Take Me Home, Country Roads," Rider strums away:

> *"Almost heaven, her Levi jeans*
> *Third-rate small town*
> *Middle of nowhere*
> *Life is sad here*
> *Sadder than a teardrop*
> *Sadder than a broken heart*
> *Broken Spoke*
>
> *City girl, take me away*
> *To the place I belong*
> *New York City, Manhattan girl*
> *Take me there, city girl."*

So Rider *did* notice my Levi's. I blink a bunch of times and try to hold back my tears. He really did notice me; my shoveling manure wasn't a total waste. I start a slow clap and don't look away from Rider. He gently puts down his guitar and crawls toward me. Closing my eyes, I feel his lips on my own.

And then in the middle of the lip lock, I hear a distinctive voice, Bubby's voice, calling, "Manhattan, Grandma and Grandpa want you home before it's dark. Hurry before you turn back into a stiletto."

Pulling back from Rider, I spot the Neanderthal getting closer. I want to tell Bubby to get lost because I am in the middle of the most romantic moment of my *entire life*.

"It's okay," Rider says. "You should go. I need to work on the rest of your song."

I stand up to leave. Waverly always says act like your interest in a guy is a seven, even if it is really an eleven. And I am so calling Waverly the *second* I get home. I wish I could've iPhoned her that kiss.

Bubby just shakes his head at me. "A city girl like you sweet on some wannabe rock star. I thought you'd be smarter, Corrinne."

"And I didn't think you knew my real name," I reply, following him to Hands's truck and trying desperately to resist my urge to turn my head back to Rider. Never look back, Waverly says. You can undo all your hard work at playing it cool in just a single glance.

I arrive at Grandma and Grandpa's doorstep at 12:05 a.m. My head's still a little fuzzy, part warm beer hangover, part I-just-fell-in-love. Crossing my fingers that my preteenlike curfew has a few minutes' leeway, I am relieved to see the house is pitch-black.

I fumble my way into my pitch-black room.

"Hi, Corrinne," a familiar voice says from the sheets.

"Holy shit!" I stumble and fall onto the bed. "Hi, Mom."

"You smell like cheap beer," my mom says, and shakes her head.

"And you arrived unannounced," I say, making my way under the covers.

"Apartment officially got sold," she says. "And I took the next flight out. I've missed my kids, so put on your pajamas and tell me about Texas since you don't return my calls."

All I can think is Rider, Rider, Rider, world tour, magazine photo spreads, free clothes, swag, the end of this recession . . . but I indulge my mother. My phone call to Waverly will have to wait; she's probably busy getting to know Vladlena anyways. I slip off my dress and put on my pajamas.

"I hear you have a job," my mom says as I wiggle underneath the covers. "I am proud of you, Corrinne. I didn't know you had it in you."

And maybe, just maybe, my mom meant that nicely, but it didn't sound nice. I yank the comforters to my side and flip over to face the wall.

"And I didn't know that you were a Rodeo Queen that dated someone named Dusty and then left town because you thought you were too good," I say, and close my eyes. "Good night, Mom."

"Corrinne," my mother says sternly as she yanks back on the covers. "That's not true."

"Hmm," I whisper. "You'd better call the newspaper and get them to write an editorial then because that's how everyone remembers you, Jenny Jo."

My mother sits up straight in bed, as if waking from a nightmare.

She reaches across me and turns on the bedside lamp.

I quickly cover my eyes with my hands.

"Are you trying to blind me?" I shriek. "You've taken everything else, and now you are taking my eyesight."

Flipping onto my stomach, I envelop my head with a pillow.

"Corrinne," my mom says loudly, "don't talk about things you don't know."

I fumble for the light and switch it back off.

"Maybe we're just talking about things you want to forget," I say, turning over onto my back. "Why don't you check out that box in the closet tomorrow? I think a few of Grandma's tears might still be in it."

My mom falls back into a lying position.

"What box?" she says.

"Oh, just the box with flower clippings, dress patterns, and recipes. You know, for the wedding Grandma planned for you, the one you shunned for the Plaza. But as you said, it's nothing I know anything about. Night night," I say, and roll back onto my stomach.

"Corrinne," my mother starts, but I don't answer.

"Oh God, she's still talking about the wedding. That was twenty frickin' years ago," my mom mutters to herself.

Lifting my head from the pillow, I say chipperly, "See you in the morning. Just in case you also forgot, Grandma doesn't believe in coffee."

Nothing is going to ruin this night, not even sleeping in a full-size bed with my mother. "Almost heaven, her Levi jeans," I softly sing to myself as a little lullaby.

Chapter 11

Back in the Saddle

WAKING UP TO AN EMPTY BED, I hope that the Return of the Momster was just a nightmare and that she didn't really barge back into my life on my most romantic night ever. Unfortunately I find Mom at the kitchen table, drinking a Diet Coke at nine a.m. Where'd she get that? Grandpa and Tripp are also at the table, both chowing down on pancakes. Grandma's perched at the stove, as per usual.

"Morning, Corrinne," Grandpa says between bites.

"Corrinne," Grandma says, "do you want chocolate chips in your pancakes?" And she holds up a tablespoon of chips over the batter.

"Yes, please," I say. "Pumpkin or banana today?" I ask. I notice my mother's mouth hanging wide open at me.

"I didn't think you ate carbs, Corrinne," my mom

says, eyeing my shape. "You're looking thin too."

"Watch it, Jenny Jo," Grandma says in a stern voice. "We don't do the oxygen diet under my roof."

"That's not what I meant, Mom," my mom says. "It's just surprising since she looks like she's been dieting. From what I remember, your cooking isn't exactly low-cal."

Grandma walks to the table and noisily sets down another platter, then gives Mom a look. Love it.

"Oh, Mom," I say, "I got this new bod with a thing called a job. Manual labor. You should try it," I say. Old grudges die hard.

"You used to eat pancakes when you were her age too if you remember, Jenny Jo," Grandpa pipes up between bites.

"Dad, don't call me Jenny Jo. It's J.J. now," my mom says, almost drooling over the pancakes.

"Grandpa," I ask, "will you drive me to the barn? I promised Ginger that I'd help out today." This is a total lie. I don't work Sundays, but I am just hoping that Rider might be there. If it means I get to hang out with Rider, I'll gladly shovel manure for free.

"To Ginger's?" my mom asks, picking a bite of pancake off Tripp's plate. "I'll take you there."

"Can I come too?" Tripp begs.

"No, Tripp," I say. "And stop asking me that. I'm sixteen, you're twelve. We're not friends."

"Corrinne—" my mother starts.

Grandpa interrupts, folding up his paper and tapping Tripp on the head. "I am sure what Corrinne means is that you can't go because me and you are going on a farm call. There's a tractor that needs fixin'."

"It's okay, Grandpa," Tripp says. "I am used to Corrinne never wanting to do anything with me. Luckily she's not *that* sweet, so I really don't care. Tractors will be cool instead."

Great, I am finally enjoying something—okay, some-*one*—in Broken Spoke and Tripp's giving me big-sister guilt. But I am not giving in to it.

"I'll drop you ladies off first," Grandpa says.

I realize quickly that I need to stop this. My mother is not invited to my romantic afternoon with Rider.

"Mom," I say, carefully syruping my pancakes, "why don't you stay with Grandma and get adjusted? Maybe you can go with her to church. I don't think that's a place you've visited in a while. I really need to concentrate on my work."

My mom totally lifts her eyebrows at that last comment and Grandma, Grandpa, and Tripp laugh. But what do I care? I am in love and about a millimeter away from becoming famous.

Rider's not at the stables when I get there. I am Bummed-out Betty.

"You aren't on the schedule today," Ginger says, coming out of the barn.

"U-um," I stammer, watching Grandpa and Tripp pull out of the parking lot, "I just came to help out."

Ginger's eyes get really big.

"Wow," Ginger says, not hiding her surprise. "That's kind. No offense, but I originally didn't take you as the volunteer type." She points to the horse in the pasture, a beautiful chestnut with a white patch on his face.

"I know that rodeo ain't your thing, Corrinne. But how about you take Smudge for a ride? He needs some exercise."

Although I made my pact to remain faithful to Sweetbread, I agree anyway. Riding a horse, even if it's Western style, has to be better than shoveling manure for free. Plus, I am doing it for work, not pleasure, so Sweetbread would understand.

"Where's the saddle?" I ask. "I'll go get it."

"Ain't one," Ginger says, and shakes her head.

"Wait, bareback?" I ask, and my mouth gapes open. This idea totally freaks me out since I've never done it. Hell, I've never even ridden a horse in jeans! This is a long way from my stable in Connecticut.

"When in Texas," Ginger starts, "do as the Texans do."

There's only one Texan thing—okay, Texan—I'm

interested in, but I filter myself and duck under the fence to the pasture. Surprisingly I manage to climb over the top rung of the fence and get myself onto Smudge's back.

Ginger whistles. "Maybe there's a cowgirl in you yet." Once on Smudge, I totally feel like I am cheating on Sweetbread. And though I don't want to admit it, being in the saddle again feels fantastic even if there isn't actually a saddle.

Ginger opens the gate, and I trot Smudge into the ring. "Just ride him around a few times, try to get his heart rate up. I am going to check on some stuff inside." Ginger slips into her office in the barn.

"You should try the barrels, Levi's," a familiar voice says. I look back. Holy Holly Golightly, it's Rider. Sitting up straight and brushing the wisps out of my face, I give a tiny wave. Like Waverly says, present yourself like everyone's about to take your picture, chin up, suck in, and smile.

Now, I had seen the barrels done a couple of times when I was at the barn last week. To me, it looked like a deathtrap. The horse gallops at a breakneck pace and makes a quick turn around the barrel. There's no beauty to it, just a lot of dust and danger. No way I'd do it unless the boy of my dreams asked me to, which he just did. And really, how hard can it be? I've ridden for years. I'm capable of making a horse dance.

"Hi, Rider," I call. "If you say so . . ."

I give Smudge a big old nudge. And with that kick, Smudge takes off like the 5 Express train.

"Eek!" I scream as I shoot backward.

I end up soaring in the air and landing with a hard thud. My face goes red. My first thought is, Where's Rider? And is there any way he might have missed seeing that catastrophe? I spot Rider, just standing at the corner of the ring and watching me. Flying straight out of the barn, Ginger runs toward me.

"Corrinne, you okay? I heard a lot of commotion. Did something spook Smudge?" Ginger asks, out of breath.

Ginger ducks into the ring and grabs onto Smudge.

I try to push myself back up. "Holy shit!" I scream. It feels like an elephant just sat on my wrist.

"What's wrong, Corrinne?" Ginger says.

"My wrist!" I wail.

"Rider!" Ginger beckons. "Come get Smudge so I can look at Corrinne."

Unable to get out of what I now recognize—and smell— as manure, I sit and swear softly. Talk about cursed: Just when I think my life is getting better, all of a sudden I am sitting in shit in front of the one boy who makes Broken Spoke feel more destined than doomed. And I am also pretty sure I've broken my wrist.

"Let me see," Ginger says after passing Smudge on

to Rider, who has yet to begin behaving like my knight in shining armor.

"Yup," Ginger says, looking at my contorted wrist. "You did a number. C'mon, I'll drive you to the hospital. I am an old hat at this."

Now I decide to just let my tears fall. How can a man resist his woman's tears? Gazing at Rider through blurry eyes. I wait for him to scoop me up, carry me to his truck, and heal me with kisses. But Rider still just stands there, holding on to Smudge and staring.

"Feel better, Corrinne," Rider calls as Ginger gently stands me up. "Facebook me later. Sorry—I am just more musical than medicinal. That stuff freaks me out." As I put pressure onto my legs, everything goes black. . . .

After I came to at the stable, Ginger forced me to go to the ER. I must have passed out again because now I am in a hospital bed. My mom, my grandparents, and Ginger are all standing around and staring at me. When they see me open my eyes, they get really hush-hush. A doctor steps through the crowd.

"Hello, Corrinne," he says. "I am Dr. Sullivan. You had us scared. What's the last thing you remember? We need to make sure you don't have a concussion."

I want to think this whole thing's been a dream, that I am still in New York, that the recession didn't happen, that I don't smell like shit, that I didn't break my wrist, that my last solid memory wasn't Rider rejecting a total potential hero moment. However, I can see my arm is in a sling, my wrist is throbbing, and I am still wearing my cowboy boots, so I figure that this is real. And of course, my doctor isn't even hot like on TV. If he were on TV, he'd be called McNotSteamyorDreamy.

"I don't have a concussion, just a serious case of are-you-kidding-me-is-this-my-real-life-itis," I say.

"The pain from your wrist caused you to pass out for a few seconds," Dr. Sullivan says, making notes on his chart. "We'll keep you for a couple of hours for observation in case you do have a concussion, but you should be just fine. And your wrist is only sprained, so it could be worse."

Worse? Really? How? My phone, I think. Where is it? Maybe Rider texted that he's bringing flowers. Maybe we'll still be rock royalty.

"Where's my phone?" I ask, searching the room for it with my eyes.

"Kids and their technology." Ginger laughs, rifling through her jeans back pocket to retrieve my iPhone.

With my one good hand, I scan through my text messages. Three messages. All from Waverly.

> Waverly: Vladlena's a Russian goddess. She's been in Russian *Vogue* 3 times.

She definitely showers daily.

Waverly: Call me. I want to hear how my cowgirl's doing.

Waverly. OHMIGOD. Smith fb'd me to ask if I need a private tour of the school. OHMIGOD. What should I wear? Underwear or no underwear?

OHMIGOD. I might as well stay checked into the hospital indefinitely. My life stinks.

"What can I get you, Corrinne?" my mom asks just as my phone rings.

I am ready to silence it because I assume it's Waverly with another message about how awesome her life is with her new BFF Vladlena and hottie-tottie Smith. But then I see it's Kitsy, so I answer in an attempt to ignore my mother.

"Corrinne," Kitsy screeches. "Are you okay? Rumor is you fell off a horse. I am headed to the hospital with a Sonic Blast. I'll be there in ten. Don't die on me."

Before I can say anything, Kitsy has hung up.

"Kitsy," I say to Grandma and Grandpa.

Grandpa laughs. "Kitsy talks even faster than a New Yorker. You remember Amber, Jenny Jo? She was a few years younger than you. That's Kitsy's mom."

My mom whips her head toward Grandpa and asks, "Amber from high school? The Mockingbirdette Amber? She's still in Broken Spoke?"

"Not everyone ran away and married money,"

184

Grandma says. "She's got a daughter and a son now. Corrinne is friends with Kitsy, who is a real sweet girl."

"Now, now," Grandpa says. "How about we leave Corrinne with her momma?" Grandpa starts heading toward the door with Grandma and Ginger at his heels.

"I'll make something special for tomorrow morning, Corrinne," Grandma says, "Pancakes, French toast, muffins. You name it. You rest now."

"Next time you want to do the barrels," Ginger says, "just ask. I'll be happy to teach you like I taught your momma." And Ginger gently shuts the door behind her.

"Oh, honey," my mom says, pulling up a chair and stroking my head. "How do you feel?"

"I feel like just when my life started not to suck," I start, "you show up, I almost break my wrist, and now I am stuck in a hospital room with you. And don't even get me started on how some Russian heiress is sleeping in what should be my XL twin bed at Kent."

"I see you haven't lost your dramatic flair," my mom says. "I called your father to let him know about your accident. He said he was sending flowers. I tried to explain to him that Broken Spoke doesn't have a florist. But you know how he doesn't really understand life outside Manhattan."

That makes two of us, except I don't understand life outside of Manhattan or inside the recession.

"Oh," I say, fumbling for the TV remote to tune out my mother. "Did they leave any painkillers at least?"

"It's only a sprain," my mom says. "You were probably just a bit dehydrated from your late-night adventures. *That's* why you passed out."

I *adore* how my mom thinks that everything, even this, is my fault. She probably blames the whole recession on me.

"Knock, knock," Kitsy squeals. Opening the door, she's wearing her cheerleading uniform. In one hand, she's got the promised Sonic Blast and in the other, she's got her pom-poms. Of course.

"Oh, hi," Kitsy says. "You must be Corrinne's mom. I feel terrible I didn't bring you a Sonic Blast."

"A Sonic what?" my mom says, eyeing the soupy chocolate and peanut butter ice-cream mess.

"Sonic Blast," Kitsy says. "You don't have Sonics in Manhattan? Excuse my manners; I am just so pleased to meet you, ma'am."

"Ma'am," my mom repeats. "I left Texas before anyone ever called me that. It makes me feel old." Then as if remembering something, my mother extends her hand "Excuse my manners, I'm pleased to meet you too, Kitsy," my mom says. "Are you a Mockingbirdette?" my mom asks, pointing to her pom-poms. "God, I haven't seen those uniforms in forever. They look exactly the same."

Kitsy blushes. "I'm team captain. First sophomore

captain ever. I think you knew my mom, too—she was a few years younger."

"How is your mother?" my mom says, and gets up to give Kitsy her chair.

"She's fine," Kitsy says. "She'll die when she hears you're back in town."

My mom pauses and frowns. "Well, I'll mosey down to the vending machines and let you girls chit-chat. Call me if you need anything, Corrinne."

Kitsy plops down on the chair. "I'll spoon-feed you," she says. "It's what I do when my brother's sick. What happened anyway?"

"I fell off a horse . . . in front of Rider," I say. "Into a pile of manure. And he didn't even help me. Ginger was my heroine."

We both laugh. "Bubby's the one who told me you were here. I have no idea how he found out. I think he has Corrinne radar," Kitsy says before stuffing my mouth with ice-cream deliciousness. "After the dance, I am sure he's sweet on you—everyone thinks so, even though he won't admit it. Hands told me that Bubby said that you were a looker, for a city girl."

"Kitsy," I whisper, "I couldn't tell you in the truck last night and then my mom showed up and then this happened . . . but Rider kissed me. On the mouth. With tongue."

Kitsy rolls her eyes and takes a big spoonful for herself. "You go, girl! I knew you'd get Rider. . . . Bubby actually told me about the kiss too. He says that you'll realize that Rider's a tool soon enough, though, and come around."

Come around? Really, that kid is as dense as Grandma's chocolate pound cake.

Kitsy continues, "I told him that he seems pretty concerned for someone who supposedly isn't sweet on you. Watch out, though: When Bubby does set his mind to something, he gets it—that's why he's so good at football and reporting."

"Even though Rider didn't exactly have hero moves today, I'll still choose the rock star over the hometown hero," I say. "I don't look particularly good in a football jersey; rock star really matches my look better. Thanks for coming, Kitsy," I say. "Nice to have someone other than my mother to hang out with. She's been here a day, and I already feel like I am overdosing on her."

"I have the opposite problem with my mom," Kitsy says, flipping on the TV. "Let's watch some infomercials."

After watching a robot that folds your clothes, I laugh hard enough to almost forget about my wrist, Rider the antihero, and Waverly, my insensitive best friend. My phone bings again with a text.

Daddy-o: Heard about the accident. ☹ Instead of sending flowers, I emailed Waverly's mom to see if Waverly can visit you for her fall break. I'll use my miles for the ticket. Feel better. ☺

Waverly, here in Broken Spoke? That would equal social ruin . . . unless I could get Rider to serenade me in public with paparazzi in the wings. That might keep my PR afloat enough to cover up this whole year-in-Texas ordeal.

Kitsy must've watched my face drop because she grabs my hand. "What is it?" she asks gently.

"Oh, it's okay." I sigh. "My best friend from home might come to visit."

Slowly Kitsy pulls her hand away and stands up. "Oh," she says. "That's—um, that's great. We'll have to think of fun stuff to do if it happens. I gotta run, I'm meeting the Mockingbirdettes. We have a team picture! Let me know if you need anything."

When my mom comes back in after Kitsy leaves, she reclaims her chair.

"Did you hear the good news?" she asks. "Your dad wants to use his miles so Waverly can visit."

Once again I get the sickening feeling that I am not sure this is good news.

"Mom," I ask, "are you sure they don't do morphine for sprained wrists?"

"Oh, Corrinne," she says. "Your drug jokes are getting tired." And she looks up at the TV and watches for a few seconds. "Is that robot folding clothes?" she asks.

And we both laugh. "I might just have to buy that," my mom says. "It will help me out since I am now our housekeeper."

"How recessionista," I say. "For three easy payments of thirty-nine ninety-nine, we could have one."

But knowing now what it's like to earn only $7.50 an hour, buying a folding machine doesn't seem like a good investment, even if it means never having to fold again. Although it might be very helpful, considering that it's impossible to fold with one arm. Then it hits me: I need to figure out how to shovel with one arm shot—otherwise I am going to miss out on quality time with Rider.

Chapter 12

Who's Kate Spade?

I STAY HOME FROM SCHOOL ON MONDAY. Why not use this sprained-wrist thing to my advantage? But by Tuesday, I am ready to go back. You can only watch so much *Gossip Girl* with your mother. She asks too many uncomfortable questions about who has slept with who and why. Plus, Rider added me as a friend on Facebook and sent a message that said,

"Levi's, I didn't know you could fly. Doesn't surprise me, though. Come back to school soon. Since we're both going to Ginger's after school, want to ride with me from now on?"

I know that isn't a sonnet in iambic pentameter, but it's the closest I've ever come to getting a love letter. Daily one-on-one time with Rider in enclosed spaces? Sign me up!

My mom has to help me dress on Tuesday, which is obviously awkward, especially the snapping-the-bra part.

"I miss helping you, Corrinne," my mom says, pulling a shirt over my head.

"But Mom, you're the one who always taught me to be independent. You can't have it both ways. Besides, I should be at boarding school by myself. Instead here I am in Texas, partially handicapped, being dressed by my mother."

"I really should have put you in theater," my mom says. "You're fabulous at being dramatic."

"Yes," I said, "you should have. I could've been a child star and supported you guys, and then we would not be in this mess. Of course, the second you tried to steal my money, I would've sued for emancipation," I say with a straight face.

"That I believe too," my mom says. "You have a good day at school, honey. Be careful with your arm."

Looking in the mirror, I think that for having to wear a sling, I still look okay.

During Spanish class, Bubby walks to my desk in the back.

"Manhattan," he says, "city slickers shouldn't be riding bareback."

I pucker my face.

"I actually am a good rider," I say. Or I was, I think.

"The horse just got spooked or something."

"Mm-hm," Bubby replies, and nods as if to say "Surrrre." "It had nothing to do with a certain boy that was there?"

Giving him the evil eye, I open my Spanish book and fake study.

"Just so you know," Bubby says before returning to his seat, "if I had been there, I would have carried you to the hospital on my back."

On the way out of class, Bubby offers to take my books, and I let him. Maybe he isn't a complete Neanderthal, especially since he finally shaved that stubble.

After school Rider and I take his car to pick up Tripp before we go to the barn. While I wasn't keen on having Tripp be the third wheel to our twosome car dates, I realized I need Tripp since I am crippled. He promised to do all my dirty work for half my pay. So basically, Tripp will do my job, and I will get paid to hang out with Rider. That part is genius, I know.

When we arrive at Tripp's middle school, he jumps right into the car.

"What's her name?" he asks Rider.

"Name?" Rider repeats.

"Yes," Tripp says. "Grandpa's truck is Billie Jean, and that Hands guy has Banana. So what's this car's name?"

"It doesn't have one. Only hicks name their cars," Rider says.

Tripp's face deflates.

But I don't say anything. Rider is right, after all.

Maybe Rider senses Tripp's hurt because at the stop sign, Rider turns right and pulls down a side road.

"Hey, Tripp, have you ever seen our state flower?"

"The bluebonnet," I answer. Thank you, Texas State History.

"We hate the Bluebonnets," Tripp says. "They're our biggest rival in football. They are the same team that almost beat Grandpa's team for State fifty-two years ago. Final score: forty-two to thirty-five. It was a close one."

"That's true," Rider answers. "But the actual flower is incredible—it grows to like a foot high. They usually don't last until fall, but I know where some still are. A popular Texas tradition is to take portraits with them. Want to become an authentic Texan and get your photo taken, Tripp?"

"Totally," Tripp says. "I am half Texan by blood. And we can make a Facebook album."

Ducking under a fence, Tripp, Rider, and I walk into a green field. In a shaded corner, a few bluebonnets still stand triumphantly.

If a fashion designer saw this, bluebonnet would totally be the color of the year.

Tripp plops down into the flowers. I pull out my iPhone and he puts on a photo shoot. I don't even make fun of him for his ridiculous poses because I like this big-brother side of Rider. It almost makes up for him leaving me in the manure.

On our way back to the car, Rider picks me a bluebonnet, and I tuck it behind my ear. I am so pressing it in my geography book tonight. No one has ever given me flowers before except for corsages that were obviously picked out by my dates' mothers, not my dates.

As we drive up to the stables, Ginger comes out of the barn when she sees me.

"You are full of surprises, Corrinne," she says. "But I am not exactly sure how you are going to work with one hand."

"That's why she brought me," Tripp pipes up. "I am going to help her—like an intern."

"What a brother you are!" Ginger says, and claps her hands.

"Well, I am working on my résumé and work experience," Tripp says. "The business world is shaky these days, and you can't start too young." We laugh because Tripp is serious. It makes me miss my dad a little bit. He'd be proud: two employed children.

"Okay, Tripp," Ginger says. "Follow Rider into the

barn. Teach him well, Rider." And without even a good-bye, the two of them leave me with Ginger.

"You, girl," she says, pointing her finger at me, "are going to help me get ready for the rodeo. You can't break anything doing office work."

I want to scream and run into the barn to be near Rider. But, as Waverly always says, make sure the boy knows that you have a life too. So I decide to be a working woman and embark on my first office job. I follow Ginger into a small structure that houses the gift shop (lame T-shirts and key chains) and a tiny office.

Ginger points to her messy desk, complete with towering piles of paper that make the Leaning Tower of Pisa look like it has good posture.

"You are going to go through the submissions for the rodeo and enter the applicants into the database. This is how we'll make the program for the different events—the Rodeo Queen, the barrel racing, the mutton busting, et cetera, et cetera."

Two hours into being a secretary with only one good hand, I am miserable. Maybe there's an infomercial where I can buy a robot to do my job. Ten thousand butterflies collide in my stomach when Rider steps into the office.

"Hey, Levi's, it's quitting time. Your brother's a hell of a lot better at shoveling than you are, but I missed the view. You do look cute behind a desk too, though."

I try not to blush.

"Oh, Rider," I say, rolling my eyes at all the paperwork. "I didn't realize how monumental the rodeo is. There's like twenty events and a zillion competitors."

"Yeah, it's the number one moneymaking event in town, after the football concessions, of course. The profits keep this place going," Rider says. "My band's playing, too. It's sorta amateur, but we can't give up a chance for publicity."

"You guys will be great," I say as I slip by Rider and accidentally (okay, not accidentally) touch his hand. "But I thought you were going solo."

"Harder to get a solo gig," Rider says. "Hey, did you know anyone in the business back in Manhattan?"

"What business?" I ask, heading to Rider's car, where Tripp is waiting.

"The music business, Corrinne," Rider says, exasperated.

Oh, I am so dumb.

"Of course," I say, happy to be able to impress him. "My friend's dad is 212 Degrees's agent."

Rider stops dead in his tracks. "Your friend's dad is Phil Porticelli?"

"Yup," I say, and smile. One hundred points for Corrinne.

"That's amazing. He's legendary." Rider is almost

gasping for air when he gets into the car. "Could you send my demo to him?"

OMG, I think. I am just name-dropping. I haven't talked to Phil Porticelli's daughter, Portia, since middle school. And I was slightly responsible for her getting blacklisted from the Sexy Six when we decided to become the Fab Five. No way would she or her dad ever be willing to help me.

"Sure," I lie. "I'll see what I can do."

Rider leans over—with Tripp in the backseat—and kisses me on the cheek. "Thanks, Levi's."

"Sick," Tripp squeals. "I want to go home." But I pay no attention. My life just got back on track.

I finally get Waverly on the phone. We've barely talked since I left New York. We text, we Facebook, I follow her tweets about Kent this and Kent that, but there haven't been any epic calls like we usually have when we are apart. Now, this might be due to the fact that I don't want to hear about her Holy Trinity: Kent, Smith, and Vladlena. But I do want to tell her about Rider and my song. I also need to figure out if she's really coming to Broken Spoke so I can go into crisis-control mode.

"Waverly!" I squeal when she picks up before voice mail.

"Cowgirl," she says with a fake Texan accent. "How

y'all doing?" I let the "y'all" thing slide. She'll figure out Texan grammar once she visits.

"Did your mom get my dad's email?" I say, and pause. "About you visiting?"

"Yup," she says. "My mom and your dad even booked my ticket. Everyone goes away for fall break, and I am happy not to go back to the city. NYC is so boring this year; everyone is staying home all the time and saving money. Besides, Smith's going on college visits, so it's perfect."

Waverly in Broken Spoke? She's going to feel like Dorothy when she first steps into Oz, except Texans aren't as cute as Munchkins. And they don't sing. And wait, how does she know that Smith's going on college visits? She totally boynapped my Prince Charming.

"Waverly," I start, making sure my door is locked so my mom won't barge in, "are you with Smith?" I don't really want to know the answer because until Texas happened, I thought it would be me who was his arm candy.

"God no," Waverly says. "We're just hooking up. You know how it is."

And of course I do. Neither Waverly nor I has had *real* boyfriends. I am hoping that I'll be able to call Rider my boyfriend by the time Waverly shows up. Finally, I'd be the first at something.

"What should I pack?" Waverly says. "What department stores do you have there?"

Um, I think. How do I put this gently? Broken Spoke is the heart of darkness for department stores. The horror, the horror. "The town's actually having a big event that weekend, so we probably won't have time to shop. Just pack as much as you can."

"Well, duh," Waverly says. "I am thinking about emergencies. What's the big event? Charity gala?"

This is going to be harder than I thought. Waverly hates horses, even my Sweetbread. How am I going to tell her that her visit coincides with the town rodeo?

"It's, uh, a performance-slash-concert. The guy I'm crushing on is going to play," I lie.

I hear a loud knock on my door. "Corrinne, dinner," my mom calls.

"Wait," Waverly says. "Did your mother just call you to dinner like they do on TV?"

"Something like that," I say. "I'll call you later. Can't wait to see you."

"Me too," Waverly replies. "I am off to some society meeting."

I quickly hang up before Waverly can elaborate on the society meeting or ask more questions about why my mom's calling me to dinner. I have become so accustomed to eating actual family dinners that I almost forgot I haven't always lived this way. There's got to be a name for what I have: Stockholm Syndrome, right? That's when you *almost* forget that you've been kidnapped and taken to Texas against your will? Of course, your best friend from your past life will make you remember this all too quickly. This is especially true when you have to take her to a rodeo.

The office job turns out not to be too terrible. It's better than the manure gig. I bring my own laptop to Ginger's because I got exhausted by her turtle-paced computer, which takes up almost the entire room. Plus, Ginger's computer crashes even more often than the stock market.

Ginger comes into my office and hands me a copy of last year's rodeo program. It's black-and-white and totally amateur.

"Ginger," I start slowly, "do you think I could update this?"

I don't add "to the twenty-first century," but I am thinking it. I am getting better at filtering every day.

"What are you considering?" Ginger asks, looking it over.

"I could attach a picture to each event," I say, becoming inspired. "A sheep on the mutton busting, a barrel for the barrel racing, and so on. It'll be simple and chic. Think Kate Spade."

"Who's Kate Spade? Does she live in Broken Spoke?" Ginger asks. Before I can answer that she's a famous designer, Ginger says, "Do what you want, sweetie, but remember, we can't spend any money on it. The whole purpose of this rodeo is to keep our doors open. And if I had any extra money, I'd spend it on equipment to help kids with handicaps get to ride. The worst thing ever is when I have to turn kids away just because I can't afford the stuff that'd make it safe."

And then I have a flash of business genius.

"How about a silent auction?" I ask. "It's free to put on and every good party in New York has one. The money raised can go toward buying the equipment you want for the kids."

"What a nice idea!" Ginger says. "But auction what? Everyone around here is pretty strapped these days."

I think for a moment. What would anyone want from Broken Spoke?

"Sonic," I answer. "My friend Kitsy works there. And I bet Chin's would donate too. And my grandpa's a mechanic, so he could offer services. Plus, we both know Grandma likes any excuse to bake. Maybe she could do cooking lessons."

Even I am surprised with my ingenuity. Of course, the items aren't a week at the Ritz in Cabo or dinner with the mayor, but it will still make the rodeo a bit more glamorous and give it a philanthropic element.

"Sure, girl," Ginger says. "I love the way you are

thinking. And it would be great to finally be able to have all Spokers ride here."

I don't admit my sprucing up the rodeo is mostly because I don't want Waverly to think that Broken Spoke's totally primitive. Even though it won't be like a gala for the opera, I am most certainly going to make it the best rodeo this town has ever seen. And I can add it to my college application if I am not touring with Rider full-time by then.

With Rider working in the barn and me working inside the office, I only see him during our car rides. Since Tripp's there, the romance factor is in the negative, especially considering Tripp hums the *Twilight Zone* theme every time we get close. Besides, Rider keeps asking about Mr. Porticelli and Portia, and I have run out of excuses. *I Facebooked Portia to ask. She's spending the semester abroad. I don't know how Internet access in Bermuda is. . . .* I am hoping that Waverly will help me solve this one. Maybe she's met some other music mogul's kid at Kent.

Rider's having a concert in his garage over the weekend, the same garage where his band all started. His parents won't be there, and it's happening after the game, literally Friday Night After the Lights. I wonder if Rider would ever sing my song in public. Hopefully he'll save that for Waverly's visit, so she'll be jealous of *something* in Texas. My grandpa's going to drive with me to the airport to get Waverly, and I am pumped for her to see me behind the driver's wheel. She's going to totally flip. If she doesn't have a heart attack then, she's definitely going to have one when she sees Grandma and Grandpa's house. Thank God Mom agreed to sleep on the couch that weekend.

"So that's where the term *garage band* comes from," Waverly says over the phone as I explain that tonight I am actually going to a concert in a garage.

I am standing outside the stadium (Spoke won again), chatting with Waverly and waiting for Kitsy.

"Yeah," I say, turning it over. "I always thought it was a type of music like pop or rap. But I guess not."

Waverly's been calling a lot this week, and I am looking forward to actually seeing her. She asks a lot of questions about the Spoke, but avoids my questions about Kent. I am not sure if it's because she's doing things with Smith that she'd rather not say or because Kent doesn't live up to the pretty pictures in its brochures.

"Texas sounds so . . . interesting," Waverly says. "I can't believe it's already October and that I'll see you—and it—in a week. We still really need to talk packing list. I am so glad that Ralph Lauren did Western chic for the past four seasons."

Looking to avoid explaining about how Broken Spoke wear and Ralph Lauren couture are a bit different, I happily spot Kitsy running over.

"I gotta run because Kitsy's here."

"What's a Kitsy?" Waverly asks.

"My friend; that's her name," I answer, waving Kitsy down.

"Weird name," Waverly says. "And I didn't think you had friends in Texas."

"Okay, *Waverly*," I say back, and roll my eyes even though Waverly can't see me do it. "Love ya, x and o."

I end the phone call and smile at Kitsy.

"I liked the new cheer," I say.

And I did; it was a totally creative version of the song "Mockingbird."

"Thanks! Let's go find Hands," Kitsy says, humming the tune under her breath. "It's not like I am *not* excited for the party, but I have to say that my ears still hurt after your crush's *last* concert."

"Fair," I say to Kitsy, remembering the torturous lyrics. "I wonder if rock star girlfriends ever think that way. Like, 'If I hear that song one more time, we might have to break up.'"

"I feel like that with football sometimes," Kitsy admits. "If I hear one more time how the right tackle should have gone left instead of right, I might go catawampus. But don't tell Hands; it would hurt his feelings."

Kitsy and I head toward the parking lot. Unfortunately,

we're sharing a ride with Hands *and* Bubby. Just like with cabs in NYC, you don't always get to choose who drives you place to place. I am just happy to get wherever I'm going.

Rider's garage looks just like Grandma and Grandpa's garage, except it's packed with all his band stuff. There's not enough room inside for the audience, so we hang on the driveway.

There are a few folding chairs that face the garage, so I go and sit in one.

Bubby follows me.

"I had fun at the dance, surprisingly enough. And we still need to rematch in horseshoes. Last time I think I was just tired from, you know, being a football star and all. Plus, it's a one-arm sport—it'd be good for you."

"I thought you didn't like Rider's music," I say, not looking away from the garage.

"I don't," Bubby says. "But I like the scenery," he says, staring at me and winking.

"Sick," I say, looking down.

"One day, Manhattan," he says. "I know how these stories go. Girl falls for music boy. Music boy breaks girl's heart. Girl falls for good boy."

"Funny," I say, watching Rider tune his guitar. "I always thought it was girl falls for football jerk, football jerk breaks her heart, girl falls for a dork."

"But I am all of those: the football player, the good boy, and the dork," Bubby says, and stands up to leave. "So what happens to me?"

"I don't know. You're not in my story," I reply, happy to see that Bubby's going.

"All righty then, I am going to have some actual fun," Bubby says, and covers his ears with his hands. "Hopefully, you brought ear plugs."

"Oh, Bubby," I say. "My best friend is coming next weekend. She likes a good project. Maybe she'll take you on for charity. She can use it as a tax deduction, right?"

"I wouldn't want you to get jealous," Bubby says, and heads back to his friends.

Kitsy comes down and sits with me. After about twenty minutes of the concert, I am convinced that being a musician's girlfriend isn't any better than being a football player's wife. Rider's really talented and everything, but the songs get old, especially since I think the apocalypse inspires them. Plus, Rider's barely looking at me. Finally, Kitsy says, "How about we do a lap around the party?"

"Agreed," I say, standing up. Rider keeps playing without noting our departure. Waverly always says watch out for men who love something more than themselves or you. Their passion can be your prison. I never really got that piece of advice until I realized to what level Rider was into his music. Even if I was naked in the crowd, I still don't think he'd turn away from the music.

Kitsy looks back at Rider and shakes her head.

"Sometimes I think that all the music goes to his head," Kitsy says, looping her arm with mine.

"I hope that's it," I say, trying not to sound too disappointed. Waverly says to never wear your emotions in your voice.

"What does Waverly like to do? Let's plan something fun for her. This might be a first: two Manhattan teens in the Broken Spoke. Hey, it's totally like that retro show with Nicole and Paris traveling to small towns."

Except this is not reality TV and neither Waverly nor I is getting fame, publicity, or a paycheck for this. Building an itinerary for Waverly in Broken Spoke would be a travel agent's biggest nightmare. Not only do I have to drag her to the rodeo, but I also have absolutely nothing else planned for her visit. Plus, it doesn't look like Rider is going to be as good a show-and-tell as I thought.

"I have an idea," Kitsy says. "Let's design T-shirts for the rodeo and sell them. And we can give the profits to Ginger for the kids. Waverly can run the table while you do the auction, and I can help my brother with his mutton busting."

Giving Waverly a job is an interesting proposition. While Waverly is most certainly not industrious, she does love power and a good sale. And I do need to find something to keep her occupied.

"That's a good idea, Kitsy," I say. "What should the T-shirts look like?"

"I am thinking something funny," Kitsy says as we move away.

"Like how funny?" I say.

Kitsy suggests: "How about 'Just Rope It'?"

"That's good," I say. "How about this one? 'Real Cowgirls Ride Bareback.'"

Kitsy and I both look down at my sling.

"I'm so happy I get this monster off, just in time for the rodeo," I say. "Could you sketch out the T-shirt?" I ask.

"Sure," Kitsy says. "Let's hope my makeup skills transfer to T-shirt design. This year's rodeo will be so much better than last year's." Kitsy looks over to Hands and waves. "You know, Corrinne, it's clear that you aren't too happy to be in Texas. But I want you to know that it sure has made my year so much better."

And the rodeo is making my year better too. Of course, I know that the rodeo won't be like some of the parties and dances that I've attended, but the parents and professional party planners always organize those. Super Secret: It's a tiny bit of fun to actually get involved. It keeps my mind off my life in New York, my MIA dad, and oh yeah—Rider.

≈⁓◈⁓≈

I look back at Rider, who is still singing in the garage even though not a single person is watching. And then I look over at Bubby, whose doing a one-handed handstand. It doesn't look like tonight will be my night with Rider. So I take Kitsy's hand and march over to the group.

"How about we all play some football?" I say to Bubby, tapping his butt as he attempts to stay in his handstand. "You boys are only undefeated because you haven't taken on true competition."

"I thought you'd never ask," Bubby says, steadying himself back onto two feet.

"But I am only playing if it's touch football."

And all the other football boys elbow one another and grunt.

"Okay," I say, "but be nice, I've only got one good arm."

Even though I've never played with a football, I hook the ball under my non-slinged arm and start trotting off with it. Bubby gently grabs me around the waist and pulls me to the ground.

"Touchdown," he whispers.

Of course, I am totally not into Bubby, but it feels good to get the attention from someone. Even a Neanderthal. And you know what, I was even able to throw a spiral by the end of the night.

Chapter 13

Welcome to the
Broken Spoke, Waverly

THE WEEK OF THE RODEO and Waverly's big visit comes in an instant. Between getting the pamphlets ready, the auction organized, and the T-shirts designed and printed, I have no time to Waverly-proof Broken Spoke. On the day of her arrival, I find a Tibi dress in the back of my closet and spend considerable extra time getting ready. I don't want Waverly to think that just because I left New York that I let myself go. You know, like what college freshman girls do.

Grandpa picks me up early from school, and he lets me drive the entire trip to the Dallas airport. Driving is a lot easier now that I am sans my sling. I'm glad I am healed because I don't think Waverly would believe that slings are the newest "it" accessory.

I forgot how desolate the drive is. My stomach gets butterflies thinking about what Waverly will think of it all: the cows, the stretches of nothingness, the truck stops, Broken Spoke in general. And my whole pull-the-Rider-card idea to make Waverly think life in Texas isn't all terrible has not been going well. The majority of the time Rider and I have talked recently, he just asked me about my music contacts. If I weren't so fun and pretty, I'd think he was using me.

When we get to the airport, Grandpa and I idle in the cell phone lot, which is for people waiting to pick up passengers. With each passing second, my anxiety grows. What will Waverly think? What will Waverly say? What will Waverly do?

"How are you feeling, Corrinne?" Grandpa says, turning from the passenger seat to look at me.

"Fine, Grandpa," I lie. "Just tired from getting ready for the rodeo." This isn't exactly true, but how do you tell your grandpa that you're worried his life won't be up to your best friend's standards? You can take Waverly out of the city, but you can't take the city out of Waverly.

"You know, Corrinne," Grandpa says, fiddling with the radio, "you've surprised me with how much you've built a life for yourself in Broken Spoke."

I don't want to let Grandpa down. Granted, postrecession, I have managed a job, some new friends, and a crush, but this is pretend life, like summer camp. Eventually, it'll all go back to how it was before. You forget all about how you thought you changed, how these are your new best friends, and how showering daily isn't necessary.

But what if I can't ever go back to my real life because Waverly has such a bad time in Broken Spoke that I can't face her or the East Coast again? Since Waverly is my only liaison to my other life, the one I left behind, whatever she tells people about my time in Texas will be the word. I am hoping the narrative focuses on Rider's hot factor rather than the fact I live in a place where Sonic is the only alfresco dining.

My iPhone bings with a text.

Waverly: Texas welcomes Waverly. Just landed. Had to check my bags. Will meet you outside.

I start up the truck engine. Momentarily, I am thrilled for Waverly to see me behind the wheel. But then I remember that I am no famous movie star, and this is no convertible.

By the time we maneuver through airport traffic, Waverly is waiting at the curb with a porter. She has not one, not two, but three Louis Vuitton bags, one of which is a hatbox. I sure hope it's a cowboy hat she packed. Waverly's wearing tight black pants and a cashmere wrap. She looks like a page out of *When Celebrities Fly*.

When Waverly sees me behind Billie Jean the Second, she does a double take. She looks at the porter, looks back at me, and then looks up to the sky as if to ask if this is happening. Grandpa reaches over and honks Billie Jean's horn. Half the people on the curb look over to watch this strange scene unfold. A glamorous girl gets picked up by unglamorous car. Déjà vu.

Haphazardly, I pull to the curb, crookedly park Billie Jean, and tumble out to hug Waverly.

Waverly hugs me tightly back while saying, "Are you for real? Were you just driving? Were you just driving that thing?" I honestly can't tell if it's admiration or disgust.

Grandpa jumps out and tips his hat to Waverly.

"Pleasure to meet you," he says.

Waverly, the consummate flirt, bats her eyes at Grandpa and says, "I see Corrinne's good looks came from you."

He blushes. I think this trip might work out after all because as long as there's someone for Waverly to flirt with, she'll be okay anywhere.

Grandpa heaves Waverly's luggage into the truck's flatbed while I reassure her that it'll be just fine back there. She hops in the middle between Grandpa and me. Before I pull away, Waverly squeals, "Ohmigosh, I've got to take a picture. I always thought I'd be the first to drive. My dad even said that he'd get me a car next summer to practice on Nantucket, but that's months away. And here you are driving in a foreign state. I can't believe this is happening."

And for a second, I can't either.

Grandpa takes over driving after half an hour. Waverly pesters me with questions about what driving is like, what it feels like. I am happy that she's intrigued, but it worries me what she's going to think of Broken Spoke if she's this freaked out about me driving.

I tell Grandpa that we'll give Waverly the tour of Broken Spoke in the morning. To be a Forthcoming Frances: I am buying some time before she sees the strip and how little Broken Spoke has to offer. When we show up at the grandparents', Tripp is waiting at the front door. He races to the car the second we hit the driveway and opens Waverly's door.

"Waverly!" he says. "How are you?"

Waverly tussles his hair. Waverly will flirt with any age, and Tripp harbors a major crush.

"Are you so excited for the rodeo?" Tripp asks Waverly.

Waverly looks at me, puzzled. "What rodeo, Tripp?"

"Oh," I interrupt before Tripp can say anything more. "That's the event I told you about. It's a rodeo."

Waverly takes a deep breath and follows Tripp to the front door.

"I wish that you were more specific, Corrinne, because I did not pack for a rodeo. Cashmere blends with Navajo influences aren't exactly what I imagine one wears to a rodeo," Waverly says.

"I am sorry," I apologize, "I figured you'd realize that

215

Broken Spoke, Texas, is a bit more casual than the grassy Kent quad."

Waverly gives me a how-would-I-know-anything-about-a-place-like-this look, and then continues. "Don't people wear, like, those leg pads and spikes on their boots? We need to go shopping so I can get some. Number one pet peeve: being fashionably unprepared. You know this, Corrinne."

Timidly, I follow a few steps behind her.

"Those leg pads and spikes are called chaps and spurs. And you don't need to wear them unless you are an actual cowboy. Anyways, it's not just a rodeo," I say quietly, feeling like my worst fears are happening. "And I actually have a T-shirt for you to wear. It's blue and brown, your favorite colors."

"T-shirt?" Waverly stops and looks back at me. "Like what you wear to bed when you are alone?"

Luckily, my mom steps outside, interrupts this awkward moment, and kisses Waverly on both cheeks.

"Waverly," she says, ushering her into the house, "I am so glad that you are here."

I turn and watch Waverly as she takes in the surroundings with big bug eyes. My grandparents' house, which had started to feel cozy, is back to feeling cramped. I wish I had convinced my mom to hide just a few of the knickknacks, especially the pillow that says, "A house is made of wood and beams, a home is built with love and dreams." I can already hear Waverly making fun of that one back with our old friends.

My mom continues, seemingly oblivious to Waverly's shock. "We've got dinner on the stove and candy in the cabinets. My mother and I just finished baking pumpkin chocolate chip bread."

Waverly blinks three times fast and regains her manners. "Thanks, Mrs. Corcoran," she says. "I never knew you were a baker."

"She's not," Grandma pipes in. My mom's face drops, but Grandma goes over and gives my mom a friendly squeeze.

Admiring the bread, Waverly shakes her head. "I am actually on a diet. Dorm food is the worst; it's totally fattening. Corrinne should at least be happy about missing out on that," she says.

Like a knife to my stomach, Waverly's comment settles into my gut. Oh yes, Waverly's here because I am now in Texas instead of at Kent. And she's about to see just how far Broken Spoke is from everything we ever knew.

"You might change your mind about the diet once you taste Grandma's food," Tripp pipes up. He's already seated at the kitchen table.

"Corrinne loves to eat now. No more miso soup for her." Tripp shakes his sandy hair.

Grandma brings over the steaks from the stove to the table. Waverly looks horrified by the generous slabs of meat, but she pulls up a chair next to Tripp and sits down.

"I thought that you went vegan," Waverly states. "And you look so thin."

Sitting down next to Waverly, I am not sure if I should tell her my next atomic bomb: I have a job doing physical labor. So I decide to keep that one to myself.

"So what's boarding school like?" Grandma asks.

"Hard," Waverly says. "It's way more competitive than Corrinne's and my old school." Waverly picks at her food with her fork and looks at me. "You are almost lucky to get to go to public school."

"Lucky?" I question back, but my mom gives me a look that says, Don't launch into a poor-me tirade at the dinner table.

"Do you have nice friends?" my grandpa asks.

"They're okay," Waverly says. "My roommate's a model, which isn't good for my self-esteem. It would have been better for my ego if Corrinne and I could have roomed together."

"Excuse me?" I say, unable to filter. While I may not be a Russian model, I don't want to think that my appearance feeds others' egos—especially not my so-called best friend.

"I mean, we've known each other forever," Waverly

says. "So you don't intimidate me and you haven't been in magazines. That's all I mean. Really."

I give Waverly a look but decide to drop the thread. No use making this trip any more difficult.

"Any good stories?" my mom chimes in.

"Nope," Waverly says, and looks down at her plate.

C'mon, Waverly, I think. Give us a bone here. I know this isn't the most glamorous dinner ever, but you could at least try at conversation.

"You are going to love it here," Tripp says. "And the rodeo's going to be awesome."

"I am sure it's a nice place," Waverly says. "It's kind of cool to go somewhere that no one else knows exists, like the Maldives before the celebrity invasion. Well, kind of like that, except Broken Spoke isn't tropical or elite," she says.

And by the way Waverly says cool, I know it's going to be a long weekend.

By the time we clear the table, I just want to go to bed and pretend this has all been a bad dream. And I haven't even started to tell Waverly about what a rodeo entails.

When Waverly yawns very loudly after turning down a Hello Dolly! bar, I am happy to suggest that we just have girl time in my room. I grab a bag of candy from the shelves and drag Waverly's mammoth bags into my tiny room.

"So you sleep here with your mom?" Waverly asks,

looking at the full-size bed. "This room is much smaller than Vladlena's and my dorm room. Did I tell you that my mom sent in her interior designer? She did the room in fuchsia, which actually turned out great."

"I thought you hated pink," I said, flopping down on the bed with the bag of candy. Even if Waverly didn't want to emotionally eat, I did.

Waverly stretches out beside me.

"Fuchsia is not exactly pink," she argues. "So tell me more about this Rider kid whose picture you sent me."

I had emailed Waverly the hottest band picture of Rider in hopes of making her jealous. I am pleased to see at least something is working according to my plans.

"It's still going," I lie, and unravel another mini Reese's Peanut Butter Cup. "He's playing at the rodeo tomorrow. You'll get to meet him. He, like, zones out with the music."

Hopefully, Waverly will mistake Rider's zoning out for his love of music rather than what I now perceive as the devastating truth: He's just not that into me.

Reaching into the bag, Waverly pulls out a mini Reese's Peanut Butter Cup. Then she flips over the bag, studies the nutritional information, and puts the gold-foiled candy back. Forty calories is too much, really? Live a little, Waverly.

"I am excited for you, Corrinne," she says, watching me unpeel another candy. "You've been such a good sport and have such a great attitude. All everyone does now is bitch about the recession. Here you are in the worst situation ever, and you are doing a great job staying positive," she says.

The way Waverly says *the worst situation ever* makes me want to gag. Of course, she's right, but I just don't like how she rubs it in.

"Tell me about Kent," I say between bites. I don't really want to know about it, but I want to put the attention off of my Broken Spoke misery. "I think I'll be able to come for winter semester," I lie again.

"Usually, they don't let in transfers in the winter," Waverly says, getting her silk pajamas out of her bag. "But maybe because of your circumstances, they'll change their mind. Kent's fine, though. Smith's hot. School's hard. End of story. Do you mind if we go to bed now? The time change has me exhausted," Waverly says, and does a dramatic yawn.

Even though it's not even ten o'clock and it's only a one-hour time change, I still agree. And unlike old times, Waverly and I don't fall asleep talking and giggling until we can't keep our eyes open. I go to bed with the certain knowledge that the only thing worse than today will be tomorrow.

Chapter 14

Not Unless There's a Helicopter to New York in It

I WAKE UP DREADING THE DAY AHEAD. Luckily Waverly's still sound asleep, so I tiptoe into the kitchen. Grandma's already whipping up two stacks of pancakes.

"Sleep well, darling?" she asks. "I saw the rodeo program on the table, and it's terrific. You really have a talent for design. That one for mutton busting is adorable."

Wow, Grandma and I are having a bonding moment. The front door opens, and Grandpa and Mom walk inside. They are carrying three take-out cups from the supermarket.

"We got some coffees," Grandpa says. "We thought today might be a good day to break the caffeine rule. Of course, Grandma and me ain't going to drink them. Why start a bad habit now? But we thought you city girls might like them."

Mom sets the cups down on the table. "The town's a-buzzing about your rodeo, Corrinne. Everyone's excited about the auction, and I already see some out-of-towners making their way in."

I want to get excited, but all I can think about is the sleeping city princess in the other room.

"I am just glad that it was planned for Saturday," Grandpa says, picking a pancake off a stack and eating it with his hands. "This way no one has to choose between the rodeo and football. Will that friend of yours Bubby be there?"

"Bubby is not my friend," I say, picking up one of the forbidden coffees. "Bubby—good ole Dusty's son by the way, Mom—Bubby is just always around like a fly. If only I could find a flyswatter big enough . . . "

And as I say this, Waverly emerges from my room, wearing a robe over her silk pajamas. "Who's Bubby and who's Dusty?" Waverly says, rubbing her eyes. "Are they horses in the rodeo?"

Mom gets red and Grandpa, Grandma, and I laugh.

"You'll see today at the rodeo, Waverly," I say.

Waverly spies the coffee, takes one, and says, "I think there's a lot I still have to learn about Texas."

Waverly is less than thrilled to wear a T-shirt.

"I mean, they are cute, but isn't this rodeo a big deal? I think we should dress up; we can wear the T-shirts underneath something cuter. We'll still technically be wearing them; that counts, right? And what type of media will be there? You know Kent has a few kids from big Dallas oil money families, and I don't want to show up in some Texan publication in a T-shirt."

"Don't worry," I say, handing over the T-shirt. "You won't be showing up in any society pages wearing a T-shirt that reads 'Just Rope It.' In fact, you won't be showing up in any society pages. We're in Broken Spoke: It's not exactly a socialite Mecca."

Waverly concedes and puts it on.

"It's so"—she pauses in front of the mirror—"comfortable." She finishes with a scrunched-up nose.

Waverly is even less enthusiastic about working the T-shirt table.

"What do I do if they want to pay by credit card? Or checks? I am not sure people still write checks, but they might in Texas. Small towns are notoriously behind the times. Maybe we should ask someone," Waverly says.

I look at Waverly with big eyes. Is she serious?

"Don't you worry about it," I reassure her. "It's a rodeo, not a foreign currency exchange bureau. It's cash only."

"I am just nervous," she says, and straightens out her T-shirt. "I don't want to mess it up because I know that you've worked really hard on the carnival."

I decide not to explain to her that a rodeo is not a carnival.

Biting my tongue, I also don't launch into how the Rodeo Queen wins an entire college scholarship and how barrel racing and roping are professional sports. They are practiced by professional athletes who make their living off of the prize money. Or how this rodeo will make the thousands of dollars that Ginger needs to buy the equipment to help handicapped kids ride.

We arrive a half hour late to Ginger's stables. We're late because Waverly locked herself in the bathroom to do her hair and makeup. Typical. Luckily we still have an hour before the rodeo starts.

As we walk around, the rodeo's almost in full swing: the booths selling popcorn, hot dogs, and rodeo souvenirs are all set up. Cowmen, cowwomen, and cowchildren alike are all reading their très chic programs. Horses are lining up in all the rings. The high school debate team is face painting horseshoes and cowboy boots as a fund-raiser. There's a level of energy that doesn't usually exist in Broken Spoke other than at football games. We find Kitsy and her brother, Kiki, moving tables around. Kiki's wearing a blue flannel shirt, Wrangler jeans, and his required helmet for mutton busting.

"Hi, y'all," Kitsy says, extending her hand. "You must be Waverly. Corrinne always talks about you. We're all worked up to meet you. Right, Kiki?" Kitsy says, and playfully taps him on the helmet.

"And you must be Kitsy," Waverly says, and weakly shakes Kitsy's hand. "Is that a family name?"

Kitsy laughs. "It was my mom's first doll's name, her first cat's name, and her first daughter's name, so I guess it is a family name. You are sweet to come all the way to Texas to visit Corrinne."

"Well, I want to be supportive of her during this tough time. I know she doesn't really have friends or like it here," Waverly says, checking Kitsy up and down.

OMG, Waverly. I am clearly aware that my life is somewhat a reverse *Princess Diaries* story, but why does she insist on insulting the few good things I have going on? Next, she'll probably tell me that Rider isn't hot.

Kitsy pauses briefly and then goes back to moving tables with her brother.

"Why don't you two set up the auction table?" Kitsy says over her shoulder. "I'll get the T-shirt table set up."

Pulling out the auction sheets from the box, I admire each one. For the donated Sonic Blasts, courtesy of Kitsy and her manager, I cut out an image of a cone with three ice-cream scoops. Of course, this isn't Christie's or Sotheby's, but it's also not totally bootleg. I even think they look kind of chic.

"So," Waverly says, looking at the cards, "I always wanted to do the paddle thing. My mom bought our Degas drawing at an auction. My dad totally flipped because the bidding got so high. But you know how my mother feels about losing. What are the prizes? Anything I'd want?"

I snatch the cards back from Waverly.

"It's a silent auction. No paddles. And the prizes are locally donated, so you probably wouldn't want them. There'd be no chance to use them in Connecticut."

"Whoa, Overreacting Ophelia," Waverly says. "I was just asking and thinking how I could help this little town's cause."

Then Waverly turns to survey the scene of people pulling up to the barn with their trailers and horses.

"So where are all the boys—especially, you know, that one guy you keep talking about? I know you are obviously just doing this for a guy. I mean, why else would you volunteer for a circus?"

"His name is Rider," I answer as I begin straightening the auction pages. "He'll be here soon because he and his band have to set up too."

Doing this for a guy? Please. I first started working to avoid being grounded; Rider has just been an added benefit. Besides, I actually liked getting ready for the rodeo, way more than all my silly college-application-padding activities back in New York.

"Good," she says. "Will he bring booze? That might take the fun factor up a notch to slightly bearable."

I look in the other direction.

"Uh," I say, thinking this is all going worse than I thought, "Rider doesn't drink. But I bet we'll all go out to the field afterward to party."

"What's the field? And Rider's already done rehab? That's so typical," Waverly says, propping herself up on the table and getting my papers messed up. "Music guys are always going to rehab," Waverly says, and rolls her eyes.

"Waverly, let's finish this up, and then we'll help Kitsy with the T-shirts," I reply, and pretend to focus intensely on my work.

"Okay," Waverly says. "One more thing: Why is Kitsy's brother wearing a helmet? Texas is totally weird. It's more foreign than Vladlena's country. Remind me to call her later. I don't want her to go through roommate withdrawal. All the juniors tell us that happens over fall break."

Even though I am positive that I know more about withdrawal than Waverly, I keep quiet and focus my eyes on the table, making it into a work of organized art. If I even look at Waverly, I will burst into tears or make throwing your old best friend into manure a new rodeo sport.

The rest of the setup doesn't go any better.

Kitsy, Waverly, and I are chatting and Waverly loudly announces:

"Rodeo is such a cute theme. Maybe we'll do this for school formal, and we can all dress up like rodeo characters. I am going to be a clown," she says. "But a sexy one if that's possible."

Mind you, there are no clowns around.

Kitsy attempts small talk.

"Hope you are having fun. I'm glad that you came to Broken Spoke," she says. "I'd love to come to New York, and maybe even work in makeup. I did Corrinne's for a dance."

"Oh, you want to come to New York to do makeup? That's so cute," Waverly responds. "That's like all the girls that come to do modeling but then have to become call girls. Makeup's probably more realistic. You probably won't have to become a call girl."

"Waverly," I say, "I know that you think you're funny, but Kitsy doesn't know you, so maybe no call girl jokes." Turning to look at Waverly, I grit my teeth.

Kitsy laughs. But really? That's beyond low, even for Waverly, especially since the rumor is her grandma Wilhelmina *did* start out as a high-paid call girl. Like the actual inspiration for *Breakfast at Tiffany's*.

Waverly turns to face Kitsy. "I apologize. Because you and Corrinne are such good friends, I thought I could tease you, too. Apparently, Corrinne's gotten a bit more uptight since her life didn't turn out how she thought it would. Is she always like this now?" Waverly asks. "It's sad; she used to be so much fun."

Kitsy's eyes pop out. "No, no, Waverly," Kitsy says.

"Corrinne's probably the most fun girl in Spoke. All the boys here are falling all over her. And there's one of them now. . . ."

Rider saunters up to the group. I quickly introduce Waverly to him. At this point, I am not that interested in impressing Waverly before she leaves. I am more focused on making sure she leaves alive, although I did appreciate Kitsy's effort to make me look like the hottie of the Spoke.

"Pleased to meet you," Rider says, smiling and tucking his hair behind his ears. He lingers when he shakes Waverly's hand. Flipping fantastic. Rider flirting with Waverly—just one more thing to add to the list of why this day sucks.

"T.M.F.G.," Waverly says, looking back over her shoulder at Rider as he walks away. "Now, I see why you haven't thrown yourself under a horse."

"What's T.M.F.G.?" Kitsy asks.

"Total Material For Gossip," I say, feeling silly about our old acronyms.

"I like that," Kitsy says. "Okay, I am going to get Kiki ready for his big event. Good luck with the T-shirts and the auction." Kitsy heads toward the mutton busters that are lining up.

"Wish Kiki good luck from me," I call back. "Tell him to ride that sheep!"

Waverly just looks at me with big open eyes. "Ride that sheep! I didn't think I'd ever hear those words out of your mouth."

I laugh. "I didn't either, Waverly. Good luck selling the T-shirts. I'll come get you when the auction's over."

"Fine," Waverly says. "But I am putting this on my college application as work experience."

And before I am even out of her sight, I catch Waverly staring at Rider and his band as they warm up.

Once the rodeo gets under way, I almost forget about Waverly and the natural disaster this visit has become.

Checking the auction sheets, I see that someone bid three hundred dollars for Grandpa's services. I can't wait to tell him. And even Kitsy's ten Sonic Blasts are going for over a hundred dollars, way more than the actual retail price.

Once the bidding slows down, I announce "Five more minutes" over the megaphone. A few people return and put in final bids.

Reading off the sheets, I ask the winners to meet up after the auction to pay and collect their prizes. I really like using the megaphone. Shocking, I know. Totaling everything up, we made way more money than I expected. It's not pre-recession Barneys shopping money, but it'll certainly pay for some of the equipment Ginger needs.

I run over to where the mutton busters are competing,

hoping to catch Kiki, and find Mom and Kitsy watching from the fence.

"Hey, Corinne," my mom says. "I am impressed. Maybe you'll go into event planning. I've seen million-dollar galas that haven't run as smoothly as this."

"Has Kiki gone yet?" I say breathlessly.

"No," Kitsy says, not taking her eyes off the ring. "He's next. The record's at twenty-four seconds."

Kiki gets onto the sheep; since he's small, he needs to balance his weight. As the gates open up, the sheep takes off, trying its hardest to throw Kiki from his back. Who knew sheep could buck? For what seems like a lifetime, Kiki holds on, shifting his weight and even hanging off the side. Finally, he drops off onto the ground. The sheep hightails it for the other side of the ring. PETA would definitely not like this.

"Ohmigod," I say, hugging Kitsy. "That must've been like three minutes."

Kitsy looks down at her personal stopwatch. "Thirty-five seconds. I don't think anyone will beat it, though, so it might as well be three minutes. He's going to be psyched. It's a blue trophy and fifty dollars," she says.

After we all hug and congratulate Kiki, Mom disappears to go find Ginger. I figure I should find the Wicked Witch of Manhattan. Hopefully, she's melted. When I approach the T-shirt table, I find no Waverly but rather

Bubby. I look around and notice that Rider and his band are also missing from their area.

"Hey, Manhattan," Bubby says. "Not bad for your first rodeo. I hope you don't mind, but I sold most of your T-shirts for you."

I realize there are only a couple shirts left on the table, and the boxes underneath are empty.

"Where's Waverly?" I ask, scouting for her among the rodeo crowd.

"She doesn't exactly have the best work ethic," Bubby says. "She and Rider ran off like the dogs were after them. So I took over. You should have asked me to sell these since I am a local celebrity. I thought a city girl like you would know the power of a celebrity endorsement."

Like the dogs were after them? I am never going to get Texan language down.

Shaking my head, I laugh. "Thanks, Bubby," I say. "Waverly's visit hasn't turned out exactly like I hoped. I should've expected she'd bolt." And then I realize that Bubby's managed to pull a T-shirt over his jersey. It's way too tight, but it's probably the cutest I've seen him looking.

"Take the T-shirt for free," I say. "It's the least I can do."

"Oh, I could think of some other things that you could do," Bubby says, and raises his eyebrows. "Go enjoy your rodeo. I still have the last T-shirts to sell. And Manhattan, it was awfully nice of you to do that auction."

"Thanks," I say, and head toward the Rodeo Queen competition, where I find Rider and Waverly talking against the fence. Rider's head is tipped toward Waverly's, and he's brushing a hair out of her face. Really, people? This is a rodeo, not a bedroom.

"Hi, *y'all*," I say, coming up right in between them. Rider immediately drops his hand.

"You know, Rider," I say, "I am not sure that Ginger's paying you to take breaks." Rider gets flushed and walks away without saying anything.

"Nice one," I say to Waverly, shaking my head. "Apparently, you don't want me to even have the one hot thing in Texas."

"Please," Waverly says, avoiding my eyes, "Rider's a total douche. He was just asking me about music contacts. And he's not that hot. Texas is just going to your brain."

Kitsy bounds up at this moment and grabs my hand. "Did you hear?" she asks. "Your mom's going to ride in an exhibition and then crown the new rodeo queen."

"What?" I squeal. I grab Waverly's hand and almost forget about her flirting with and nearly kissing Rider. "This we need to see," I say, and I drag her to the fence where Grandma, Grandpa, and Tripp are standing.

"Did you know about this?" I ask my grandparents. Still in shock, I watch my mom, in a bedazzled rodeo queen shirt complete with a Miss Rodeo Queen 1985 sash, get up and mount a horse—Smudge, to be exact.

Grandpa and Grandma shake their heads. "I have been dropping her off at Ginger's during the day," Grandpa says. "But I just thought she was lonely and wanted to catch up with her old friend."

Waverly stares at me in total amazement. "Your mother is wearing jeans and is on a horse," Waverly says. "And is her shirt bedazzled?"

"I know," I say, double taking to make sure it's not a mirage. "I guess she used to do the barrels before modeling, before New York, before my dad, before me."

Before Waverly can ask about the barrels, Mom nudges Smudge and takes off. Dirt envelops the ring, creating a cloud of dust. Luckily, my mom handles Smudge with much more grace than I did. She goes left, she goes right, making tight figure eights through the barrels. In a flash, she's completed the course. The crowd that's gathered hollers and hoots.

Someone behind me whispers, "Jenny Jo's back five minutes, and she's already stolen the spotlight again."

I ignore them; it ain't worth it.

"Our princess back on her throne." Grandpa whistles and smiles.

"No, Grandpa," I correct him. "She's a queen. A Rodeo Queen."

In my loudest voice, I cheer, *"Vive La Reine,"* which means long live the queen. Thanks, Marie Antoinette and French history. I guess I didn't totally forget everything from my prep school life.

Then Grandma hugs nearly the whole town and accepts everyone's congratulations on my mother's return to the ring.

Mom dismounts the horse, and she helps to crown the newest Rodeo Queen, a girl from Broken Spoke High named Angela.

Mom's still beaming by the time she makes it back to us.

"Wow, Mrs. Corcoran," Waverly says. "If Fifth Avenue could just see you now . . ."

My mom looks down at her shirt and laughs. "Funny how things work out. Who knows, Waverly? Bedazzling might just make a comeback; there's certainly something fun about it." Mom turns to me. "I am going to call your father. He's the one who encouraged me with this little secret," my mom says.

Apparently, there's a lot that I don't understand about my mom, her past, and my dad. I guess Grandpa was right that day in the car. My mom isn't boring after all.

Kitsy looks at Waverly and me. "So how about the field tonight?"

"A football field?" Waverly says, and flares a nostril;

it's not a pretty sight. "I don't do football," she says. "I'd much rather get hot and sweaty with a boy than watch them do it together."

"No, a different field," I say. But I figure the last thing that Waverly and I need to do is participate in another Texan rite of passage. It's about time that we talked, really talked.

I look at Waverly and say, "We need to have a chat, so we'll probably skip the field."

"For sure," Kitsy says. "Y'all chat. I am going to tend to my own knitting and take Kiki to Sonic to celebrate. Call me when you get back from the airport, Corrinne. Nice to meet you, Waverly."

Waverly responds, "I didn't know you knitted. That was in vogue in New York for, like, a hot moment. Bye now, Katsy. It was such a fun experience to meet a real Texan."

Kitsy turns back around to face Waverly.

"It's Kitsy, Waverly," she says. "Kitsy Kidd. And by the way, you'd look a lot better in purple eye shadow. Blue doesn't really do it for you."

Waverly just stands and watches Kitsy go. Activating my filter, I stifle a laugh and only silently agree that Kitsy's totally dead-on about the blue.

"I need help with putting away these tables; then we can go," I say to Waverly, who's eyeing the parking lot.

"Finally," Waverly says, taking off her T-shirt to reveal just a skimpy tank top. "How do you live in this sauna?"

I don't answer.

In silence Waverly and I carry the fold-up tables back to the barn. Ginger's standing inside, and she bear hugs me.

"Best rodeo ever," she says. "Everyone thinks that we should do a spring rodeo too. Thanks for all your work. I think with this money, all Spokers who want to ride will be able to. Corrinne, you do remind me a lot of your momma, but you must have gotten that business savvy from your dad."

My dad, I think. I'll have to send him some pictures, but not for pity this time. I am proud to be part of this Texan scene.

I smile big and nod while Waverly rolls her eyes.

On the car ride back home, I ask Grandpa to drop Waverly and me off at Chin's.

My mom gives me twenty dollars for dinner. "Thanks, I'll call you when we need a ride."

"Are we eating here?" Waverly says, looking at Chin's advertisement for a $7.99 all-you-can-eat lunch buffet.

"Yes," I say, and open the door. "It's good. I ate here before a dance with Bubby. New York doesn't hold the patent on Chinese food. Or anything else for that matter."

"I seriously distrust your taste these days," Waverly

says, and pauses before she follows me in.

Mr. Chin sits us in the back of the restaurant, and I am glad to be out of sight from the other customers.

Looking at her menu, Waverly says, "I am not sure if I can eat anything here since I have to fit into my clothes when I get home. T-shirts and jeans don't exactly cut it at Kent, especially when everyone's going to come back all tan from their exotic fall breaks."

"Shut up, Waverly," I say, and slam my menu shut. It makes a loud smacking noise. "All you've done since you've gotten here is complain and make me feel bad."

"Please, Corrinne," Waverly says, from behind her menu. "This visit hasn't been all champagne and roses for me. Does this place at least have good sake?"

"No, they don't have sake. One, Broken Spoke is a dry county. Two, it's a Chinese restaurant, not Japanese," I say. "Three, you are so ignorant."

Waverly slams down her menu. "Ignorant? Oh, sorry, Corrinne," she nearly shouts. "I forgot that you moved to the middle of nowhere and that makes you worldly. I don't really remember you of all people as the educated one. I am pretty sure I always had the better grades, and well, better everything."

Timidly, Mr. Chin approaches the table.

"Girls, what would you like to eat?"

"Um," I say, noticing the other customers have begun

to stare at us. "We'll take egg rolls and General Tso's chicken with a side of fried rice."

Waverly looks up at Mr. Chin. "And we'll take that to go."

Mr. Chin retrieves our menus. "Okay then, I'll get that as quickly as we can." He almost breaks into a run on his way back to the kitchen. I think Waverly's New York attitude totally freaked him out. Hell, she's even freaking me out and I *am* a New Yorker.

"I guess I'll call my grandpa to pick us up, then," I say.

"And I'll call the airline to change my flight to tomorrow," Waverly says. "I really can't be here any longer, and Monday's too far away."

"Do whatever you want," I say, and get out my phone. "It's all about you anyway, right?"

Waverly stands up from the table. "I'll wait for you outside," she says, and shoves in her chair.

"Terrific," I say, already dialing my grandparents' home phone.

After a car ride in silence, Waverly and I sit down at the kitchen table to eat our Chinese food. Mom, Grandpa, Grandma, and Tripp just watch us from the couch as if we were a reality program. *Teen Manhattanites in Texas.*

I reach into the bag to pull out the fortune cookies.

"Do you want your fortune cookie, Waverly?" I ask, holding it out to her.

"Not unless there's a helicopter to New York in it," Waverly says, not even looking up from the fried rice.

Has Waverly always been like this? Some best friend she is. And all I did was take her to a rodeo!

"I'll take the cookie," Tripp pipes up from the couch. I toss it to him, and he breaks it open.

"Waverly," Tripp says, "your fortune is 'Tough times don't last, tough people do.' Can I eat the cookie?"

"Sure," Waverly says. "If you don't mind, I am going to shower today's adventure off of me and go to bed. I've lost my appetite."

"Whatever," I say. Turning around, I announce, "By the way, we need to take Waverly to the airport tomorrow instead of Monday. She changed her flight."

The eyes of everyone on the couch perk up. My grandparents look at each other, Mom looks at me, and Tripp looks down at the ground. Waverly gets up from the table, throws her food out, and heads for the bathroom.

"Tripp," my mom says, "why don't you go to your room?"

"I always miss the good stuff," Tripp says, and follows my mother's directions.

Grandpa does a dramatic stretch. "You know," he says, "I am tired myself. I'll head to bed too." Grandpa stands up and walks over to me. He puts his hand on my head. "Corrinne," he says, "what a rodeo! I am so proud of you."

Looking over at my mom, Grandpa says "Jenny Jo, it was really great to see you back on the horse."

After Grandpa leaves the kitchen, Grandma walks up to the stove. "How about some hot cider, girls? It's that fall time of year."

"Thanks, Mom," my mom says, and comes to sit with me at the table. "What's going on, Corrinne?"

"Waverly hates it here so she's leaving," I say, and try not to tear up. "She's going to tell everyone how I am now the star of a reverse *Beverly Hillbillies*. A debutante gone redneck."

"I am sorry, baby," my mom says, rubbing my back. "This has been a bad fall, huh?"

"Bad?" I say. "I think you need to seriously expand your vocabulary. It's been unfathomably depressing."

"You know," Grandma says as she puts the hot water on, "your bad luck has turned into the best luck I've ever had. I got to spend time with my grandchildren and I got to see my daughter back in Broken Spoke. I am starting to like this whole recession."

"And I did get to ride again and mend some broken threads from the past," my mom says, and winks at Grandma. "You've also really, really impressed me with how much you've grown up, Corrinne."

"So?" I say. "I've lost my best friend, my horse, my city, my life, my future. I really cannot get very excited about my maturity."

"C'mon, Corrinne," Grandma says as she prepares three mugs of cider. "Tell me that you have hated it all, that you did not enjoy the rodeo, or that you don't like Kitsy or that Bubby kid. Lie to me that you are unhappy here."

"Grandma," I say, "I've just lost my best friend of ten years. Waverly and I grew up together in the city. Now we have nothing in common."

"Corrinne," my mom says, getting up to help Grandma bring the cider to the table. "Let me tell you something that I wish I knew earlier. Just because you change doesn't mean you need to give up all the things that once made you who you were. I don't think you realize that *you're* the one who changed. Waverly is the one trying to get used to the new you."

Grandma and Mom walk over to me and sit down on either side of the table.

"She's right," Grandma says. "Me and your mom wasted a lot of time because I was mad at her for growing up and making her own decisions. Just because Jenny Jo wasn't in Broken Spoke didn't mean that she and I had nothing in common. I should've made more of an effort to get to New York and learn that new part of Jenny Jo—or rather J.J."

Mom sips her cider and touches Grandma's shoulder. "And I should've honored where I came from more and remembered that I am still that girl, too, the one who danced to 'Billie Jean' in this kitchen before going on dates with a guy named Dusty."

And when my mom mentions Dusty, I feel relieved that it didn't work out a) because I wouldn't have been born and b) because Bubby's getting cuter and nicer, and that would've made him like my brother or something.

As happy as I am to see Mom and Grandma patch up their mother-daughter quilt, I am not sure how this will help me convince Waverly to still be friends and still like me even though I am new hick and nouveau poor.

"Just think it over, Corrinne," my mom says. "Being disappointed and surrendering are two different beasts. I think you've learned that recently."

"Thanks for the advice," I say, and put on a big smile. "Maybe things will be better in the morning. I am going to shower and head to bed."

Leaving my mom and Grandma to their Hallmark commercial, I go to my bedroom, where I find Waverly already tucked in and asleep. I am totally relieved.

Chapter 15

Swimming What?

AT SEVEN IN THE MORNING, I hear a knock at my door. Both Waverly and I sit up in bed and look at each other.

"Who is it?" I say.

"Grandpa," the voice answers through the door. "Get Waverly packed up, put on y'all's swimsuits, and meet me in the car in ten minutes."

"Swimsuits?" Waverly questions. "Thank God this is almost over. I now see why the Midwest is a fly-over zone."

It's too early for our next battle, so I decide not to correct Waverly's geography. Texas is about as Midwest as Mexico City.

"Let's just try to be civil," I say. "The North and South already had one war."

As if she were packing for a surprise all-expense-paid

trip to Tahiti, Waverly throws all of her clothes back into her bag at a record pace.

"I didn't pack a swimsuit since this wasn't a vacation to Cancun," Waverly says. "And I haven't exactly seen any water."

"Just indulge him," I say, and throw her one of my bikinis, an old faded one in orange, Waverly's worst color. Orange is to Waverly what pink is to me. It's a small moment of revenge, but it buoys me nevertheless.

She gives the bikini a once over and flares her nostrils, but she slips it on anyways. "This is so Texas *Twilight Zone*," Waverly says.

"That we can agree on," I say.

Waverly says some quick good-byes while Grandpa heaves her luggage into Billie Jean the Second; then we set off for who-knows-where. Grandpa won't tell, and I am afraid we've been signed up to be on a reality show about trying not to kill your ex-best-friend in the middle of Texas.

Since we're taking twisty back roads, I have absolutely no idea where we are. Finally, Grandpa pulls down one last road. He pulls out a picnic basket and two towels from the backseat, and points down a dirt path lined with oak trees.

"Go down that path," Grandpa says. "I'll be back in an hour, and we'll head to the airport. And by the way, it's very deep and completely safe. People having been doing it for more than fifty years."

"What is deep and safe, Grandpa?" I say. "This is just weird."

"Not to mention creepy," Waverly adds, and looks suspiciously at the path ahead of us.

"Fine," Grandpa says, and reaches to take the picnic basket away. "Give me back all Grandma's muffins and doughnuts. We'll just head to the airport now."

"No," I say, hearing my emotional hunger growl. "We'll go."

Grandpa hops in the truck and drives away. Waverly and I slowly start down the road.

"This reminds me of that time we tried to run away from summer camp after the counselors confiscated our gossip magazines because they weren't camp-appropriate," Waverly says. "We only got to the gas station before the director caught us. Remember having dish duty for a week after because of it?"

"What were we supposed to do?" I say. "What if major celebrities broke up when we were away and we missed it?"

"Not to mention the mosquitoes; they were out of a sci-fi film. And the food was inedible. Thank God we hid candy in that old stuffed bear," Waverly said.

"We were pretty genius for eleven-year-olds," I interject.

"We totally were," Waverly says. "Nothing was going to keep us from chocolate. We weren't as weird about eating back then."

Waverly and I had been quite the troublemakers as kids. I had forgotten how much fun we used to have.

After a few minutes, we reach the end of the dirt road. We keep walking straight through a grass field. Then the grass stops. And far below us is a sea blue pond.

"Wow," I say as I back away from the edge. "There is water in Texas."

"How high do you think we are? Like diving board high or tenth-story high?" Waverly asks.

"It's totally Empire State Building high. No way I am jumping from that," I say.

"It's actually pretty, in a nature-hugging way," Waverly says, and steps closer.

"At least there's one thing you like about Texas," I say, bringing the picnic basket over to an old bench made out of a fallen tree. "Well, this and Rider."

"Corrinne," Waverly says. "First of all, nothing really happened with Rider. All he did was talk about music contacts. Second, he seemed to me like someone who uses people like us."

"People like us?" I say, and shake my head. Was my mom right? Was I the one who changed? Did I used to be like Waverly?

I take out three Ziploc baggies of muffins from the basket.

"This is the thing, Waverly. Maybe I've changed, and I get that. But I hate how you judge everything here; you even said the coffee tasted second-rate."

"Me?" Waverly says, and pulls off a muffin wrapper. "Judge everything? You are the one who keeps telling me how much you hate it. Why do I have to be the small-town cheerleader? You have Kitsy for that." Waverly shakes an imaginary pom-pom, and I catch myself before I laugh. "Let's face it, this isn't what you want," she accuses.

"Want?" I say. "No. But this is my life now and I want you to see it. I don't want our friendship to exist solely in the past. My life's never going to be like how it was, Waverly."

"I just don't know what we have in common now," Waverly says.

"Me neither," I whisper, not knowing what to say next. Maybe Waverly's and my relationship was defined by our zip code and our lifestyle. Maybe we never did have anything in common beside that. I pop an entire muffin top into my mouth.

"Why did your grandpa drop us off here?" Waverly asks. "He didn't really expect someone like you, a Scaredy-cat Susie, to jump off a cliff, did he?"

I pour each of us a glass of juice in an attempt to

dislodge the poppy-seed muffin top from my throat.

I swallow. "He's old," I say. "He probably thought the fresh air would mend our friendship. Grandpa is from that whole we-walked-ten-miles-to-school generation. He believes that the great outdoors and a little exercise can cure anything."

We laugh.

"Maybe he's right," Waverly says. "There's not much great outdoors in New York and everyone there is totally nuts. I bet that's why all the rehab facilities are always in the country."

Pointing to the edge, Waverly asks, "Do you want to jump first or second? You aren't too chicken to be first, are you?"

I forgot how competitive Waverly is. But then I remember it was Waverly who challenged (forced) me to do the high dive, to ride a roller coaster, to take a helicopter. I used to be way phobic about heights. Without Waverly, I don't think I would've ever seen above street level.

"Oh, please, Waverly," I say. "I am a recessionista. That's pretty damn tough. A cliff is nothing compared to this fall."

"That's it." Waverly snaps her finger. "I am used to being the brave one. And here you are enrolled in public school, riding on circus animals, and hanging out with cowboys and wannabe rock stars. Somehow you became the brave one. I guess that's why this is hard." Waverly pauses and then raises her eyebrows. "C'mon, recessionista, I'll race you to it." We both get up and run to the edge. Waverly makes it first. Of course. She's never let me win.

"Okay, boarding school girl," I say, refusing to look down. "Let's see it."

"Two things first, Corrinne. One, if I die, I love you— even the Broken Spoke version negative three-point-oh Corrinne. Two, take my picture. I've got to Facebook this."

Grabbing Waverly's iPhone, I get ready for her picture. Waverly steps to the edge and then stops. She looks back and grabs my hand.

I put the phone down.

"We're jumping together," she says, and drags me over. "You may be a recessionista, but you are still afraid of heights. And you still need me, even if only for this."

I want to let go of Waverly's hand, but I hear Grandpa's voice repeating "deep and safe." And isn't there a saying that if all your friends jump off the Brooklyn Bridge, you should too? Before I remember the actual answer is "No, you shouldn't," Waverly and I are flying through the air, still clutching hands and plunging under the cool water. When we push through to the surface, we squeal collectively.

"Awesome," Waverly says as she treads water. "Maybe your country grandpa has some street smarts after all. One more time, Corrinne?"

I look back up to the edge, "Only if you hold my hand again," I tease.

"I'm only holding it again if you promise to control your palm sweating—that was gross," Waverly says.

After our next big leap, I look at my watch and realize that we were supposed to meet my grandfather ten minutes ago.

"We have to go, Waverly," I say. We dash back to our clothes and run back down the road.

As we run, Waverly grabs my arm and says, "Boarding school kids are so uptight. I bet half the girls there wouldn't have jumped because they are worried about their hair. Thanks for doing it."

"Waverly," I say, trying not to pant. "I really appreciate you coming, making me jump off the cliff, and being you, even though you are sometimes obnoxious. And thanks for letting me change and still be my friend."

And we slow our pace to a power walk.

"I know this hasn't been easy for you," I continue after catching my breath. "If you reinvented to Goth or something, it'd take me a while to get used to it too. But think twice before you do that: I am not sure how you'd look with a chin piercing."

"I am not going to completely rule out Goth," Waverly says, thinking it over. "Wearing all black is so slenderizing and a lot easier than going on a diet."

At the end of the road, Grandpa's waiting in Billie Jean the Second.

"How was it, girls?" he asks with a coy grin.

"Memorable," I say. And I mean it. I guess my mom and her late-night lesson was right. Sometimes disappointment and surrender are two different beasts. That's another saying Grandma needs to embroider.

"Refreshing," Waverly adds as she rings out her hair. "Mr. Houston, will you take our picture in front of Billie Jean the Second?" Waverly says. "I want to show my roommate back at school a picture of Texan Corrinne and me. I only have pictures of New York Corrinne."

"Sure," Grandpa says. "I am proud of you girls. Not everyone would jump into a pond infested with swimming nutria; that takes a real friendship. Especially since it would definitely take both of you to fight the nutria off."

Grandpa holds up the camera, and we strike a pose. Like all of our pictures since we were little girls, Waverly curls her arm underneath mine before she sticks out her chest and butt and poses for the camera.

"What's nutria?" Waverly asks, just before Grandpa takes the picture.

"Oh, just swimming rats," Grandpa says. "This is Texas, girls. We are not known for clean, fresh, or rat-free waters. Our water is like your subways."

And before we can reply or scream, Grandpa presses down on the button. "Say cheese," Grandpa says with a chuckle.

Click. In this picture, our mouths hang open wide. Swimming rats? How's that for an anecdote?

Waverly and I create a scene at the airport. I may be a recessionista now, but I'll forever be a drama queen.

"Don't worry, Waverly," I yell through the throngs of travelers as she moves toward the terminal. "We'll never let a recession or a rodeo come between us. Love is stronger than that."

"And I'll get a friend who can tolerate furry creatures to check on Sweetbread," she hollers back. "I'm titling my Facebook album 'Ain't Nothing Broken About It.'"

I decide to take that as a compliment. Back in Billie Jean, I put my head against the window and sleep for a while.

When I wake up, Grandpa is humming to the radio and admiring the view. Now that I've done the drive a couple of times during the daylight, I must agree there's a little bit of truth to the saying that Texas is God's country. While I wouldn't go as far as agreeing with Hands's bumper sticker, which says "American by birth, Texan by the grace of God," there's something to be said about farmlands.

"You awake, Corrinne?" Grandpa says. "That cliff jumping must have knocked you dead tired."

"Not as tired as Waverly made me," I say, and smile. "But she's always been tiring. That's part of her charm."

"I'm proud of you, grandbaby," Grandpa says, and squeezes the back of my neck. "You are growing into one fine lady."

"C'mon, Grandpa," I say. "Don't get all sappy on me. I might not be a city girl anymore, but I am no softie."

We both laugh.

"How about I finish the drive home?" I say.

"Home?" Grandpa repeats as he pulls to the shoulder.

"Yes," I say. "I heard on a TV show that whatever strange place you find yourself, make that your home."

Grandpa gets out his door and comes around to my side.

"You calling the Broken Spoke strange?" he probes.

"Oh, it's definitely strange," I say as I walk around the truck to the driver's side. "But it's still home. Or one of my homes. And what was our deal again? When exactly does Billie Jean the Second become mine?"

"I thought you'd never ask," Grandpa says with a side wink. "I've already been checking out her successors. How about I go with red this time? A nice fire engine red truck for my three-quarter-life crisis. Not sure if Grandma will like that, though."

❧❧❧

And it turns out, I hit my first traffic jam around Dallas on the way home due to a Cowboys game. Grandpa keeps telling me to be calm, and I tell him that I have had plenty of practice staying calm after this last fall.

By the time we get home, everybody is in his or her rooms, getting ready for bed. I crawl into bed in the dark and hear a crunchy noise underneath me.

My mom sits up in bed and turns on the light.

The crunch noise is revealed to be a piece of loose-leaf paper with a note written in Tripp's perfect cursive. I didn't think they even taught that anymore, but somehow Tripp's handwriting looks as good as a schoolteacher's.

"Hi, Mom," I say, and hold up the paper. "What's this? Does Tripp still believe in the tooth fairy?"

Tripp is such a good kid that he even writes the tooth fairy thank-you notes.

"You've really got to tell him she's not real. He's got enough going against him with the chess obsession," I say, looking her dead in the eye.

My mom waves a finger and takes the note.

"I think he still does actually believe," she says, reading the paper. "Good thing I have one child who's not a total cynic. But that's not what this letter's about. Tripp's teacher gave it to me at the rodeo."

"Did he get his first bad grade?" I say, and my voice perks up. Maybe Texas is turning him into a human after all.

"No." She laughs. "We're still waiting on that. It's about you, actually. Why don't you take it someplace to read alone?" my mom says, and she lies back down.

"Like where?" I ask. "The bathroom?"

"Sure," my mother mutters, already half asleep.

Sitting on the toilet—with the seat down, of course—I start to read.

Across the top, Tripp titled the paper "My Hero."

My hero is my sister, Corrinne. Anyone who sees her knows that she is pretty, and she's even funny when she isn't being too mean. But that's not why she's my hero.

When we moved from New York to Texas, I was worried. Corrinne and me have never been very close, and she's always too busy for me. I didn't know Grandma and Grandpa well, so I thought I would be alone in a place I never visited. And at first, that's how I felt. I made some friends, but I missed my parents and New York.

But then little by little, Corrinne started to be nicer. She let me work with her, and she even sat with me and my friends at a football game. And a couple of times, I was pretty sure that she was even listening to what I had to say. Even though she's never let me drive with her or taken me to Sonic, she's still my hero because she finally became the sister I always wanted to have. . . .

Me, a hero? I most certainly don't have any superpowers, like blowing fire or running at super speeds, and

I don't think that I have ever been purposefully nice to Tripp. I only sat with him at the game because it was better than sitting with my grandparents. I am starting to get a stomachache, and I am fairly certain it's not just from the MSG last night. Tripp has no good reason to think I am his hero because I am not even a good sister.

Getting out my phone, I text Kitsy.

Corrinne: Is Sonic open for brother-sister bonding?

Kitsy: Sure. Hurry.

I go to Tripp's room and wake him up. He's in pajamas emblazoned with cartoon characters. I figure I can give the fashion lesson another time.

"Is everything okay?" Tripp asks as he rubs the sleep from his eyes.

"Everything's great," I say. "We're just doing something we should have done earlier. Tiptoe."

We both quietly sneak into the living room.

Now, I know heroes aren't supposed to break laws, but sometimes they do. Think about Robin Hood. So when I grab Billie Jean's keys, I know it's for a greater cause.

Opening the door slowly, I am relieved it doesn't squeak.

"No way," Tripp says as I open the truck door for him.

"Hey," I say, "aren't brothers and sisters supposed to have secrets? This will be ours."

"Way cool," Tripp says, buckling up. "This is better

than the time you paid me five dollars not to tell Mom and Dad about your party."

"And we're not done yet," I say as I put the car into reverse. For once, Billie Jean doesn't sputter. She takes off without a sound.

"Where are we going?" Tripp asks as he peers out the window.

"You'll see," I say with my eyes on the road. This would almost be worth the arrest except my hair looks funky from my swim in the lake.

When we pull into the Sonic parking lot, Kitsy is cleaning off tables inside.

Glancing at her watch, she says, "I'm fixin' to close. Well, I was supposed to close four minutes ago. But y'all are worth it. Let's make it quick, though."

Kitsy goes into the kitchen and puts her Sonic cap back on.

"Next," she yells from behind the counter.

Tripp bounces up as if we were at the Pearly Gates.

"What'll you have?" Kitsy asks.

"Reese's Sonic Blast," he says, looking up at the menu again. "And French fries," he adds.

"And I'll have a chocolate milk shake," I say, and pull out my wallet.

"It's the recession special," Kitsy says. "Free."

Kitsy works on our ice-cream treats and Tripp and I

sit in a booth. We're the only customers left in the whole place.

"So, Tripp," I say as I pull out napkins from the dispenser. "How's everything going?"

Tripp grins. "This has been the best weekend ever."

Reflecting back on Hurricane Waverly, I am not sure I can agree. But there've certainly been a lot of memorable moments.

Balancing the food on a tray, Kitsy walks over to set it down at our booth.

"We'll actually take it to go," I say, and hand Tripp his goods. "We've got to get Billie Jean back before anyone notices she's disappeared. And we need some time to talk too."

Tripp heads out the door, but I linger with Kitsy for a second.

"Kitsy," I start, "thanks for everything this weekend. I can't apologize for Waverly, but I know she just acts like that because she's jealous of our friendship. Please forgive me for bringing all my northern drama south."

"No worries," Kitsy says. "Broken Spoke can use some Manhattan drama; it was pretty boring around here before you New Yorkers came and stirred it up. Anyways, she's big hat, no cattle."

Tripp and I exchange confused glances. We still aren't fluent in Texan.

"She's all talk, no action," Kitsy translates. "Don't worry about it at all."

Well, that's certainly true in any language, even Texan.

As I push open the door into the darkness, I look back at Kitsy, who is already wiping off our table.

"Thanks," I say before shutting it again. As hard as it is to now remember life pre-recession, it's even harder to remember life without Kitsy.

Pulling into the driveway after talking about sixth grade politics and the thirty-two reasons why the school needs a chess club, I decide I need to fess up.

"Hey, Tripp," I say, "it was totally sweet that you wrote about me being a hero. But here's the thing: I am not a good choice for a role model. I am moody, conniving, and selfish. There are better inspirational figures out there."

"Corrinne," Tripp says, unbuckling his seat belt, "you are all those things, but you have some good qualities too. And I just wrote that essay to practice my creative writing. No offense or anything. But after tonight, you are my hero. We just broke like fifteen laws. Sweet."

Way to a twelve-year-old's heart: lawbreaking. Lesson learned. I'll remember that every time I feel like a bad sister.

Shutting our doors carefully, we sneak back into the house and into the living room without incident. I slurp down my milk shake, bury it deep in the trash, kiss Tripp on the forehead, and get back in bed with my mom.

"Mmm," she says, rolling over. "Smells like fried food."

"You must be dreaming," I say, and close my eyes.

Chapter 16

New York, New York

The month following Waverly's visit passes quickly.

Via FedEx, Waverly sends me Magnolia cupcakes on dry ice as a thank-you gift. Her note says, "Bringing a little bit of the city to my favorite country girl." A totally sweet thought, but honestly they aren't as good as Grandma's Mockingbird cupcakes, which have been in high demand since the football team is still undefeated.

Before her visit I could barely get Waverly on the phone, and now she constantly floods my inbox with texts.

Waverly: OMG. Smith made out with Vladlena.

Waverly: How do you make yourself exotic? Do you think I could learn Russian?

Waverly: Can I come back to the Spoke? The boys are hotter there. How's that loser Rider?

I text back:

> Corrinne: You were right. Rider just wanted music contacts. No more rock stars for me.

I don't add how could I never trust him when he goes on tour when I can't even trust him with my best friend in Broken Spoke. His band wound up placing second in the Dallas Battle of the Bands, so now as Kitsy puts it, "He thinks the sun comes up just to hear him crow." (Yankee translation: He's got an ego problem.)

For Thanksgiving, Mom, Tripp, and I are going to New York to meet up with my dad. We invited Grandma and Grandpa, but they said that we should have time for just our family. Thinking about it, I actually really miss my dad, and I can't believe it's been three months since I've seen him. He'll be happy that I am getting all A's and never followed through on my plans to run away from Texas. Of course, it's going to be weird because we are staying in a Midtown hotel and eating Thanksgiving dinner at the Plaza. I'll almost be a tourist in my own city—except I will never wear one of those I Heart NY shirts. Talk about tacky.

Plus, I get to see my baby: Sweetbread. Shakespeare was right: distance does make the heart grow fonder.

In Spanish class while we are supposed to be independently filling out verb sheets, Bubby leans over and asks if I am coming to Houston to see the State Championship game at the big dome.

"Corrinne," he whispers, "you are my good luck charm. We haven't lost since you've been here. So if you don't come and we blow it, I am going to have everyone blame you, not me. We'll call it the Curse of Corrinne."

Blushing, I whisper back, "I can't come because I'm going to New York for Turkey Day. Aliens have to return to their mother planet at some point, you know."

"Sucks," he says. "And no, some aliens decide to stay. My planet does football a lot better than your planet. And you are missing the biggest thing that's happened here in fifty-two years."

Kitsy turns from her front-row seat and says, "Tell me about it. The game's even going to be on local TV, and you aren't going to see the boys play or me cheer. What if I get on the JumboTron? I want to wave to you."

"I'll be there in spirit," I say. "And Kitsy, Waverly emailed; she said you were right about the blue eye shadow thing."

Kitsy rolls her eyes. "Ah, Waverly."

"What blue eye shadow thing?" Bubby asks.

"Girl talk," I answer.

Señor Luis claps his hands and points at the three of us.

"*Hola!*" he says. "Back to conjugating verbs. Corrinne, if you are going to flirt, do it in Spanish and practice your *español*."

Flirt with Bubby? Get serious. Although he is definitely looking cuter and I did accept his Facebook friendship. But flirt? Please, I am not going native again, especially not after the Rider fiasco.

Flying over Manhattan at night reminds me exactly why I miss it. The city looks like a jewel box that's all lit up. Who knew that steel and electricity could be so beautiful? A pain shoots through my chest, and I feel genuinely home-sick for the first time in a while. It's harder to be happy about Broken Spoke when I see the city again. My mom peers over me to look out the window. She squeezes my hand. Sharing a bed has made us a lot closer, apparently.

"You've really missed it?" she asks.

"Yes," I say, anticipating the smell of chestnuts on the street and Barneys holiday windows. Shopping won't be nearly as much fun without a credit card, but I am looking forward to just being out in the crowds and seeing more trends than just Western.

"Thank you," my mom says.

"For what?" I say.

"For being a good sport this fall," Mom says, looking away from the window and at me. "You impressed me. You helped me get through all this. I know the high road isn't always the paved one, but you found it nevertheless. Something I haven't always been good at myself."

I stare at my mom as I realize that Broken Spoke's been really good for our relationship. Even I have to admit that. I bet she'll even be nice and let me borrow her clothes—and they will actually fit now, since all the shoveling shrunk me to her size.

We take a taxi instead of a limo from the airport. Waiting in the long taxi line, I wear my winter coat for the first time in months. At first it feels good to be cold, and then it just gets annoying. It's almost hard to remember why people live in the North.

When we get to our hotel, my dad's waiting in the lobby. Tripp runs at him with the speed of a barrel racer.

Mom and I quickly follow and join the group hug. Taking in my dad's cologne reminds me of all the Thanksgivings I spent on his shoulders watching the Macy's Thanksgiving Day parade.

"Corrinne," he says, looking down at my jeans and sweater, "you look so old and so, so casual." Checking myself out, I nod. Texas has done a lot for my comfort level.

After dinner at our old neighborhood's bistro, I meet Waverly and all of her boarding school friends at her apartment. Since she made the effort—however drama inducing it was—to get to know my life, I figure I should do the same. Vladlena's visiting for the holiday since Russia doesn't exactly celebrate Thanksgiving. Apparently Smith moved on from her, and Waverly forgave her for the whole ordeal. Vladlena turns out to be super nice and keeps asking about Broken Spoke and the rodeo. After she saw Waverly's pictures, she decided she must make it to Texas soon, so she can meet a real-life cowboy too. Ah, people and their Texan stereotypes.

All the kids sip cocktails, and I have a beer. It feels strange to drink anywhere but the field. After a while, everyone heads out to a karaoke place, but I decide to call it a night since tomorrow's Thanksgiving and I'm seeing Sweetbread in the morning. Plus, my dad told us that he has big news. Three months later, I'm still recovering from his last piece of big news, so I decide to get my beauty sleep.

Even though both my mother and Waverly, the horse-hater, volunteered to come with me to visit Sweetbread, I decide to take a town car alone a) because I think Waverly's just trying to make nice after that near kiss with Rider and b) because it's really my and Sweetbread's time to see each other.

I hope Sweetbread hasn't forgotten me. Last night Waverly told me horror stories about her boarding school friends' dogs not recognizing them. "Just trying to prepare you, Corrinne. Animals are not as smart as humans,"

Waverly said. "They don't have long-term memories."

But when I duck into Sweetbread's stable, she neighs, like, eight times and pushes her head into my chest. Just like I thought, nobody could forget Corrinne Corcoran.

My trainer is away for the holiday, so I can't ride Sweetbread because of, like, four thousand insurance laws. But I am happy just to talk: I am not sure why anyone pays for therapy when there are horses. Although therapists' couches are probably a lot more comfortable than a barrel of hay and their offices probably don't reek of manure either. But other than that, Sweetbread is as good a therapist as Sigmund Freud.

Brushing out Sweetbread's hair, I confess my secret: "So there was this horse named Smudge, and I was riding him for work, not pleasure. And then there was this boy—okay, not just any boy. A rocker. And then I ended up in the hospital. So basically I learned that I shouldn't jump on the back of just any horse that'll have me. It's dangerous."

Talking with Sweetbread, I wonder if that's what love is: the ability to go away and to come back again as if nothing has changed, even though everything has changed.

After telling Sweetbread about Kitsy, Sonic, and everything Broken Spoke–related, I say to her:

"Okay, here's the deal. I am not exactly sure about the future. I did mention to Ginger about you coming there.

And she said we could work something out, which means I'll be shoveling a lot of manure. But I'd do it for you. Hell, I did it for Rider. Big mistake. But Ginger's barn is a bit different from here. A little less country club, a bit more country. When you come, I'll introduce you to all your crazy, rodeo Texan cousins, even Smudge. Hey, maybe we can even start a dressage program down there."

Sweetbread neighs again. Waverly was so wrong, animals are smart.

"I have to go, Sweetbread, but thanks for not forgetting me. I'll be back."

Kissing Sweetbread between the eyes like I always did, I head back to the city for Thanksgiving with the family.

The Plaza puts on an extremely elaborate buffet, and there's even a kid's table in honor of the Plaza's most famous resident, little Eloise from the children's books. Of course, Tripp beelines for that table and decides that he'll have a Thanksgiving dinner of chicken fingers and fries. Mom and Dad don't care, they just seem happy to be a foursome again.

Once we all sit down, Dad says, "I want to give a toast before I tell you the big news."

We all hold up our glasses (Tripp has a Shirley Temple, and I have a Diet Coke).

"To getting through a really tough time," Dad says.

"And to remembering that family's stronger than any recession."

The family clinks glasses, and Tripp manages to spill most of his drink on the white tablecloth. Typical but charming in a cute-little-brother way.

But I honestly am impressed that we made it to Thanksgiving. One hundred and some days without Barneys, Starbucks, my dad, and all the other elements of my old life, and I somehow survived.

"The big news is," Dad says, "I am opening the New York office for my company. While the company's not recession-proof, this is still a big job that pays well. Corrinne, I worked it out with the headmaster and you can start Kent in January. And Tripp will re-enroll at Mann."

"What?" I say, looking at Mom to confirm that this is happening.

"Your father, being resourceful as ever, somehow made this fall into an opportunity. We're certainly not back where we were, but frankly no one is. Y'all were a big part in making this happen by being willing to go to Texas for a while," my mom says.

"For a while?" I say, still confused by this news. I guess I figured that I'd go back to New York eventually, but now that it's happening I feel strange—like I am almost unsure which place I'd rather be.

Dad gives a thumbs-up. "Go ahead," Dad says. "Text

Waverly. It's totally okay. You can break with good manners for this."

"But what about Grandma and Grandpa?" Tripp says, mashing one of his fries into the plate.

"I haven't told them yet," Mom says. "We'll visit a lot more, though. I should've taken you guys to see the Spoke long before this all happened. But of course, Grandma and Grandpa will stay in Texas; that's their home."

Their home? Although I never got used to the Barbie-size closets, Grandma and Grandpa's did feel like my home too—at least recently.

My dad makes eyes at my mom.

"Aren't you guys excited about this?" Dad says. "Isn't this what we all want?" Tugging on his ear with one hand, he quickly finishes his champagne.

"Of course," I say. "It's just sudden." Looking down at my stuffing and cranberry sauce, I start to feel a bit queasy.

My dad stares into his empty champagne glass.

"I just don't get it, J.J." my dad says. "Didn't you guys miss me, miss New York? Corrinne made it sound like Texas was a penitentiary. You should have seen some of the texts she sent me. Sometimes she even attached photos of bizarre barbecues in parking lots."

"Tailgates, Dad," Tripp says.

My mom looks at both Tripp and me. "Of course

they're excited, Cole. They've just had a lot of changes recently."

Over dinner, my mom and dad go over the details about getting a new (smaller) apartment and how they were able to re-enroll us in our schools. And how the new Nantucket place might even sell, which will free up a lot of cash.

None of us goes up to the buffet for seconds, and Tripp and I stay pretty much mute for the rest of dinner.

When I turn my phone back on, I have four texts from Kitsy.

Kitsy: I am thankful for you.

Kitsy: Come back! I am getting nervous for the BIG game.

Kitsy: How's New York? I looked for you at the Macy Parade.

Kitsy: Call ME!!!

Oh, Kitsy, I think. How I am going to tell Kitsy that I am going to Kent? She's going to be totally depressed. To be honest, I am randomly depressed too. I don't even call Waverly to tell her the news. Without saying much to each other, Tripp and I both go to bed early. We don't even order any movies off of the hotel TV.

The next day my mom asks if I want to go shopping. Now that we sort of have money again, my mom's evidently begun to loosen up the purse. While it's totally like going home again when I step into Barneys, I have sticker shock, nearly fainting when I see all the prices. Dividing everything by $7.50 to figure out how many hours it would take me to earn it makes me not want to buy anything, even with Black Friday prices.

After some browsing, my mom can tell that I am not into the crowds or the sales.

"Want to go on a walk in the park?" my mom says. This is something that we haven't done together in a long time.

"Okay," I say, happy to leave the chaos of the shoe sale.

In the park, a light snow starts to fall.

"I forgot about seasons," I say.

"I know," my mom says. "It seemed like winter would never come. And here it is."

"And back in Texas," I say, "it's probably seventy-five degrees and sunny." Pulling out my iPhone, I say, "I have to take a picture for Kitsy. She's never seen snow, she'll totally freak out. I would bring her back some if it wouldn't melt."

My mom holds out her glove to catch a snowflake. "Kitsy's become a really good friend," she says.

"Yeah," I say. "She's actually nice, which is more than I can say about most of my friends."

Waverly's got her pluses, but no one would ever check

the "nice" box when describing her.

"Kitsy must be excited about the big game," my mom says, examining her snowflake.

"Excited?" I ask. "Having a heart attack is more like it. I think the only person more excited is Grandpa. He asked me to get him Bubby's autograph. Thinking about the game makes me almost sad to miss it."

"Corrinne," my mom says and stops walking. "Do you want to go?"

I halt dead in my tracks. "Go where?" I ask, even though I know she means Texas.

Watching the snow melt as it hits the pavement, I get a rush. "You know, Mom, now that we're leaving Texas, I'll get to see Dad all the time. I do want to go. Can I, though? It's, like, tomorrow."

My mom claps her gloves together. "It's settled, then," she says, and reaches into her purse for her phone. "Let's get your flight changed to Houston for tonight. If you want a chance of making it, you have to beat the real snow. We're supposed to get three inches tomorrow."

For the first time since I heard Dad's big news, I smile. Ripping off my glove, I furiously text both Kitsy and Bubby.

> Corrinne: Good luck charm heading to Houston. See you at the game.

My mom looks at me and asks, "Would you care if

I came too? I kind of want to see Broken Spoke history made."

"Grandpa would love that," I say. "But promise me we can get hot chocolate after this walk. New York is freezing!"

Chapter 17

The Best Day of Our Lives

SINCE THE GAME'S IN HOUSTON, we get a hotel right by the stadium. Grandma and Grandpa drive down and get a room too. No one wants to take a chance of missing the game.

My mom tells my grandparents our news over continental breakfast.

"I am not surprised," Grandma says. "Your husband has always been resourceful. And your family should be together. Corrinne, you must be happy about Kent."

Grandpa wipes his eyes a bit. As always, he's a bit more emotional. "Y'all promise that y'all will visit more often."

"For sure," I say. "And you guys have to come see me at Kent. I must admit, though, equestrian competitions aren't as fun as the rodeo. And Grandpa, maybe we can even drive Billie Jean the Second cross-country. She is mine, right?"

"Of course," Grandpa says. "A promise is a promise."

I picture myself driving onto the grassy knolls of Kent in the pickup truck as soon as I'm old enough to get my license; everyone will at least know for sure who I am: the Manhattanite-Texan hybrid that drives stick. That's hot. Or so my grandpa says.

"Corrinne," my mom says, and snaps me out my daydream, "let's talk about this after you actually get a license."

"Have you told Kitsy?" my grandma asks, her voice full of concern. "She's the one who's going to be really devastated. That Kitsy grew on me, and so did you, Corrinne, especially after I convinced you to eat carbs."

"I am waiting until after the game to mention it," I say. "And I am only telling Kitsy if Broken Spoke wins."

"We're definitely going to win," Grandpa says. "Your friend Bubby is no small part of that because he really took this team to another level. And he's only a sophomore. Broken Spoke will finally have a good few years."

"Dad," my mom says, and shakes her head, "how many times does Corrinne have to tell you that Bubby isn't her friend?"

"Actually," I say, spreading cream cheese on my bagel, "Bubby's okay if you are into that star-of-the-football-team-good-guy thing."

"And are you?" Grandma says with her eyebrows raised.

"Depends on if they win," I say.

The Houston stadium is huge and it's packed. I have never been to a Super Bowl, but I doubt that they are any more exciting than this.

My mom insists that we get hot dogs at the stadium even though it's an eleven a.m. game.

"You have to eat hot dogs at a football game," she says. "It's tradition."

Before the game starts, I make my way down to where Kitsy and the girls are stretching.

"Good luck," I yell from the stands.

"Thanks, Corrinne," Kitsy yells back. "The field tonight—no matter what!"

"For sure," I say, and nod enthusiastically in case she can't hear me.

And for the next three hours of my life, I feel every heartbeat, not just mine, but Mom's, Grandpa's, and Grandma's.

At the half, Broken Spoke is down by seven.

"Okay, okay, no worrying yet," Grandpa says, squeezing Grandma's hands. "This is how it was when I won. You remember that, honey. "

After the third quarter, the game is tied. Bubby has

yet to score as the Bluebonnets have three guys defending just him. And then as if right out of a sports movie, Bubby manages to get away and score a touchdown with forty-two seconds left. In the end zone, he breaks out into his own rendition of the Mockingbirdette's dance. All of us are laughing so hard that we are crying, and crying so hard that we are laughing.

Then we get the extra point. And I throw my arms around my grandpa.

"I can't believe it," Grandpa says, hugging me tightly. "My city granddaughter's become quite the Texan after all."

And for the next thirty-nine seconds, no one breathes, eats their peanuts, or looks away from the field. With the Bluebonnets unable to get a first down, Broken Spoke wins the State Championship, the first since Grandpa's senior year.

All the students from Broken Spoke rush the field. It looks like a gray cloud. Staying back with my grandparents and Mom, we collapse into our seats for the first time since we got there.

"What a game!" my mom says as she takes off one of her heels and rubs her foot.

"What a fall!" I say, and link arms with my grandma and mom.

"What a fifty-two years!" Grandpa adds. "Never

would I have thought I'd get to watch Broken Spoke win State again with three generations of Houston women. Don't know how I got so lucky. Someone up there must like me."

We huddle together for a while and watch the excitement on the field before we head back to Broken Spoke in Billie Jean the Second.

Hands pulls his truck up to the field, just as the orange sun sets into the November sky. Kitsy, in true form, is still in her Mockingbirdette uniform. Hands, Kitsy, and I jump out, and I look around for Bubby. To be a Truthful Tabitha, I was a tidbit disappointed when Hands told me that Bubby got a ride with someone else. And not just because he got named Most Valuable Player of the game, although titles are totally sexy.

"Tell me all about New York," Kitsy says when we approach one of the dozen kegs.

"Oh," I say, "it was fun. But listen, Kitsy—can we talk?"

"Sure," Kitsy says. "Something wrong? Is it Waverly?" She grabs two cups of beer for us.

"No, she's fine. Still Waverly," I say, walking toward the woods where Kitsy first taught me to pee cowgirl style. "It's actually about me."

We sit down cross-legged in the grass. I am still in a

Broken Spoke High T-shirt, jeans, and my mom's boots, something I would've never worn three months ago. And I am sitting with a girl who has turned out to be my best friend, something I would've never believed three months ago.

"Well, what is it?" Kitsy says. "This is not a sit-and-talk night, this is a party night. I mean, *hello*, we just won State. In football. In Texas."

Before Kitsy can break into a song and dance, I interrupt her with the news.

"I am leaving Broken Spoke after the semester ends," I confess. "Stuff changed with my dad's job and I can go to Kent after all. Mom, Tripp, and me—we are all going back."

"Oh," Kitsy says, and sips her beer. "Guess the day was going too well. I don't know what to say. Congratulations?" she sputters before her words get caught in her throat.

After a moment, Kitsy finds her voice again. "I am happy for you because I know how much you love New York." Playing with the strings of her pom-poms, she stares down at the grass.

"Kitsy," I say, fighting my own tears, "you're the best. You're responsible for making Broken Spoke okay for me. No, you made it actually great because you made me realize that the company you keep is the most important part of life. And yes, I know that my grandma has a teacup that says that, but it's actually true. You were there for all the stupid Friday Night After the Lights concerts and Hurricane Waverly. You taught me how to be a recessionista. I even wore my discount dress to a party in New York and got tons of compliments."

"That's the thing," Kitsy says, and wipes her tears. "I am not a recessionista. I know that's the it-word right now. But that's me. I live like this all the time. This has been my life, this is my life, and this will always be my life."

Holy Holly Golightly, Corrinne! Even when you are trying hard, you can't manage to filter yourself and end up hurting your best friend.

"Oh, Kitsy," I say. "I like it here. It's a good life with good people like you and my grandparents and Hands."

Kitsy gulps down her beer. "It's only interesting for you, Corrinne," she says, "because you've seen other things. I'll never go anywhere else or even eat anywhere but Sonic or Chin's. And now you are leaving, so I won't even get to hear about the other places there are. Cable will become my only outlet to the world again."

"But great things happen here," I say, and stand up. "Broken Spoke just won State; that's, like, every Texan city's dream. Anyways, you don't have to stay here for the rest of your life."

Kitsy pushes herself up off the grass.

"I think I will be here," she says. "That's how it goes when you are from Broken Spoke. I'll marry Hands, we'll be semi-happy, and we'll wait another fifty-two years to win another State Championship, so we can feel really happy again. I'll be, like, a grandma by then. Meanwhile, you'll be fabulous and successful in New York. And one day you are going to come across me on Facebook and be like, 'Oh yeah, Kitsy Kidd.' And then you'll unfriend me because what's the point of being friends with some girl you knew for four months once."

Kitsy starts to walk back to the keg.

Where did my ra-ra, pep-and-go cheerleading friend disappear to, and who is this girl? I never realized the magnitude of Kitsy's fear of being stuck here, but then again I never asked.

"Whoa, Kitsy," I say, chasing after her. "You can go to college too. Maybe even in New York. We could be roommates. And then you could help me with my makeup every night. And I'll help you with—well, I don't know what I'll help you with, but I'll think of something."

I try to grab Kitsy's hand, but she pulls it back. Over the past fall, I've never seen Kitsy sad, never mind crying. And on the State Championship day. I feel like a monster.

"Really?" Kitsy says, and stops walking away.

"Yes, really," I say, and I mean it too. I know just how unexpectedly life turns out. "Let's go have fun. We still have all of December and the holiday formal. And you can visit me on your spring break. I'll get a job at school and save for the ticket. Then we can go to the city and to the MoMA, even though I hate museums. We'll still be friends, Kitsy. If anything, I am loyal. You did meet Waverly, right? If I'd stick by her, why wouldn't I stick by you?"

"Oh, that Waverly," Kitsy says. "Thanks, Corrinne. I've got to fess up: I originally liked you only because you were from New York, but now I just like you for real."

"I figured that," I say, and dust the grass off my jeans. "When I got here, I wasn't exactly bursting at the seams with likable qualities. So where's that superstar Bubby? I have a congratulatory hug for him." And I wink at Kitsy.

"No way," she says. "No freaking way. Now that you are leaving, you like Bubby?" she asks. "That's absurd. Why didn't you crush on him, like, two months ago? It would have saved me from having to hear Rider sing—or whatever he does with that mike—quite a few times."

Kitsy keeps yapping, but I see Bubby, surrounded by half the females of Broken Spoke, at the keg.

"Hold that thought, Kitsy," I say, and put my cup down. "By the way, we'll always be friends. This is chapter one."

As I am walking over to Bubby, a familiar car pulls onto the field: Rider's car. We've pretty much avoided each other since the rodeo except for two more attempts on his part to get Phil Porticelli's number.

Rider rolls down his window: "Hey, Levi's," he calls out.

What I should do? Ignore him and keep walking toward Bubby, the guy who sold T-shirts for me at the rodeo? Or head for the guy who attempted to swap spit with my friend?

What I actually do: walk right up to his car.

"Hi, Rider," I say, standing a safe distance from the car. "Big game, huh?"

Rider sighs deeply before exiting his car. "Thank God you're here, Corrinne. I came because what else is there to do in Broken Spoke, but this scene is totally pathetic," Rider says, looking around with a snarl. "How is everyone okay with the fact that today is going to be the greatest day of their entire lives and they are only in high school? It's so small-town depressing."

And I can't blame Rider for thinking that way because I thought that way not long ago.

"I kind of know what you mean," I concede, meeting his eyes. "But here's the thing: So what if this is the greatest day of their lives? Or even our lives. It is magical to actually belong somewhere and get to celebrate its successes."

Feeling part of that is worth all the stuff that led up to

this, even the part when my credit cards got frozen.

Rider inches closer. "I thought you were different, Corrinne. For a while I felt sure that we met on another level, one that wasn't about Sonic and the field and the Spoke. I thought it was about music and connection. I guess I was wrong. Go have fun with the other Spokers. I see Bubby looking at you now," Rider says, pointing toward Bubby and the kegs.

"I will have fun," I say, backing away from Rider and his car. "And Rider, I don't think it's going to work out with Mr. Porticelli. You see, I am pretty sure he only works with musicians who actually have potential for commercial success. I am not exactly sure who your market is. There're enough emo musicians out there. Maybe if you were a bit more hometown hottie. And speaking of hotties, I have to go," I finish, and turn to finish my walk toward Bubby.

Okay, okay, I haven't completely mastered the filtering concept, but Rider's a douche bag; he totally used me.

Maybe if I read more, I would have seen that whole rocker-woos-girls-with-lyrics-and-flowers-because-he-wants-to-use-her-for-contacts cliché happening. But the thing about being in the middle of a cliché is that when it's happening to you, the experience feels so unique that you can't imagine anyone else has felt anything like it. Ever.

Walking toward Bubby, I wonder if he really likes me

or if it's just another cliché: boy wants girl because girl doesn't like him. Girl decides she does like boy, so boy no longer likes girl. What if it's all a game to Bubby, just like it was with Rider?

But you can't live life on the sidelines, so I saddle up next to Bubby, and I pull a key chain of Manhattan's skyline out from my purse. I bought it at the touristy "I Heart New York" airport shop.

Dangling the chain in front of Bubby's eyes, I say, "Here's a charm of Manhattan from your good luck charm, Manhattan." When he takes it from me, I add, "And you owe me big for leaving New York early to come to the game."

Bubby admires the key chain before he slips it into his pocket. "Thanks, Corrinne. How exactly can I make it up to you?"

"You can answer a question: Why do you like me? Is it because you are used to getting what you want?"

"No, Corrinne," Bubby says. "That's you. And who says I like you?"

"You like me," I say. "I know that. But now I want to know why." And I silently add, To make sure you aren't using me because my friend's dad has front-row Giant tickets.

"If someone were to like you, Corrinne, I think it would be because you surprise people. You turned out to be not who I thought you were, and I like that."

"So you do like me?" I say, and step toward him. "How about a kiss?"

Bubby gives me an are-you-serious? look but then moves closer.

He takes my left hand in his, raises it to his lips, and he kisses it softly. I feel more like a princess than I ever have, including the six consecutive Halloweens I dressed up as one. Finally: a true gentlemen.

In front of nearly all of Broken Spoke, I kiss Bubby. As Waverly always says, public displays of affection should be left for the big moments, only the ones that change your life, like your wedding. I figure this one has to count.

Everyone, including Kitsy with her pom-poms, cheers.

"So, Manhattan," Bubby says, "is this how the story ends? Girl gets smart and finally picks the right boy?"

"Bubby," I say, "I have no idea how this story ends, and that's okay."

Acknowledgments

To my readers, thank you for taking this journey with my characters. I encourage you all to construct something to put into the world—be it a story, a picture, a song, whatever. There's no better feeling out there.

I want to especially express gratitude to everyone who helped make a little girl's dream into an (almost) adult woman's reality. In my opinion, all great artistic endeavors are collaborations. There are many people whose names deserve cover space just as much as mine.

To my mediabistro class and Carla, thank you for being the spark.

To Leigh Feldman, your offer to represent me is the greatest gift I've ever received. And I was a pretty spoiled kid, so that says a lot. I am forever in your debt for your generosity, support, and talent.

To Catherine Onder, my amazing editor extraordinaire. You took a manuscript, which showed at best promise and heart, and you breathed life into it. I can't ever thank you enough for the time, talent, patience, and dedication you gave to my novel. Your name deserves big billing—in bright, illuminated marquee lights—for everything you did for this book.

To Maggie Herold, my copy editor, I'm sorry. I know I didn't make your job easy. Thank you for polishing my rock into a gem. I wish I could somehow grant you the recognition you deserve for your role in my novel.

Thank you to all my friends. In the words of Brian Andreas, the inventor of the beautiful StoryPeople collection, "Don't you hear it? she asked & I shook my head no & then she started to dance & suddenly there was music everywhere & it went on for a very long time & when I finally found words all I could say was thank you."

And Leah, I like to think that somewhere you are enjoying this at least 1 percent as much as you liked *Harry Potter*.

And finally, thanks Mom, Dad, and Aliceyn. You dug me a foundation of concrete, but you also helped me build wings as light as feathers. Please know that wherever I fly to, I will always return home, which has been many physical places but is always with you all.

7 3 1 3